Visioners2

Into the City

WALKER BUCKALEW

PUBLISHED BY FIDELI PUBLISHING

12   11   10   09   08   07   1   2   3   4   5   6

ISBN: 978-1-948638-75-3

Edited by
Frances O'Cherony Archer
Cover illustration by Paisley Hansen

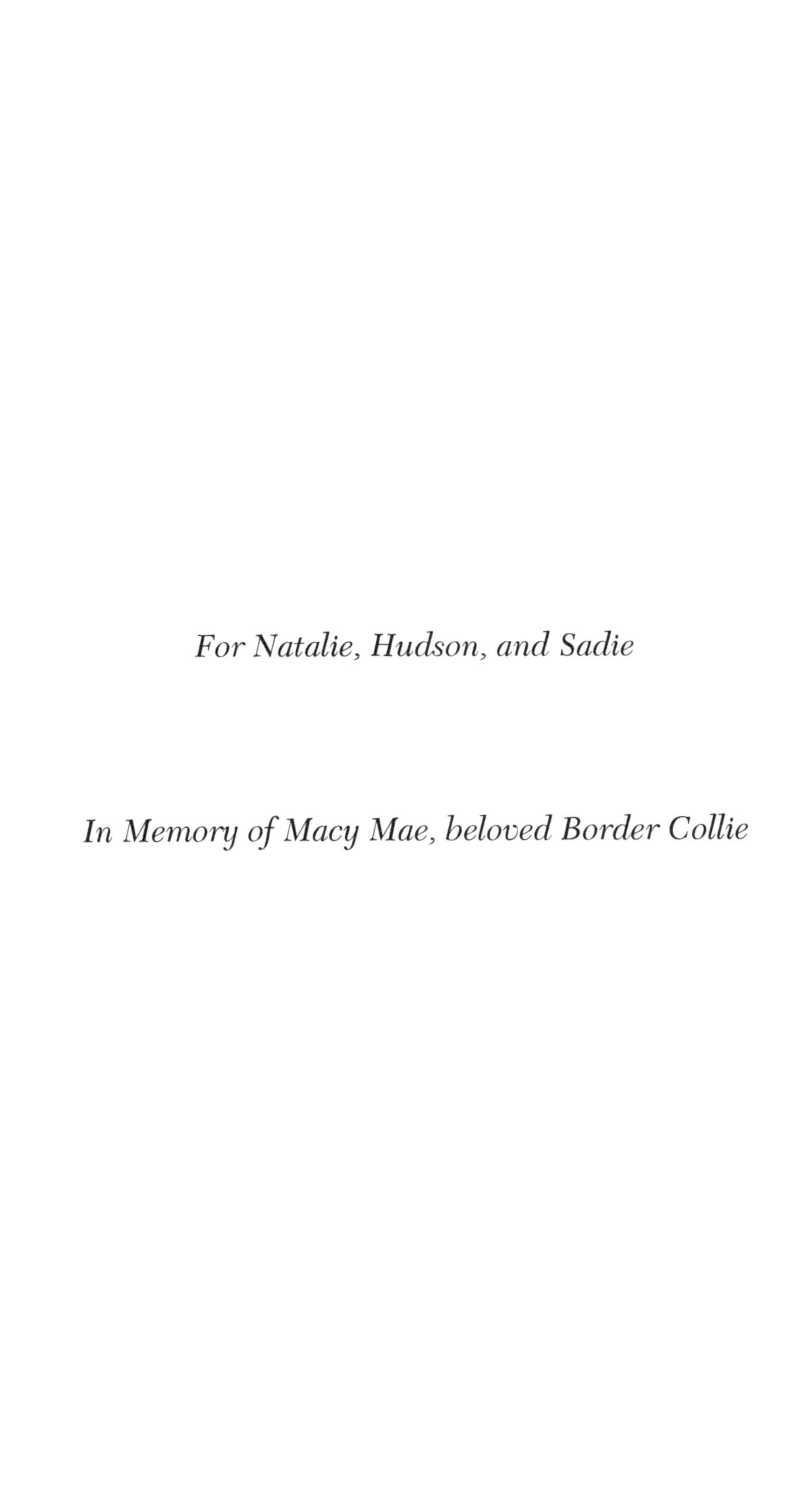

For Natalie, Hudson, and Sadie

In Memory of Macy Mae, beloved Border Collie

Chapter One

1

This is a story I did not want to be telling so soon after the first one.

I'm in New York City and I'm riding on top of an open-air, double-decker tour bus. I'm sitting with my twin brother, Samuel, and my Welsh boyfriend of four whole weeks, Gareth Morgan.

He and his parents are hanging on every word our tour guide speaks. They're rubbernecking all the time, twisting around to see the buildings and theaters and parks and bridges and churches, while my brother is obviously just bored.

But me … I'm feeling desperately embarrassed, and more so every minute. Embarrassed because I'm spoiling the bus tour. And on my way to spoiling the whole day, maybe to spoiling the whole New York visit, all because I'm so terrible at hiding my feelings when I'm … as Mum says … *seized* by distress. That's how she puts it: *seized* by distress. Not only am I *seized* by distress, I don't have Flurry, my border collie, to help me get away from this thing I'm being seized by.

It's not that I'm in distress just because I don't have Flurry. I've been without her for four days now, but we're nearly halfway through our visit to the United States, and I'll be home in London soon enough and with her again. No, it's just that Flurry helps me out of distress just by being who she is, always there, always looking me in the eye. Just loving me. I'm in distress for a different reason.

It's the dreams.

I'm so afraid that this is the start of another outbreak, another flare-up of the danger that came — just *weeks* ago — to me and my new boyfriend and my brother and my parents and my boyfriend's parents and who knows how many other people. I thought the dreams were over, at least for a long while. I didn't know they might come back so soon. I mean, it's only been a little more than a month and here the dreams are again, two of them this time, both in the same night, if you can imagine.

True, I can't know for sure if these are the special dreams, or if these are just regular dreams that are especially vivid and that I should just try to ignore. I so much don't want to ruin this trip for Samuel and Gareth and his parents, and so I am keeping this all to myself. I'm *trying* to keep this to myself, I should say.

But already Gareth and his mum, Mrs. Morgan, are starting to look at me out of the corners of their eyes. It won't be long until one of them, probably Mrs. Morgan, asks me what's wrong, and I won't be able to say, "Oh, nothing, Mrs. Morgan," in a way that will convince her that I'm being truthful. She'd know immediately that I'm not, and so would Gareth. And they'd just look at me until I finally say what the thing is, until I say why I am seized by distress.

So, like a small child instead of a reasonably grown-up 14-year-old, I turn my face away from them and pretend to stare up at the buildings. We're on Broadway right now, and there is plenty to look at. So, I do, not fooling either of them for a minute. Not fooling myself, either. My mind is *not* on the buildings.

When the danger finally ended earlier this summer, my mother warned me that it — the danger — would almost certainly be back, sooner or later, at some point in my life. I knew she was serious. I knew she spoke from her own experience. I just didn't think she meant so soon. I was 14 when the danger came. I'm still 14.

I honestly didn't know that Mum meant that in just weeks, not months or years, I might face this same kind of thing again. I thought she meant … maybe … once every five or 10 years. But no. She meant now. Right now.

So, I'm feeling more than just regular, ordinary distress. Regular, ordinary distress is the kind you get when you forget your homework or forget to prepare for the test that you thought was tomorrow but turns out to be today. *Seized* by distress means that you are *frightened,* that distress has gripped you in talons that you cannot get away from no matter what you try to do. The harder you try, the tighter the grip. The harder you try, the worse it gets.

You're caught.

2

This is summer vacation and my first trip out of England ever. Samuel's, too. Gareth's, too. I'm supposed to be relaxed and seeing new things and reading the books I brought with me in my e-reader and getting to know my boyfriend better than we could during the danger times back at the start of summer.

Our families — Gareth's and mine — had made such good plans when we left Wales last month. Both sets of parents had agreed that we would meet somewhere between Carmarthen, the Morgans' home, and London, where we live — maybe near Cardiff, the Welsh capital — and probably in late July. We would have lunch somewhere, and then Gareth would get in our Volvo with me and Mum and Dad and we'd drive back to London. We hadn't decided, then, whether Samuel would go with us, but we agreed that, if he didn't, there would be room in our car for Flurry.

As it turned out, Samuel was going to have a soccer match on the day, and so Flurry would have gotten to come. Honestly, if I could have my way about everything, she would always come. Things are so much easier when Flurry is with me. I don't have to think of things to say. I don't have to make conversation. I can just pay attention to Flurry, and people seem to understand that that's what you do when you have your dog with you.

You talk to her and put your hands on her furry head and rub her chest and belly and everything is better. Everything is easier.

Our plans were so good and so right, I thought. Gareth and I had already chosen two books each — two fiction and two nonfiction — to read in advance of our meeting, so we'd have something to talk about. We were both afraid that, if we didn't do that, we'd just sit uncomfortably with each other and secretly wish we were somewhere else. We're both shy, and better at being alone than with people.

The first time we were together, at the start of the summer, there was so much happening and so much confusion and so much danger we never had a chance to be absolutely paralyzed by our shyness. We had to talk about what to do next. We *had* to talk. There was no choice.

But that doesn't mean that we had no time to be embarrassed. Each of us was constantly looking down and looking away and blushing and, in my case, giggling about nothing at all. Horrible.

Horrible, yes, but also exciting, at least for me. That's because I'd never had a boyfriend before. I'm too long and skinny and awkward, in addition to my shyness, to have boyfriends. My clothes never fit, and my hair, though it is very long and absolutely jet black like Mum's, is nearly always tangled and confused.

Even worse, in addition to looking odd, I'm always reading or writing or playing my violin or playing with Flurry. I had just assumed my life was not going to include boys, at least not in that way, until I got much older and stopped looking so … well … so unfinished.

So, I was amazed when it became obvious that Gareth somehow thought I was pretty. He's a lot like me; very tall and thin and unathletic. Like me, he's much more at home with books, and, unlike me, with electronic things, than he is with people. But I gradually got accustomed to his liking me. Really *liking* me. Thinking of me as his *girlfriend*.

I'm still amazed just to remember how that eventually became obvious to me. And, to our continual embarrassment, obvious to everybody else, too. But I just accepted the fact finally that a boy liked me, and that I liked him, and that we'd just figure everything out as we went along. And when the danger was over and Dr. Cameron Stafford and his people had been arrested and taken away, we made our plans.

But plans, as you see, can change.

The change intruded itself at home, in London, at dinner one evening. All at once, with no preliminaries and no warning, Mum informed me that Gareth was no longer coming to visit us. No longer were we — he and I — going to have a chance to visit London museums and the other parts of the city that our family likes best. No longer were we booked to attend the matinees we had chosen. Nothing that we had planned was going to happen.

Mum told me that Gareth's mum, Lily Morgan, had decided that she would accompany her husband, the Reverend Cecil Morgan, to a business conference being held in New York City. Not only that, Mum explained, but the Morgans had been invited by some American friends to use their apartment, which was vacant during the summer, on the west side of Central Park for the whole 10 days of the conference. Plenty of room for five, those American friends had said, and wouldn't Gareth love to come, too, and bring a couple of his friends?

Would you like to guess which friends Gareth picked?

Mum and Dad had said yes to the invitation without even talking to Samuel or me about it. When at dinner Mum informed us of all this and saw our look of astonishment and dismay, she at first shrugged and said, "Joanna, Samuel … sometimes you have an opportunity that you just have to take advantage of. This is a chance to experience the United States and New York City while you're still in your early teens. You can't let this pass by."

She and I saw Samuel shrug his shoulders as if to say, *sure, why not?* Samuel doesn't really worry about anything very much. And he's not afraid of anything at all.

But Mum saw the color drain from my face. She studied me.

I timidly watched her as she studied me.

I want to remind you what Mum looks like. She is in her 40s now, but she is still the most beautiful woman in the world. No, really. She is *the* most beautiful woman in the world. She is six feet tall, straight as an arrow, has shiny black hair that falls halfway down her back, and still has the slender, strong physique she developed when she was an internationally ranked tennis player in her 20s. She still plays regularly, and she can probably beat almost any woman in the world her age.

Mum has an elegant, queenly face with high cheekbones and deep gray eyes. She also has a vicious scar on her right cheek. The scar starts near her mouth and runs in a shallow V almost all the way to her ear. And yet, the scar somehow makes her face more beautiful — more interesting — than if it were not there. I know that's hard to imagine, but it's true.

For now, I just want you to picture the two of us studying each other across the dining-room table. My face shows consternation. Her face, as she studies mine, shows her love for me. And so I know she is no longer going to speak to me the way she did a moment ago, when she said so matter-of-factly that this invitation to go to America is an opportunity we can't pass up. She is going to say something different.

Dad and my brother see exactly what is going on. They remain silent. They know this is a mother-daughter conflict. They have learned to have confidence in the outcome of these things.

Finally, Mum says, "Joanna, dear, you're afraid. Can you tell me what is frightening you?"

I drop my eyes from hers and think. She's right, I see right away. But, afraid of what? After a long silence, with each of them waiting, I eventually find words.

"Mum," I say, "I was already nervous about Gareth's coming to visit us here for a few days. I was already afraid that he'd find he didn't really like me as much as he thought. Or maybe I'd find I didn't really like *him* as much as I thought.

"But at least I was going to be here, at home, with Flurry and you and Dad and Samuel always around. I barely know Reverend and Mrs. Morgan, Mum. I barely know *Gareth*, even. And once I get on that plane for New York, there's no escaping the thing. I'll be caught. And for more than a *week*."

I shake my head, looking down at my plate.

"And you didn't even ask us, Mum," I add sadly. "You didn't even ask us."

My mother gets up from the table, walks around to me, leans over and puts her arms around me, her shiny black, sweet-smelling hair falling across my shoulders and into my lap. "I'm sorry, sweetheart," she says softly in my ear. "I did this badly."

She holds me for long seconds, and I feel her love for me, flowing into me. And I know she is truly sorry for not involving us in this decision.

I also know we are going to New York City.

3

Now — right now — on the bus, I feel Gareth's and Mrs. Morgan's eyes looking *through* me, as I continue to pretend to focus on Manhattan's sights and our tour guide's words. Mrs. Morgan is a small woman with a sweet and kind face. It would be wrong to say that her look right now is severe. The look she is giving me is not that; it's parental.

Concerned. Worried. Unsure what to do with me.

Gareth is staring, too. The two of them have by now completely stopped paying attention to the tour guide's words. Reverend Morgan is still listening attentively to the guide's commentary.

Samuel is still bored.

I think about that conversation Mum and I had at our dinner table at home. I remember how I'd said that I was afraid. Afraid to leave my parents and my border collie for more than a week to be with people I barely know. Afraid that Gareth would find that I'm not really the girl he thought I was. Afraid of everything about this trip.

And here I am. Right now. Afraid. But of something else.

Suddenly I lean forward and cover my face with my hands. I try to pray. I ask God to help me through this. I ask …

I feel Gareth touching my arm. Just a light touch. I pause in my prayer. I begin to realize, and to say to myself, that I must talk to Mrs. Morgan about the dreams. I don't have my mum and dad with me. But my family trusts this family, or we wouldn't have been allowed to come here at all. I look up at Mrs. Morgan.

I take a deep breath and say slowly to her, my voice shaky and uncertain, "I had two dreams last night, Mrs. Morgan, and I don't think … I don't think they were regular dreams. I think they were … the prayer-dreams.

"I think it has started again."

As soon as I've said this aloud, it becomes real. And it's too much for me.

"I thought it would be a really long time," I say, whining, helpless.

Suddenly I burst into tears.

It's ridiculous, but I can't stop. Immediately I'm sobbing, my face in my hands again, my hair falling forward and covering my hands.

Gareth and I are sitting beside each other, facing his parents and Samuel in the tour bus's "family seating" section. I feel Gareth get up and I realize without looking out from under my hands and my hair that he and his mother have changed places. She is now sitting beside me. She reaches around me with both arms, much as my mother did at the dinner table back home.

Mrs. Morgan hugs me tightly to herself and says nothing. She just holds me. And I realize that experienced mothers somehow know exactly how to do this … how to comfort a 14-year-old who is sobbing. No words.

As minutes pass, my sobs diminish. My breathing returns to something close to normal. I give a huge, ragged sigh and stop crying. I let my hands drop. I lift my face. My hair falls away from my face, and Mrs. Morgan pushes it back behind my shoulders, using both hands. She wipes the tears from my face with her hands. She pushes her own shoulder-length brown hair back behind her head, holds it in place with one hand, and places her ear next to my mouth. "Talk to me, Joanna," she whispers.

I see that Reverend Morgan has finally stopped attending to New York City and has focused his attention on me. Gareth, too, of course, though not Samuel.

My attention is now on the two dreams. And on Mrs. Morgan, whose small physical presence envelopes me.

"I was saying my prayers last night in my room," I begin softly, aware that only she can hear me, "when the first dream started, just like the first prayer-dream in Wales last month, when Flurry and I were together in the forest. And just like that first time, I couldn't tell when my prayer had stopped and my dream had started, or even if they were two different things. Maybe my prayer and my dream were just one thing. I'm not very good at this yet."

I feel her head nod at this. She understands. Not from personal experience, but from knowing how our family's visions have played through the story of British Christianity for a long time, before Samuel and I were born, and how my own prayer-dream visions of just a few weeks ago helped to save us all from something we could never have imagined.

"In the first dream," I whisper in Mrs. Morgan's ear, "I saw Dr. Cameron Stafford."

I feel Mrs. Morgan tense at this name. She can't help it. The name has meant evil to our family for a long time, and the Morgans have by now become as familiar with the name as we are.

"I saw Dr. Stafford," I continue, whispering so softly that I feel her pressing her ear yet closer to my lips, "dressed in the same gray suit and tie he wore the only time I have ever seen him in real life. He walked toward me in my dream, looking straight at me through his glasses, but still at quite some distance from me, and I could see that his wrists were bound in front of his waist in a pair of shiny, silvery handcuffs.

"He was smiling at me, Mrs. Morgan," I say, becoming terrified at the telling, just as I was during the prayer-dream and after I awoke. "He was smiling," I say to her again, "and it was just the creepiest smile I can remember seeing in my life.

"Awful," I say, shaking my head.

Mrs. Morgan nods her head, just a little nod, to indicate to me that she hears, and that she understands. "Yes, Joanna," she whispers softly.

We are both aware that neither Gareth nor my brother nor Reverend Morgan can hear a word of this exchange. But we both sense that this story must be told in secret. It can become a five-person secret later, when we are no longer on public transportation in the middle of the great metropolis.

I continue, still whispering. "I could see behind Dr. Stafford a lot of people. They were not distinct individuals. Just vague, shadowy figures. Some carried guns. Some wore ski masks.

"I don't know how many there were, and I only saw them for a few seconds. I just know that none of them seemed to be handcuffed. Dr. Stafford was; they weren't. They seemed to be his little army, and they were free to do whatever they could, under his orders, whether he was free or arrested, in prison or not in prison.

"Horrible, Mrs. Morgan," I whisper, again shaking my head. "Horrible."

I am quiet for several long seconds, trying to recover my wits enough to speak the second dream to Gareth's mum. She just continues to hold me, comforting, silent. I sense that Gareth and his father understand that this is something they are going to learn about later, but not now. Not on the bus.

My brother's attitude is always that, if someone wants to tell him something, they will. And then he will pay attention. He doesn't try to guess what people are thinking. And he may be conscious of the fact that I'm crying in Mrs. Morgan's arms, or he may not. Either way, he'll pay attention when I ask him to. My brother loves me. Truly he does, but he's just different in the way he shows it. Flurry is much better than Samuel at showing her love for me.

Finally, I gather myself enough to continue. "The other dream," I whisper to Mrs. Morgan, "followed along just after the first one, but it was somehow separate from it. I think it was, in fact, some of the same shadowy figures that I saw behind Dr. Stafford, but they were no longer trailing behind him. In fact, he was gone.

"They were standing beside something. They were standing beside something perfectly huge. A fortress or a castle. Something large and old and made of stone. And there was water in the foreground. Big water, like part of the ocean or an enormous lake. And then the handful of figures turned and went into the fortress.

"And that was all. Just shadows moving into a fortress on the shores of a sea."

I pause, thinking.

"I think that's all, Mrs. Morgan," I whisper.

4

The bus continues. Mrs. Morgan, after continuing to hold me for some time, returns to her seat next to her husband, while Gareth comes back to the seat beside me. I feel so pitiful I can't even pretend to look at anything. I just sit back, looking down at my hands in my lap, not talking. Hardly even thinking.

The Morgans, thoughtful people, ask me from time to time what I'd like to do. I just shake my head each time, like some perplexed six-year-old, and say that I don't know. I'm half blaming Mum for insisting that we come, and half blaming myself for deciding that this was the grown-up thing to do. Of course, I know very well that I should stop blaming anyone at all, and just stiffen my backbone.

In the midst of my pathetic wallowing in self-pity and self-blame and Mum-blame, Reverend Morgan does a surprising thing. He leans forward in his seat, which is facing mine, and looks carefully into my face. He smiles his nice smile and says softly, but not whispering, "Joanna, I know you've experienced something dreadful, and you've been brave enough to whisper something about that to Lily, and now I'm sure you must feel very much alone and very much afraid."

He pauses. I nod my head, but without smiling. I can't smile. My face won't do that right now.

"After all," he continues, "we are here in this foreign metropolis, an ocean away from your parents and your beloved border collie, and something is happening to you that you did not ask for and that you don't understand."

That's when I realize that Reverend Morgan just assumes that I had prayer-dreams last night, and that I have been telling Mrs. Morgan everything that happened in them. He knows that without being told, just from knowing what happened earlier this summer when my dreams first came, and from watching what just happened. I'm amazed and grateful. Gareth has such good parents. So do we, Samuel and I.

"It seems to me," Reverend Morgan continues, "that, if we just stay here on the tour bus, hour after hour, you're going to find yourself more and more swamped in fear and worry.

"So, let's not," he says brightly. "Let's get off the tour bus, see one or two things, and then take a taxi back to our apartment. Once we're there, Gareth and Samuel and I can hear what you've told Lily, if you're willing to tell us, and then we can form a plan and, I should think, get in touch with your parents. They can help us sort things.

"What do you think?"

I smile at Reverend Morgan — my face seems to be working again — and look down once more, thinking. After a moment, I look up and ask, "What about Mr. Belton?"

Reverend Morgan looks puzzled for a moment. I think he has forgotten. Detective Sidney Belton had said he would meet us for lunch, if we would give him the name and address of a restaurant, once we'd found one we liked. He'd said he'd come right over from his office in lower Manhattan once he'd heard from us.

I should have explained Mr. Belton earlier. He is almost a member of our family. He has been involved in all the visioners' episodes our family has experienced in the last 20 years or so, including the one last month in England. When my parents and grandparents first met him, he was a member of the New York Police Department. He is retired from the NYPD now, and owns a private detective agency here in the city with a companion from one of his earlier exploits.

That companion's name is Mr. Jaakov Adelman. I know that he was once an agent with Mossad, Israel's intelligence organization. I have never met Mr. Adelman, but I am told that he and Mr. Belton look funny together. Mr. Belton is very short, and, because he is nearly crippled from various injuries he suffered over the course of his long career, he walks with a cane. Mr. Adelman, I understand, is very tall and … well … elongated. Much like Gareth and I are, only more so.

After thinking for a moment, Reverend Morgan nods to me and says, "Yes, Joanna, of course. Let's find a restaurant and phone him from there. I'll look forward to that. Lily and I have never met him, you know."

Our tour bus is one of those you can get off and get on whenever you want. You buy a pass for the day, and a whole fleet of busses circulates through the city, each one with its own tour guide. You can get off, visit a museum or church or park, then go to the nearest pick-up point and continue with the tour on the next bus that comes by.

We get off our bus near Penn Station and Madison Square Garden, famous places in Manhattan that I have read about as part of our homework for this trip. As I step from the bus to the footway and start to look at the city again, I realize that, once I finished my teary, pitiful dream descriptions for Mrs. Morgan, I'd felt relieved and exhausted at the same time. And I'm still that way. I find I'm not sure if I want to continue the tour or go back to our apartment or just sit on the curb and cry. I'm just a miserable mess of a 14-year-old right now.

I move along the footway in a daze. The dreams still hang over me like storm clouds. My parents and my dog are on the other side of the ocean. My brother is with me, but he is in his own world, and doesn't yet even know I have had these new prayer-dreams. And that reminds me that I need to tell him.

Samuel *will* pay attention, once I start to tell him. He loves me and takes care of me whenever he knows I need taking care of. I just need to be alone with him for a few minutes, so that I can let him know.

Then, at least, he will stop drifting off to wherever he goes when he is bored. Probably, in his mind, to his last soccer match. Or his next one.

Suddenly Samuel grabs my arm and jerks me almost off my feet, dragging me violently toward a broad flight of steps that descend to the underground network of shopping corridors that, 50 yards on, become part of the train station itself … Penn Station. He pulls me so fast and hard that I can't think. I can't cry out. I can't even try to speak. Every ounce of me is concentrating on keeping my feet under me as we fly down the steps, dodging around people who are going up or down the steps. As soon as we reach the bottom, Samuel pulls me even harder and faster, darting this way and that through the dense throng of people.

I know this means that someone is chasing us, but I don't want to look behind us. I don't want to see who it is, or how many of them there are. Fresh memories of the ski-mask people in the forest in Wales flood through me. The ski-mask people who kidnapped our grandmother and chased Samuel through the woods. The ski-mask people who tried to shoot and kill Gareth and no doubt would have done to me whatever they could, had not we managed to escape, thanks in great part to the prayer-dreams that were sent to me then. My first visions.

I run as fast as I can, trying to keep up with Samuel, trying not to slow him down. Sprinting, we turn a corner and he immediately pulls me into the first store we come to. Still holding my upper arm in his grown-up man's grip, he pulls me, fast, to the high shelving that fills the center of the store. We stop behind one bank of shelves, and I realize we are in a toy store. We have stopped in an aisle filled with a variety of small stuffed animals.

I see that Samuel has found a line of sight through a space in the shelving, and he is staring intently toward the front entrance to the store. This is not the time to ask anything, and so I simply stand, breathing deeply, trying to recover from our desperate scramble from the street. Others in the store pay no attention to us.

That's the way of cities, I think to myself. London or New York or anywhere in the world. In big cities people just get accustomed to seeing strange behaviors and learn to pay no attention. The same behaviors in a small town like Carmarthen, in Wales, where Gareth lives, might cause an uproar.

Finally, without moving his eyes from the entrance of the store, Samuel says quietly, "Joanna, four men piled out of a stretch limo, wearing long coats and dark glasses, pointed at you, and started toward you at a run."

He glances at me and then turns his eyes back to the entrance.

"What's happened, Joanna? Tell me quick."

I follow his eyes to the front of the toy store and see two burly men wearing long, dark-colored trench coats — absurd in midsummer New York City weather — and dark glasses, speaking to each other and gesturing up and down the shopping corridor. One of them gestures at the door to our store as if to indicate he will search our store next.

Samuel grasps my hand. His grip is amazing for a 14-year-old person, yet he tries not to hurt me. He simply takes my hand firmly in his, spins me around toward the back of the store, and pulls me, hard, toward the fire exit. He is not slowed at all by the sign that reads "Alarm Will Sound." He blasts through the exit door and starts running, dragging me with him, racing along this back corridor and then up a flight of steps to street level.

I am so exhausted from my two prayer-dreams, from talking about them and sobbing in Mrs. Morgan's arms, and, now, from running so fast and long, that I have no idea whether the exit-door alarm did or did not sound. I only know that I am running as hard as I can to keep from slowing Samuel as he dodges across a side street, darting in and out of the flow of cars and trucks, finds a narrow alley, and, entering the long alley, sprints past overturned garbage cans, torn garbage bags, and piles of debris.

There are rats in this alley, I think to myself as I run. *Big, horrible rats.*

I don't see any. But I feel sure this is what rats would love most: dirt and filth. This adds one more layer to my distress.

Halfway down the length of the alley, we come to a small tributary that runs off to our right for a short way. Samuel pulls me into the miniature cul-de-sac, stops, and asks me for my cell phone. I unzip my little waist pouch that has room for my phone, some U.S. dollars, and my passport, and pull out the little device. Samuel places the two devices — his and mine — on the dirty concrete surface, picks up a tennis-ball-sized chunk of dislodged concrete and starts smashing our phones into bits.

I stand open-mouthed, unable to say anything. When he finishes, he throws some of the bits into a dumpster. Other bits he pushes into the front pockets of his jeans. He strides back to the alley proper, looks both ways, and gestures for me to follow him. I do.

When we reach the far end of the alley, he walks to a small pickup truck, sitting empty and idle at the curb. He pulls the cell phone bits from his pockets and tosses the bits into the back of the truck. Then he looks at me and says, "We need to get to Detective Belton's office, Joanna, whether he is there at his office or not. If he's gone, his partner may be there. Either way, that's the only safe place I can think of. You?"

I nod. I can't really think of anything to say or to suggest. My mind isn't running that fast right now.

He then looks away from me and stares at something across the street. I follow his gaze. I see that he is looking at a Goodwill store. A large sign on the front reads:

SECONDHAND CLOTHING AND HOUSEHOLD ARTICLES

5

Fifteen minutes later, we leave the Goodwill store and move generally south toward Washington Square Park, the neighborhood where Detective Belton's office is located, but we stay away from the main north-south arteries: Broadway, Fifth Avenue, Park Avenue. We have studied our Google maps carefully for days, both before and after our arrival here. This turns out to be a good thing, since we no longer have cell phones.

At the Goodwill store, I had purchased a dark-blue, lightweight, long-sleeved blouse to replace the purple and yellow shirt I chose to wear this morning. I doubt that my change of top will keep these people from recognizing me, but I could find nothing in the store to replace my knee-length, yellow, pleated skirt.

Nothing really fits me very well anyway, and I know that if I wear something huge just to change my look, I will become even more conspicuous. And I have no good way to do anything about my long hair, my "most distinctive feature," as my best mate at school, Trisha Cunningham, is always telling me.

Samuel had better luck than I did at the Goodwill store. He bought a pair of jeans that are brown instead of blue, and he replaced his red knit, collared shirt with a light-blue *I Love New York* tee shirt. He actually bought several of these, two of them in my size, for later use.

I should mention that there is nothing about his short brown hair that is distinctive. My brother is a very nice-looking teen, but he looks quite like many other average-height, brown-haired, brown-eyed, athletic boys.

With his brown jeans and blue tee, he really does look different from the boy who was running away from four men at Penn Station. But the fact that he is walking beside a too-tall, terribly awkward, ridiculously gangly teen girl with very long and very black hair doesn't give him much cover, as they say in the detective movies.

I still have not had a chance to explain to Samuel anything about last night's prayer-dreams, but I'm sure he already knows what *kind* of thing I must have dreamed, even if he does not yet know details. And even if he has not guessed any specifics, he certainly knows, as we all do, that just because Dr. Cameron Stafford and his closest accomplices were arrested in England a few weeks ago, and will stand trial there eventually, that does not mean that his organization lacks plenty of other terrible people who can act on his behalf. In fact, that very thought puts me in mind of my prayer-dream, the one that showed Dr. Cameron Stafford, handcuffed, with a legion of sinister figures walking behind him, none of them handcuffed or in any way under control of law enforcement people. Free to come at us whenever they choose.

And come at us they will, simply because our family has visioners: three of my four grandparents, my mother herself, and, to my great shock a few weeks ago, me, Joanna Clark. Yes. Come at us they most certainly will.

Now that our pace has slowed a bit, I give Samuel the highlights of last night's prayer-dreams. He is not surprised. He simply nods and continues his brisk pace, occasionally taking my upper arm or hand in his to keep me moving as fast as he wants to move. Not as fast as before, but fast.

Not everyone thinks that our visioning is a God-Thing, because not everyone believes in God. But, among our friends and even among our enemies, there seems to be a certain level of acceptance that we are given "special insight" into certain things that happen from time to time, things that matter a great deal. And, amazingly to me, Dr. Cameron Stafford and his people seem *certain* that we have this special insight. To me that means that they believe that our special insights are from God. But that belief somehow does not make them believers.

Very strange. They seem to believe God sends us special dreams, special messages, special warnings … and yet they embrace evil.

In any case, now that I have given Samuel the highlights of last night's prayer-dreams, I need for him to know that I need to go to a church and pray. And not just to any church. To a particular church.

Before leaving England, the Morgans had decided to take us to visit Grace Church, at 10th and Broadway, sometime during our New York visit. That's an Episcopal church, and I remember thinking it was so thoughtful of Reverend Morgan, pastor of a Methodist church in Wales, to plan to take us to visit an Episcopal church, knowing that those are so very like the Anglican church that our family attends in London.

"Can we get to Grace Church, down on 10th Street, safely, on our way to Mr. Belton's office?" I ask as we continue to walk east from the Goodwill store. "I need to pray, Samuel. I need to pray in *that* church."

He understands immediately. He nods quickly. "Yes," he says simply. Samuel nearly always understands me, often without my even saying anything. He is a wonderful brother.

As we begin our slight detour toward the church, I ask, "What do you think happened back there at Penn Station, Samuel? And Gareth and his parents … what should we think?"

We cross Broadway, traveling east before turning south, staying huddled within the masses of pedestrians. Once we reach 29th Street, with traffic going one-way in the other direction, he replies.

"Those men pointed just at you, Joanna," he says quietly as we walk briskly along. "They wanted you, not the Morgans. Probably not even me. They want the visioner, Joanna. They want to get you away from the rest of us."

I know this is true. That's what our enemies have always wanted. They have wanted to capture or even kill my mum, her parents, my dad's mum

… the visioners. We are always in their way. If they can get us, they can execute their plans much easier than if we remain free.

"Yes," I say, "but what do you think happened back there after you pulled me down the steps and into the underground corridors? What do you think the Morgans thought? What do you think they did? What are they doing now?"

The more I say, the whinier I become. I hate when I whine. But sometimes I just can't seem to stop myself. Right now, I keep imagining Gareth watching Samuel dragging me away with four strange men chasing us. I keep imagining how frightened he must be to see me chased like that.

Gareth really likes me. I'm not sure why, but I know he thinks of me as his girlfriend. He must be devastated right now.

And the Morgans! They feel completely responsible for us, of course. They asked our parents to let us come with them to the United States, and suddenly we are gone and in obvious danger, and they have no way to do anything to help.

After we navigate our Sixth Avenue crossing, still tucking ourselves in among the crowds of people, and continue east on 29th, Samuel finally answers my question. "Well," he says, "I'd think the Morgans would go to the nearest police officer and report us missing. And I'd think they'd phone London immediately, to let Mum and Dad know what happened.

"I also think their phone call will be heard and recorded by … our enemies."

"Won't the Morgans know that?" I ask.

"I really don't know how aware Reverend and Mrs. Morgan are of what technology can do, Joanna, and I don't know how aware they are of what our family has been facing for all these years … how danger always waits, not very far from any of our visioners, including you and Mum."

"But they know what happened a few weeks ago in Wales," I say, starting to whine again.

"Honestly, Joanna," he says, "I think Gareth knows a lot more about the danger and the history of it and the possible future of it than his parents do, and I'm certain he knows more about technology. I think it would be fairly easy for his parents to think of the events last month as a one-time thing. I can imagine their thinking that this trip would be a good way to move their family past it all, and to get back to normal."

I decide to think about this for a while, and so we walk without speaking for a very long time, crossing the large avenues while tucked in among the throngs, and sticking to the small west-to-east streets as much as we can. Finally, not far from the East River, we start south toward lower Manhattan.

Less than an hour after leaving the Goodwill store, we finally approach Grace Church from the east, along 10th Street. We find, as we hoped and expected, the church is still open from the noonday service. We unhesitatingly walk in and take our seats on the left, in one of the rear pews. The sanctuary is cool and, where we sit, near the very back, quite dark.

We sit close to each other, thrilled to be in the holy silence of the sanctuary. For long minutes, we just sit quietly on the wooden pew, soaking in the sacredness of the nearly 200-year-old church.

Eventually, starting now to feel calmer and stronger than I have since I sobbed on Mrs. Morgan's shoulder and we left the tour bus, I move forward onto my knees, letting my knees sink into the soft padding of the kneeler cushion, my elbows now resting on the back of the pew in front of us. I gratefully close my eyes in prayer, purposely not yet forming thoughts or words.

I'm a girl who always says *morning* prayers. And I sometimes say nighttime prayers, too, but not always. I did say nighttime prayers last night, which is when the prayer-dreams came. And, of course, I say little prayers of thanksgiving many times a day, and little prayers asking for help whenever I need to.

When I said my morning prayers today, I asked God for His help in knowing what to do about the two prayer-dreams I had had just hours before. I felt, after some time had passed, that I got an answer. A real answer. I felt I was to go to Grace Church, maybe today, maybe tomorrow, but soon — to this church Reverend Morgan had suggested, and which we had read about in our New York materials — to go here, where I am right now, and pray. And so, here I am, ready to pray, ready to listen.

I begin my prayer, thanking God for His greatness, for His mercy on us, for my family, for Flurry, for holding us in His hands. I continue for several minutes in this fashion, no longer aware of my brother's nearness, no longer aware of my fears, no longer aware of my worries for the Morgans.

And then, as I thought it might, barely perceptibly, it begins. In the cool darkness and quiet of the sanctuary, and in the quiet of my praying mind, I begin to sense the approach of the One Who loves us.

It's going to happen again. It's coming to me. Again.

If you have ever felt something overpowering coming toward you, then you know a little of what I mean. It's something that scares you and gladdens you at the same time, like your first day trying for a new team, or for a new choral group, or for a new drama production … something you've looked forward to and yet dreaded at the same time. Something you are so very excited about, and yet you think, just before the moment that it is to begin, *Why did I ever say yes to this?*

You know that the thing is going to be scary, but you allow yourself to hope that the experience will have good parts, too, and that you will learn new things that will make you wiser and better and readier for what the world will bring to you. And you hope not to fail. You hope not to disappoint yourself and the others.

Or, in this case, the One Who loves us.

So, this anticipation is like that, and yet it's not like that. It's not really *like* anything else at all, because it's what people call a God-Thing. I know that can sound a little irreverent, but I don't mean it so. A God-Thing happens when you know God's involvement is there. It's just so obvious, especially when you think back on it.

And when you experience a God-Thing, you experience something that can't be compared to anything else. You just know what it is. And it may scare you, and you may wish every second for it to be over, but you know when it's finally, truly over that you are, as I just said, wiser and better and readier for what the world will bring you.

And suddenly it is upon me. The Divine Intrusion, as Mum sometimes says. I have learned to recognize the sensations. I know what is happening to me, and I know what I am to do. I am to open my mind and heart to God and remember everything, every part of the prayer-dream. I know that the dream will be what our family will call "the data." It will become a set of Heaven-sent facts that will let us know how to think and how to act in whatever crisis comes to us. These Heaven-sent facts will shape our decisions and plans, if we will simply attend to them and not be too afraid to act.

And now it is here. Slowly, gradually, the image of a wall begins to form in my mind, seemingly inside my closed eyes. It's just a wall. An interior wall, of the sort you'd see in a Sunday school room, although I don't think this is really a church that I'm being shown inside my eyes. The wall, wherever it is, is light-colored, a soft white. It remains in front of my closed eyes. Just being itself. A soft white wall.

And then I realize that words are beginning to form on the face of the wall. I can't see how they are being formed, or by what. They just gradually come into focus, the block letters taking shape without anything seeming to cause them to be there. At first, they are indistinct, blurred. Then the focus sharpens.

And suddenly they are there. Sharp and clear. Three three-word commands.

I stare at the words. I know that I am to remember these words, without fail. This is what is required of me. And so, I simply concentrate, and I pledge to myself and to God not to forget and not to fail and not to change a single word.

ATTACK THE CASTLE

BAPTIZE THE SCRIPTURE

CLEANSE THE CHURCH

Chapter Two

1

When the prayer-dream ends, I find myself emptied. I can't keep kneeling, even though I want to, because my muscles won't work. I slump straight back onto the pew and then lower myself onto my right side, away from Samuel.

I close my eyes and pull my legs up onto the pew. Then I pull my knees up to my chin and fold up into a ball. I'm in a fetal position.

I'm certain that Samuel is looking at me, worried, but I just don't care. I can't care. I can't move. I can't reassure him. I know that the church is very dark and that hardly anyone is still present, and I am glad of that. But, even if the pews were full, it wouldn't make any difference. I feel sleep coming, overtaking me.

Blackness.

Suddenly I realize Samuel's hand is on my arm, shaking it gently. I try to open my eyes, but they won't open. I hear my brother's voice.

"Joanna," he says softly, "you've been asleep for more than an hour. We should leave. We need to get to Detective Belton's office."

My eyes open. I push myself up into a sitting position on the pew. I feel groggy. I rub my eyes and try to clear my mind.

"How long did you say?"

"More than an hour," Samuel replies.

I shake my head incredulously. *"Seriously?"*

"Yes," he says.

Then, after a moment, "What happened, Joanna?" he asks, a trace of urgency in his voice. "I know you've dreamed. What was it?"

The prayer-dream comes back to me.

"Oh!" I cry involuntarily. "Oh, Samuel!"

"What is it? Tell me now."

"The writing on the wall," I say. "The message."

I pause for a moment, pulling the words from my memory. I reach for the visitor's card and the pencil on the back of the pew in front of us. "I need to write this down," I say, "before I forget any of the words."

Samuel reaches out and stops me, gently taking hold of my wrist. "No, Joanna," he says. "No. You know what Mum has taught you. Never write your prayer-dreams down. Never record them electronically. Just remember them."

"Oh, right," I say. "If we are caught …"

"Exactly. Tell me the words," he says, "and two of us will have them."

I look at him.

"Three three-word sentences," I say. "Three commands, really."

He nods.

I say the nine words to him. He repeats them to me.

Then we sit beside each other in the darkness, etching the words into our minds. And thinking what they might mean.

Finally, Samuel says thoughtfully, "We need to get this to Detective Belton, Joanna, and then to Mum and Dad. But first tell me last night's dreams in more detail. Let me have everything. Tell me what you were whispering to Mrs. Morgan on the bus."

I do.

He listens intently until I finish. He nods again.

"Good," he says. "Now let's go. Right now."

Without wasting another minute, we get up from our pew, walk quietly toward the side doors near the altar, and find an exit. We push the door open and find ourselves in bright sunlight, at the side of the church. After taking a moment to sort our directions, we start walking again. Walking fast. We know from our family's experiences that prayer-dream messages demand immediate action.

After walking for 10 more minutes, we turn onto Washington Square North and approach the address we long ago committed to memory: the address of *Belton and Adelman Private Detectives,* as the agency is listed on their website.

As we turn onto the street, I see in the distance the tall figure of an elongated adolescent boy. I stop and gasp.

"Gareth!"

Samuel, stopping beside me, follows my gaze with his eyes and then smiles in Gareth's direction.

"Very impressive," he says admiringly to himself. "Very, very impressive."

"What do you mean?" I ask, looking at my brother.

"Not only did he memorize this address, Joanna, but he navigated a maze of New York City streets by himself to get here, on foot. That's good work."

Seeing Gareth turn his head toward us, I raise both hands in joyful greeting and resume walking — nearly running now — toward him. He waves and starts toward us. In seconds, we meet and he and I give each other an awkward, but grateful, hug.

Gareth and I are not good at any of this boyfriend-girlfriend behavior. Not a bit. But we do manage the hug without great embarrassment.

Samuel claps Gareth on the shoulder in his usual easy and athletic manner. Everything of that sort comes easy to my brother.

"How did you do it, Gareth? What route did you take?" asks Samuel, genuine admiration in his voice. But then he stops Gareth before he can answer.

"Wait," he says, "we need to get off the street. Let's get ourselves out of sight."

We arrive quickly at the address. I notice there is no sign on the door. Just the number. There is also a camera mounted well above the door. It points directly down at us, and so I assume Detective Belton can see us.

Samuel presses the doorbell.

Almost immediately a man's voice comes to us through a speaker, which I search for with my eyes, but can't find. The voice is not Mr. Belton's.

"Push the door open when you hear the buzzing," says the voice.

The buzzer sounds. Samuel pushes the door and we enter. We find ourselves in a small anteroom, no larger than a walk-in closet. The walls are bare.

We hear the same voice again.

"Push against the wall on your right."

We look to our right and see nothing but a plain wall. We hesitate.

"Push," repeats the voice.

Samuel pushes and the entire wall slides about two feet to the right, creating a small opening on our left. We still hesitate.

"Pass through the opening," says the voice from nowhere.

We do. An overhead light comes on in the small enclosure and the wall slides closed behind us. Then double doors somehow materialize from each side and close, covering the sliding wall entirely. We then hear a humming sound and we realize we are on a lift taking us up from the ground floor.

The lift stops after what seems to me a rather long ascent, considerably more than one floor. I recall having a sense that the building is three or four stories high, maybe more. When the lift stops, I find myself thinking we must be on the top floor.

The double doors open, and we see a very tall, middle-aged man staring at us intently from just three feet away. He strikes me as an older, taller, and even more elongated version of Gareth, just as I'd been led to expect. This is Mr. Jaakov Adelman, Mr. Belton's partner in this private detective agency. And I recall what I know of Mr. Adelman: that he is formerly an agent with Mossad, the nation of Israel's intelligence organization; that he and Mr. Belton worked together on a very dangerous mission when Samuel and I were babies; that they've saved each other's lives more than once; that they've been professionally inseparable since they first worked together.

Mr. Adelman is dressed casually in a black, knit shirt and lightweight khaki trousers. His hair is black and thinning on top. His nose is prominent, his lips are thin and seemingly set in a tight grimace. His eyes are black and deep-set, much like Mr. Belton's. He says nothing to us, but gestures for us to walk behind him into the interior of the office. He indicates that we should sit at a rather long conference table, and he asks if we would like water. All three of us, grateful for the offer, accept.

He strides gracefully out of the conference room. We hear him walking down a lengthy corridor. We hear the refrigerator door open and close, and then we hear him returning. He places three water bottles on the conference table, along with a speakerphone that he moves from a desk to the center of the table. He folds his lanky frame into a chair at the head of the table and, without any of the small courtesies that an adult often speaks in trying to place young people at ease, he looks squarely at me.

"Joanna," he says, tension in his voice, "have you dreamed?"

I am amazed. I stammer, "How … how could you know? "

"New York police radio is reporting a possible kidnapping from Penn Station a couple of hours ago," he says, speaking rapidly in slightly Israeli-accented English.

"The man reporting the kidnapping, whose British-accented voice I heard on the initial call-in, stated that two teens — a boy and a girl — were pursued by four trench-coated men, and that a third teen — another boy — fled the scene. I assume, young man," he says, looking at Gareth, "that the caller was your father.

"Sidney and I knew you three were here in New York, of course, and Sidney expected to rendezvous with you and the Morgans in early afternoon, for lunch. Not only has the rendezvous not happened, obviously, but two hours ago Sidney pressed the alarm on his Scotland-Yard-issue mobile. When that device transmits its emergency signal, it displays its location for five seconds and then electronically wipes itself clean.

"I consider my partner, the closest friend I've ever had, to be missing," he says, his voice quavering slightly, just in the instant that he speaks the word "missing."

"And I can only assume," he adds, "that whatever has happened to Sidney has something to do — no, *everything* to do — with your presence here in the city, Joanna, and with your being pursued by those four men at Penn Station.

"So," he says, now speaking sternly, and directly to me, "I repeat: have you dreamed, Joanna?"

I then tell him, speaking rapidly but, I hope, leaving out nothing, of all three of my prayer-dreams. The Cameron Stafford dream, with the handcuffed Dr. Stafford trailed by armed men wearing ski masks. The fortress-dream, with some of the ski-mask people moving into a fortress-like structure, and with part of an ocean or a large lake visible in the foreground. And now the word-dream, with three three-word commands.

I tell him everything. I see Gareth staring at me and hanging on every word, and that reminds me that he has heard nothing of the dreams I told his mother, and that he was not even aware of the third dream that I received an hour ago in the church.

As I speak, Mr. Adelman jots notes in a small, spiral-bound notepad. He asks me to repeat the last dream, so that he can be sure he has written the nine words correctly. "Is that all?" he says to me, looking at me with his piercing, nearly black eyes.

"Yes, sir," I say.

He shakes his head angrily. "I knew this was a mistake," he says. "You're a visioner now, Joanna. You can't just travel around unprotected any longer. I told Sidney that if you were to come here, your uncle Luke should be with you every step of the way. I *told* him! This trip was foolish."

I see my brother's face change. "*I'm* with my sister, Mr. Adelman," says Samuel, attempting to match Mr. Adelman's anger with his own.

"*I'm* with her," Samuel says again, "and, as you see, she is fine. Safe. Secure. I'm with her every step of the way, Mr. Adelman. And there was no way our parents could have guessed that, with Dr. Stafford and his people under arrest back in England, we'd be in danger here in New York. This was *not* foolish. You're wrong!"

Mr. Adelman smiles indulgently at this. "Samuel," he says quietly, "what do you think your uncle would have done at the sight of four large men materializing at Penn Station and moving menacingly toward your sister?"

Samuel thinks for a moment and looks down at his hands. "He would have, um, disabled them," he says thoughtfully.

Samuel looks up at Mr. Adelman. "He would have broken their faces. All four of them. And without needing to use a weapon. There would have been no need at all for us to run."

Samuel looks down, then, after a moment, up again at Mr. Adelman. "I still don't think that our parents were foolish, sir, but you're right that if our uncle had been with us, things would have been different."

Samuel now looks embarrassed. He looks uncomfortably at me, then back at Mr. Jaakov Adelman.

"I'm sorry, sir," he adds.

Samuel tugs at his right ear, his one nervous habit. I reach over and give his other hand, resting on the table, a little pat. Just a little pat that says to him that I love him and that I know he just wants me to be safe, and just wants me to be as safe with him as I am with our uncle.

After a moment, Mr. Adelman speaks to Samuel.

"I apologize for using that word 'foolish,' Samuel," he says. "Your parents are always careful with you. And with Stafford and some of his henchmen incarcerated, you're quite right that your mother and father could not have foreseen any of this.

"I'm just terribly, terribly concerned about Sidney, you understand," he adds. "But now that you are here with me, I no longer have to worry about you three young people. And that's a very good thing.

"You've done splendidly, Samuel," he says kindly to my brother. "You acted fast and decisively. You got your sister out of there and not just safely away from those four brutes, but all the way from 31st Street on the west side of the city to this office in lower Manhattan and on the east side of the city. That's an incredible achievement. Your uncle and your parents will be immensely proud of you.

"Now ... next steps."

2

My head is swimming.

In the last three hours, so much has happened. On the secure line in the detectives' office, Mr. Jaakov Adelman quickly placed a call to Mum and Dad's mobile devices and found that, to my surprise, they were already moving forward with their emergency-action plans. It turns out that Mr. Belton's distress signal from his Scotland-Yard-issue mobile device not only alerts Mr. Adelman here in the two detectives' New York City office, but also, via satellite, our parents' mobiles and our uncle Luke's mobile, too, over in England.

I didn't know any of that.

Mr. Belton's mobile generates an alerting indication to those other mobiles, those that are set up to receive that kind of signal. It transmits an emergency indication before it self-destructs electronically.

Mr. Adelman tells us that, when the signal was received here in the office, the device was transmitting from the southwest corner of Central Park. He immediately drove his auto to that location, but the drive from here, in lower Manhattan, to Central Park, through New York City traffic, takes a long time. Once he arrived there, he talked to everybody he could find, including some of the vendors, but no one could help.

Our parents and our uncle assumed that Mr. Belton's alerting signal must have had something to do with us, and so they instantly launched one of their many contingency plans. Our parents and our uncle are always ready. They know the evil never goes away completely. It comes back.

So, by the time Mr. Adelman had returned from his search for Mr. Belton, and by the time Samuel and I got from Penn Station to Grace Church to Mr. Belton's and Mr. Adelman's office in lower Manhattan, and found Gareth already here, and by the time we then contacted our parents and our uncle from the secure transmitting device here in the office, the four of them — Mum and Dad and Uncle Luke and his wife, our aunt Kory — had already driven from London to the lodge in Birmingham, a 90-minute drive. Our mother's and our uncle's parents — our grandparents on our mother's side — have lived at that lodge for decades. Mum and Uncle Luke grew up in that lodge.

To Mum and Uncle Luke, "the lodge" is home.

Our parents and Uncle Luke and Aunt Kory have "go bags" ready all the time. All they do is grab those bags and, of course, Flurry, who has her own "go bag" containing her food and her water bowl, and they're gone.

The lodge is a working hotel outside the city of Birmingham, situated well beyond the edges of the city itself. The lodge rests on a high hilltop, has a formidable, 360-degree wall with electronic surveillance cameras and motion detectors everywhere, a guardhouse at the base of its hill, and complete underground living quarters modified from a World War II bomb shelter. It is also home to a 130-pound German shepherd named Max, who is great friends with my 40-pound Flurry, always gentle with her and with our family, but a fierce presence in the face of an enemy.

In emergencies, all paying guests of the lodge are instructed to depart immediately, something that is part of the agreement they sign when they choose to come to the lodge in the first place. I would guess they will all be gone by early tomorrow morning, London-Birmingham time.

Mr. Adelman allowed us to be part of his conversation with Mum, Dad, Uncle Luke, and Aunt Kory — a "secure communications exercise," as Mr. Adelman puts it — and we were surprised and grateful to be included. Some of their conversation I could not follow, and I knew better than to ask. But one of the topics that included all three of us teens had to do with Gareth and his parents.

Gareth feels terribly guilty about running from the scene back at Penn Station, and he is miserable about the fact that his parents don't know if he is safe. Mum, Dad, Uncle Luke, and Aunt Kory feel badly for him, but they are not receptive to his request that he be allowed to contact them.

They gently reminded Gareth, several different times and in several different ways, of something we all know and feel in our bones. One of Gareth's own uncles either fired a rifle at him, or permitted that rifle shot, in Wales, just a few weeks ago. Gareth is not himself a visioner, but he is not safe. He is by now so closely associated with our family that our enemies would no doubt like to be rid of him almost as much as they would like to be rid of us, the actual visioners. In his clearest moments he knows this. So do his mum and dad.

The truth is that anyone close to us is in danger almost as much as we are. And, now that I think of it, that would include Detectives Belton and Adelman.

And if something has happened to Detective Belton, who has been part of our visioners' battles from the start, then that's why. And here is one more thing I should mention about that secure communications exercise. When the grown-ups were talking about our enemies' purposes, aside from eliminating the visioners and those close to them, Mr. Adelman asked Mum if she had dreamed, just as he had asked me, when Samuel and Gareth and I arrived here at the office. Mum said no, she had not. Then he asked her if she had an idea as to why our enemies appear to be moving against us right now, if Mr. Belton's emergency alarm means what we think it does.

Mum said that she would guess that the same plan we just defeated, temporarily, a few weeks ago in England, might still be underway. She guessed that that plan might still be alive and well, even though Dr. Cameron Stafford and those who were with him in England and Wales are in jail and awaiting trial. Mum reminded Mr. Adelman that Dr. Stafford's plan was really an update of his original plot 15 years ago, when our family first faced him, and that there were probably plenty of accomplices that could move forward with the plan, even without Dr. Stafford.

"Remind me, Rebecca," Mr. Adelman then said to Mum.

"Fifteen years ago," she said, "Dr. Stafford and his people were developing reading texts for American children, texts designed to destroy children's sense of right and wrong simply by placing ideas into their basic reading books.

"It's so hard, Jaakov," Mum continued, "for reading texts to be content-neutral, you know. They have to be *about* something."

"Yes," he said.

"This summer's plan was much like the old plan, but updated," she continued. "It had two paths. One was in the direction of electronic games that would accomplish the same sort of thing: corrupting children's sense of right and wrong by what was rewarded in the format of the games."

"Yes," he said again, "I remember the general approach. Filling the children's reading material with stories that assume one choice is just as good as another choice … that it really doesn't matter how you think or what priorities you have or what habits you develop. It's all the same as long as you can make yourself feel *comfortable* with your choices and your behaviors."

"Exactly," Mum replied. "The other path involved several versions of a graphic Bible that would eliminate all references to God or to anything supernatural. One level was for very young children; a second level, for older children; and a third level, for young adults. These would have shown Jesus Christ, for example, as just another teacher with a large following. Nothing miraculous. Nothing about Resurrection. Nothing about His being the Messiah. Nothing about His being our Savior.

"Dr. Stafford's new plot, judging from what we discovered earlier this summer, seems to be better financed and better organized than the old one, and it appears designed to be electronically based, worldwide, and multilingual.

"I'd guess, Jaakov," Mum concluded, "that other members of Dr. Stafford's organization, over there with you in the United States, are moving forward as if nothing has happened. And in a way, nothing has. Evil has always had many soldiers in its army."

This is where Mr. Adelman looked at me and raised his eyebrows. I knew what he meant. He was asking me if I wanted to report my prayer-dreams to Mum and Dad and Uncle Luke and Aunt Kory as part of our secure communications exercise.

I nodded, and he gestured to the speakerphone on the table. I leaned toward it and started to speak. I was surprised how relaxed I felt doing this in front of Mr. Adelman and Samuel and Gareth, but I was.

"Mum," I said, my voice not trembling like it does so often when I'm speaking and other people are listening to me, "my prayer-dreams started again last night. Two of them came during the night, and another one came this afternoon when Samuel and I spent time praying in Grace Church. And the first one may have hinted at exactly the kind of thing you just described."

I went on to summarize my three dreams: Dr. Stafford in handcuffs followed by many shadowy figures, none of them in handcuffs and all of them seeming to follow him, ready to do his bidding. Then the fortress-looking structure with, possibly, some of the very same followers standing to one side of, and then moving into, the fortress-building, and with a large lake or part of the ocean in the foreground. And finally, the word-dream with the nine-word set of commands. And I spoke the words for them:

ATTACK THE CASTLE

BAPTIZE THE SCRIPTURE

CLEANSE THE CHURCH

Mum and Dad, and Uncle Luke and Aunt Kory were quiet while I spoke. I knew they were looking at each other, sitting at a table like this one, somewhere in the lodge on the other side of the Atlantic Ocean, giving each other the kind of meaning-filled looks people give each other when they have lived with and loved each other for a long time. For Mum and her brother Luke, that would be all their lives, because they are twins, just like Samuel and me. For Mum and Dad, that would be for nearly 20 years, when they first met, right there at the lodge.

Mum broke the silence after what seemed a very long time. "Jaakov," she said tensely, "take us off speakerphone. Young people, please go to a different part of Mr. Adelman's office, so he can speak to us without needing to decide what ideas and plans you three should hear and what ideas and plans you should not."

3

We leave the windowless conference room, and Mr. Adelman closes the door behind us, after gesturing toward the long corridor that leads to the office's small kitchen. The cramped kitchen has a window next to the refrigerator, and I see bright sunshine and am reminded that here in New York, it is still afternoon. In England, it's probably dark by now.

We prepare to sit down at the kitchen table. Gareth tries to pull my chair out for me and it scrapes noisily, then catches on a crack in the linoleum.

I've told you we are not good at any of this, Gareth and I. Samuel averts his eyes at our clumsy effort at trying to achieve lady-and-gentle-man manners. Finally seated, I smile up at Gareth, wanting him to know I appreciate his thoughtfulness. He looks away, embarrassed again.

And that's how we are. Continually embarrassed that we like each other, that we are boyfriend and girlfriend. Sometimes I think we will never get better at this.

The two boys take their seats, too, at the small round table. Gareth and I both look at Samuel, since he is the one who plans fast and first, but he just looks back at me. That's a signal that he thinks that I ought to address something before any real planning is attempted. And I see that he is right.

Samuel and I often have no need to use words. This is one of those times.

I turn my eyes to my boyfriend. "How do you feel, Gareth?" I say gently. "How do you feel about what happened back at the train station?"

He drops his eyes and is silent.

Samuel and I wait. Mum has taught us to wait, once we have asked a question that may require the other person to think for a little while

35

before replying. We have learned not to fill the air with noise, and just to give the person his time to think.

Finally, Gareth looks up at me and smiles his little smile. For the longest time, when we were first together at the start of the summer, I never saw his teeth. He seemed not to want his teeth to show, but when he finally smiled big enough for me to see them, I realized he has very fine, white teeth. I don't know why he usually smiles without showing them.

Maybe that's just part of being shy.

"Well, Joanna," he says thoughtfully in his careful way, "I feel … ashamed … at how I was back there. When Samuel grabbed you and ran, I looked around and saw what he was saving you from, and I froze. I was petrified.

"When those huge men chased you both down the stairway, I just ran away. I couldn't even think about what I *should* do. I just ran. I didn't think about Mum or Dad, or about helping you, or anything at all.

"I just ran. I ran south, but without thinking about my direction. I just kept running until I couldn't run any longer. When I finally stopped to think about where I was, I began to realize I was probably no more than an hour's walk from this address, which, of course, all three of us memorized before we left England.

"But I didn't come directly here. I began to be afraid in a new way. Not afraid of the men that chased you, but afraid to see you or anybody at all, because I'd been such a coward. Such a terrible coward.

"But I finally realized I didn't really have a choice. This was the only place to come to, the only place that made sense. I knew I'd be safe here. We're all safe in this place, but maybe nowhere else."

Gareth stops. He looks down at his hands as they rest on the tabletop. He shakes his head sadly.

I reach over and pat his hand. I feet silly doing that, but I feel right to do it, and so I decide not to be embarrassed this time. I just pat his hand and then pull my hand back and place both of my hands in my lap. I look up at Samuel.

Samuel returns my look, and then looks over at Gareth. Samuel shakes his head, just as Gareth did, but I know this means something completely different. My stomach gets tense. I know Samuel is going to scold Gareth. I can see what's coming.

"Gareth," Samuel begins, "all that self-pity is just *stupid.* Think about it.

"What about your actions a month ago in Wales, in the forest? You moved forward, in the dark, *on your own,* to help me and Uncle Luke rescue our parents from armed fighters. Those people had guns, and they were trained to use them.

"Yet, by yourself, you moved in the dark toward the danger. And by yourself, you got Dr. Stafford's briefcase away from him, the briefcase that had most of the secrets to Dr. Stafford's plots.

"And before that," Samuel continues, staring at Gareth in his you'd-better-pay-attention-to-me way, "think what happened in Swansea, after you'd been *shot at* by your own uncle, when you simply took over at the guardhouse, and made the guards understand that they should allow us onto the property at Mr. Jonathan Murphy's shipping and import-export business site.

"There are so many things you've done just in the short time we've known you, that are not the things cowards do, Gareth. So stop it!"

I decide to step in before Samuel gets too carried away.

"Gareth," I say quickly, "Mum and Dad would say that when we're suddenly surprised by something, we usually do what our habits lead us to do. In Wales last month, in the forest, in the dark, you had time to *think* about what you wanted to do … what you felt God wanted you to do … what you felt we all needed you to do.

"And then you did that. Exactly that.

"Your dad would call that being obedient to God. So would my mum. So would most thoughtful Christian people.

"Today," I concluded, "you were surprised and you ran away. Samuel didn't. But Samuel has had lots of practice in being obedient to God's expectations, under all circumstances, and so, when he is surprised by something, he doesn't need to stop and think for a while. He is practiced in doing the Christian thing, all the time.

"You — and I, too, Gareth — need to practice. We just need practice. Do you know what I mean?"

Gareth smiled his no-teeth-showing smile again. He looked down for several seconds, thinking. Then he looked up at us both.

"Yes," he said, still smiling. "Actually, I think I do."

4

In the calm that follows Gareth's response, we suddenly realize we are famished. We promptly raid the office refrigerator, although we find little that our school nutritionists would approve of.

We don't care. It all seems good enough to us. Basic sandwich-making ingredients, the usual things you'd find in a refrigerator belonging to two people who probably don't cook. I say a short blessing for us, and then we happily consume our very late lunches.

As we eat, happily silent, I take the opportunity to study my boyfriend's face. He still looks worried to me, still distracted. So, as we finish eating, I ask him to talk to us again, even if he doesn't really want to. He sighs and agrees.

"I'm so worried about my parents," he says. "They don't know where I am. They won't understand why I haven't contacted them. They don't really understand about the danger that goes with making mobile-phone contact when people have electronic means of finding out where you are.

"I can't think what I should be doing."

At that exact moment we hear the conference-room door open, and we hear Mr. Adelman striding down the corridor toward us. He stops at the kitchen door and looks at the remains of our sandwiches. He seems surprised that we have raided his refrigerator, but, after a moment's reflection, he seems pleased that we have made ourselves at home. I get the sense that Mr. Adelman gives little thought to food, and I know from experience that Mr. Belton gives none at all.

"We've reached decisions, young people," he says after a moment.

Looking alternately at me and at Samuel, he then says, "Your uncle Luke, Max, and Flurry will be on the next Royal Air Force overnight flight from RAF Brize Norton Station in Oxfordshire, home to the RAF's strategic and tactical Air Transport arm, to Dover Air Force Base in Delaware. With the time change from England, the flight will land about 3:00 a.m. in Dover. An unmarked military police SUV will be ready for your uncle's use for as long as he needs it. Luke should arrive in this area around sunup. I expect he and the two dogs will be here at the office before 7:00 a.m."

My jaw sags. I stare at Mr. Adelman in disbelief.

I look at my brother and see a smile beginning to cross his face, followed by a broad grin. I look at Gareth and see a reflection of my own response: disbelief.

All three of us look back at Mr. Adelman, who continues, speaking to Gareth.

"The twins' uncle, whom you met, Gareth, in Wales last month, is a Royal Navy reserve officer with connections both to the Royal Navy and to the Royal Air Force. He also has a sterling reputation — make that a *legendary* reputation — well earned during his active duty days, that stands him in high regard in both countries' forces. He has arranged this kind of thing before, Gareth, and, no doubt, he will again. The only novelty this time is the dogs, but military transport aircraft can haul anything up to the size of a medium tank. No problem to add 170 pounds worth of dogs.

"We considered," Mr. Adelman continues, now speaking to all of us again, "which members of the family should come, because we were in agreement that at least one of them needed to be here with Joanna and Samuel, and quickly. We knew from Sidney's alarm signal that there must be a new crisis, and that was, obviously, reinforced by the attempt to kidnap you, Joanna, earlier this afternoon.

"We know now that you, Joanna, are selected to provide visions in the crisis. We want someone from your family here with you.

"Your mum desperately wanted to be the one to come, but we all know that no one can match your uncle Luke as a combatant, which is what we need right now. And, Joanna, your mum can receive visions no matter where on the earth she may be, and, if she is also sent visions in the new crisis, she can communicate with us via the secure communications network here in the office."

We three continue to sit silent, trying to absorb this news, this news that none of us even dreamed of. And Flurry! My Flurry!

I'm overwhelmed.

For a moment I don't even realize that Mr. Adelman has started speaking again. I try to catch up.

"And we have a safe house," he is saying, "over in the Red Hook district of Brooklyn. There is a park — Coffey Park — near the safe house. That will give you a place to walk Max and Flurry. We'll move you three over there sometime tomorrow, after your uncle and the dogs arrive here in the morning."

We still stare at Mr. Adelman, speechless. This is all so unexpected. We thought we'd be riding on the top of double-decker busses every day, gawking at the New York City sights. We never imagined …

But Mr. Adelman is speaking again. Once more, I try to catch up.

"And so, Gareth," he is saying now, "since your parents went straight from Penn Station to the nearest police precinct station, I'm headed over there now to pick them up. We've agreed that they need to be here, in this office, or in the Brooklyn safe house, for the duration of the crisis. Here in the office, we've got sleeping rooms on the floor just below this one. I'll be using one of the rooms, but they can occupy one of the others. They'll be safe.

"There are also rooms for each of you on that same floor. And then, tomorrow, all six of you — you three, Luke, Max, and Flurry — will move over to the Red Hook safe house, which has more space, more room for the dogs, access to a park, as I mentioned, and a full kitchen. You'll bunk there until the crisis ends, whenever that turns out to be."

I look at Gareth and see delight on his face and relief in every fiber of his body. He closes his eyes and bows his head, and I realize his first impulse is to pray.

So is mine. I close my eyes and begin a silent prayer. *Father, thank You! Thank You for bringing us here to this place, safe and secure. Thank*

You for leading the Morgans to safety. Thank You for Mr. Adelman and his great skill in helping people like us. Please give us the wisdom and strength to do Your will in this crisis, and to help Mr. Belton in whatever way we can. Please care for Mr. Belton. Keep him safe. Help him.

And thank You, Father, for my brother and his bravery and his great love for me. Thank You for Gareth and his sweetness and … his, um, love … for me.

Please be present, be present with us, Father.

I pray in the name of the Lord Jesus. Amen.

I keep my eyes closed in the silence, certain that the other three are saying their own prayers of thanksgiving, too. I then find myself wondering if Mr. Adelman's silent prayer might be in Hebrew.

I decide to ask him, when everyone finishes. And we all look up, it seems, and at each other, at the same time.

"Mr. Adelman," I say, "do you pray in Hebrew?"

Surprised at the question, he gives me his first real smile, a genuine, wide, glad smile. "Yes," he says. "Certainly. Always. From childhood."

"Would you teach me some Hebrew prayers?" I say hopefully, completely forgetting for the moment that we are in the midst of crisis and that my questions about praying in Hebrew are just plain silly. My relief that our uncle and the dogs are coming, and that the Morgans will be safe, simply overcomes everything else in my brain.

"No time for that now," he says, still smiling, "but I know a certain Methodist minister, closely related to Gareth, who must be well versed in Hebrew."

He and Gareth share a smile at this reference to Gareth's dad.

"After this, ah, little problem we're facing is all settled," Mr. Adelman says, "that is, after we know what has happened to Sidney … after we have recovered him from … from whatever has happened to him, then perhaps Reverend Morgan would agree to give you a few lessons, Joanna."

Gareth and I look at each other and hold each other's gaze for what seems a long time. And I realize that, for once, we are not embarrassed.

Interesting.

Chapter Three

1

It's nearly noon. All of us seem to have slept reasonably well in the detectives' sleeping rooms last night, including the Morgans. We were so incredibly relieved to be together and safe that sleep came quickly for us all.

All of us, that is, except possibly for Mr. Adelman. His partner and best friend in the world, Sidney Belton, is missing. I don't know if Mr. Adelman slept at all, nor, if he did sleep, where he slept. Maybe in the lounge area just off the conference room, where there are several sofas. They're too short for him, probably, but maybe workable.

My morning prayers today were filled with thanksgiving for all God has provided, just in the past two days. And exactly as I finished getting dressed, I heard the elevator whirring, and I ran from my sleeping room just in time to greet my uncle and Flurry and Max as they stepped out of the elevator.

What a reunion we had! I don't know when I have felt such joy, holding Flurry in my arms again. She was quivering with happiness, and she still is, hours later, sitting beside me here in my uncle's unmarked SUV.

I'm sitting cross-legged in the very back. The vehicle is midnight black. Its windows are heavily tinted. This car makes me feel like we are on some top-secret and very dangerous mission.

And I suppose we are.

Flurry and Max are here in the back with me. Flurry and I don't take up much room. Max takes up quite a lot, but he tries to be thoughtful and not step on us with his huge paws when he paces around.

Uncle Luke is at the wheel. Samuel is in the front passenger seat. Gareth is sitting on the back seat, just in front of me. Uncle Luke's gear is wedged into the space next to Gareth. Uncle Luke's gear always includes a variety of weapons and tools. The weapons may sometimes include some sort of firearm, but he has a strong distaste for using guns in his work of protecting our family. He uses his hands and, if absolutely necessary, his array of knives, clubs, ropes, and straps when he has to fight. When he was in the Royal Navy, he led boarding parties that forced their way onto pirate vessels and other boats and ships carrying illegal material. Guns were not of much use.

He was very, very good at that, and, as Mr. Adelman explained to Gareth yesterday, is still well known and respected in the Royal Navy and in the U.S. Navy, too. Our dad was also a naval officer, when he was young, but he did not do the kind of fighting Uncle Luke did. In any case, when Uncle Luke is with us, I feel completely safe, even when I probably shouldn't. Right now, I probably shouldn't, but I do.

Uncle Luke has just found a parking spot along the edge of Battery Park at the southern tip of Manhattan. As I sit sideways with Flurry in the SUV's cargo area, I can see all of New York Harbor, just in front of me. We are here because Uncle Luke wants to exercise the dogs in Battery Park, before we cross the East River into Brooklyn.

Once we are in the Brooklyn safe house, he has explained, he does not want to go out again until he has conducted what he calls a complete reconnaissance of the neighborhood, including Coffey Park, where we expect to exercise the dogs every day and every evening. Here in Manhattan, Uncle Luke has circled around and through Battery Park several times, maneuvering through its intricate roadways, just to make sure our SUV has not been followed. But, no matter, he will not allow the boys and me to leave the vehicle until we get to Brooklyn.

We are content, though, Samuel and Gareth and I, together in the SUV, knowing that the Morgans are safe in the detectives' office building, and that we are in the hands of our family's best fighter and protector. And I have my Flurry, finally.

My hands on Flurry's head, and her eyes looking at me, so trusting, it's just the happiest thing I know. Flurry's presence also helps me forget that I have not changed clothes since yesterday, and that my hair is even more of a disaster than usual.

I truly like having such long hair, and, with Mum's help, it can be wonderful. But now, not only is my hair in a terrible mess, but I'm still wearing my Goodwill store blouse over my own clothing, and still wearing the same skirt I put on yesterday morning. I know how vain I'm being, and I know that my embarrassment is mostly because Gareth is with me, but I admit that I do try hard to look nice around him. I can't look beautiful, because I'm not, but I can at least look presentable.

Usually.

When we get to the Brooklyn safe house this afternoon, I'll be able to clean up and put on the new clothes that an NYPD policewoman has been charged with purchasing for all three of us. She came by the detectives' office early this morning and measured us, so she could get something that might fit, no matter how imperfectly. Very thoughtful, this police department, and I know it has everything to do with the fact that Mr. Belton served for so many years with these same people, and that they respect the work he and Mr. Adelman do.

My gaze floats across the scene — the park, the people, the ferryboats purring across the choppy water of the harbor — not really focused on anything. But suddenly my eyes grow wide and I gasp.

"Oh!" I exclaim, without meaning to.

"Oh, my goodness!" I say, also without meaning to.

All eyes, including the canine ones, turn to look at me. Then all eyes, *except* the canine ones, turn to follow my gaze. While Flurry and Max continue to stare at me, the rest of us are staring out into New York City's teeming harbor.

"What?" says Samuel from the front seat. "What is it?"

"It's my fortress!" I say breathlessly. "It's my dreamed-about fortress!"

We all stare across the harbor toward a small island. There, perhaps half a mile away from us, stands an enormous fortification, circular in shape, its sides dotted with what I take to be gunports, and exactly matching my dreamed fortress. The four of us stare, silent, at the structure. I rest my hand on Flurry's head to reassure her that there is nothing she needs to be alarmed about. Max has already begun to pace again.

I realize in seconds that Uncle Luke is on his secure mobile.

"Jaakov?" I hear him say into his mobile to Mr. Adelman back at the detectives' office. "What is this fortification we're looking at right now from Battery Park? It's on the northwest corner of a small island in the harbor. It appears to be early 1800s construction. Circular. Sandstone. Rectangular gunports. Joanna says it matches her dreamed fortress exactly."

He listens.

"Castle Williams on Governors Island?"

He listens again.

"Yes," he says, "my thoughts exactly. Joanna's second dream of the fortress with armed people guarding it. And then her third dream, the first command she was given: Attack the Castle."

Uncle Luke listens again.

Finally, he says, "Can you get schematics of the interior of Castle Williams over to our safe house in Brooklyn within the hour?

"Yes? Excellent."

Then, after a moment, he adds, "And Jaakov? You'd better bring the schematics personally, and be prepared for action. Tonight. Yes. Without question. Tonight."

And he clicks off.

That's when I know that Detective Belton is going to be rescued. Tonight.

I look at Max and see that his body is tense. He is staring at Uncle Luke. I think he actually understands that action is coming. And I realize that I would very much not want to be one of the people keeping Mr. Belton captive.

Not tonight.

2

It's almost midnight. The four of us — Samuel, Gareth, Flurry, and I — are huddled in the small, darkened living room of the Brooklyn safe house. The safe house and Coffey Park, where we exercise the dogs, are just a short distance from the eastern edge of New York Harbor, where Governors Island almost touches Brooklyn. The channel between the Brooklyn shoreline and the southeastern corner of Governors Island — Buttermilk Channel — is narrow, and, although Uncle Luke expects the current to be swift, the distance is small for the inflatable raft that he acquired this afternoon from a military supply store. He, Mr. Adelman, and Max left us about an hour ago.

Our uncle and Mr. Adelman spent much of the afternoon pouring over the schematics of the inside rooms and passageways making up the interior of Castle Williams. Then, once full nightfall had descended over Brooklyn, they took all of us to Coffey Park to let the dogs run. As soon as we returned, the two of them prepared to "Attack the Castle," as my third prayer-dream had directed. When they went out the door to get into the SUV, the two men were dressed all in black, with black shoe polish on their faces, and with bulletproof vests under their lightweight, black jackets.

Max, too, wore a bulletproof vest. He was quivering with excitement and eagerness once the vest was cinched into place.

Now we are sitting in a small circle on the floor of the living room, each of us wearing the new clothes that the policewoman bought for us earlier today. She did well, and we think we look nice in them. She explained that she is the mother of a boy and a girl about our ages, and so she just bought the kinds of things her own children wear.

I'm wearing a dark skirt and a pale yellow blouse, and I've had time to wash my hair and set it in a long ponytail, which is the only style I can really do by myself. The boys have on jeans and collared knit shirts.

I find I am extremely nervous. This entire venture is based on the assumption that my prayer-dreams are true. That they are, in fact, Divine Intrusions, as Mum says.

But what if they are just dreams? It's obvious they are not just *ordinary* dreams, but that doesn't necessarily mean they are messages directly from God. What if I am endangering our uncle and Mr. Adelman and Max — and maybe even Mr. Belton somehow — with something right out of my own imagination? Something with no connection to reality at all?

I remember asking Mum, at the end of our first set of episodes last month in Wales, why she thought Divine Intrusions would come to me when I'm so young, when *her* first visions came to her in her 20s, at a time when she was at least 10 years older than I am now. She said that, in our case, the evil had come to get *us* — to get Samuel and me — and so the prayer-dreams had needed to come specifically to one of us.

Dr. Cameron Stafford had pledged, she reminded me, when he had been sent to prison the first time, that he would come after Mum and Dad's *children,* once he was released. We had been just babies then, but he eventually attempted to do exactly that, just as he had said he would.

But why now? Why are the visions coming to me now, when, apparently, it is Detective Sidney Belton who is in the first line of danger? A tiny, high-pitched groan escapes me. I didn't mean for it to. It just did.

I begin to realize that the other three with me in the darkened living room heard that little noise and have begun to stare at me. Flurry moves closer, snuggling against my side, looking up at my face. Samuel reaches over and pats my knee. Just one little pat, but he continues to stare at me.

It is Gareth who speaks.

"Joanna," he says quietly, "it's going to be all right, you know. Compared with so many of the rescues and adventures your uncle and Mr. Adelman have undertaken, this one is simple. For them, I mean."

My brother looks at Gareth and shakes his head no.

"Joanna knows Uncle Luke and Mr. Adelman and Max can handle the mission, Gareth. That's not what's worrying her. Not really."

Both of them look at me inquiringly.

I shake my head.

"No," I say miserably, "it's not. I'm just so afraid that my dreams might not be true, or might be only partly true, or that we might not interpret them right.

"I mean," I add, my voice unsteady, "the three of them are going to that fortress with no evidence from any source other than me. They know the layout of the interior from those schematics, but they don't know how many guards they'll find, and they don't know exactly where Mr. Belton might be held, or, really, if he is there at all.

"I'm just so afraid I've sent them into danger and that somehow it's all wrong."

I say this last in my whiniest voice, the one I hate as soon as I hear it coming out of my mouth. I look down and cup Flurry's face in my hands, peering into her trusting eyes and hoping I'm worthy of her trust.

The boys are quiet for some time. We remain seated on the floor in our little circle. Finally, Gareth does something unexpected. Without rising to his feet, he scoots himself over — awkwardly, as always — until he is right in front of me, facing me, cross-legged in his new jeans. He reaches out and takes both my hands from Flurry's face and holds them in his.

This is a new thing for us, as girlfriend-boyfriend behaviors go. We have not purposely held hands like this, ever. But he seems to do it almost as naturally as Samuel would, if *his* girlfriend were here and terribly worried about something.

I blush immediately, of course. I look down at Flurry, as if she might help me. But I don't pull my hands from Gareth's.

"Joanna," he says as quietly as before, if not more quietly, since he is much closer to me now, "you dreamed of something very specific last night, and then, maybe 12 hours later, you saw, in the harbor, the exact thing that you dreamed. And the thing that you saw — Castle Williams —

was something you'd never seen and did not know existed. That doesn't just happen, Joanna.

"And then," he continues softly, "the first three words of the message-dream suddenly made sense, in the context of Mr. Belton's emergency signal and disappearance. All of that, combined with last month's episode — what you dreamed and what we then found in Wales last month — no, these are truly your prayer-dreams, Joanna. They are obviously authentic. We *know* they are the prayer-dreams, and so does the enemy. And that's why we need this safe house.

"You can be worried about your uncle and Mr. Adelman and Max, but you need to stop worrying about whether or not your prayer-dreams are true, Joanna. They *are* true. They just are."

A prayer then starts up within me, as soon as he finishes, and without my even thinking about it. I bow my head and carefully pull my hands from Gareth's. I fold my hands together and put them under my chin.

"Heavenly Father," I begin so softly that I know the boys can barely hear, *"we ask Your protection for our uncle and for his friend and for our Max. We ask that You hold each of them in Your hands and bring them back safe to us this night."*

And then, without any conscious thought on my part, the 17th-century words and phrases from our prayer book flow from me, and I hear my voice getting stronger with each word: "Stir up thy strength, O Lord, and come and help us; for thou givest not alway the battle to the strong, but canst save by many or by few."

And, after a long pause to let those words bring their full weight to us here in this small, darkened room, I conclude: "This we pray in the name of Your Son, our Savior, Jesus Christ. Amen."

3

Flurry is the first to know that the rescue party has returned. She noses me awake and I immediately hear the mechanical whirring on the ground floor of the garage door as it opens, accepts the SUV, and then closes. I quickly grab the new robe the policewoman purchased for me yesterday and pad downstairs barefoot, still tying the cord around me, hurrying through the dining room and into the kitchen. The kitchen clock reads 2:25 a.m.

Flurry and I wait in the kitchen while the men and Max exit the SUV and collect their things. The door from the garage to the kitchen finally opens and Max trots into the room, head and ears up, still in protect-and-attack mode. He stops briefly, sniffs and listens, and then visibly relaxes, having concluded that the house is safe.

He then moves to Flurry, who has been waiting at my side, and they touch noses. They quickly move together to a corner of the kitchen and sit, relaxed but alert, waiting for any instructions that might be coming.

Detective Sidney Belton is next to appear, his cane clumping along just in front of him, Uncle Luke and Mr. Adelman just behind him. Mr. Belton sees me start toward him and immediately holds up his hand as a stop sign.

"Stop right there, honey," he says in his deep, rumbling voice. "Feel like I haven't had a bath in 15 years. Feel like I haven't shaved in a month. Feel like I'm the grubbiest detective in th' history of th'world. Don't even *think* about givin' me a hug.

"Ya know what I mean, kid? Hm?"

"Yes, sir," I say, smiling at his calling me "honey," since he doesn't do that with just anybody, "but are you all right, Mr. Belton? Are you hurt?"

Uncle Luke answers for him.

"Joanna, he has been handled roughly, but I don't think he has actual wounds that need attention. We just need to get him to bed right now. You and he can talk in the morning, or in the afternoon, if that's when he is able."

Mr. Belton stops, and turns to face my uncle. I should make clear what a comical pairing these two are, as they face each other at close range. Mr. Belton is in his sixties, but looks much older. My uncle is in his forties, but looks much younger.

Aside from the actual and apparent age difference, Mr. Belton is a stooped, partially disabled gnome of a human being who has endured terrible injuries in his long career, first in the military and then on the police force. In contrast, my uncle is probably the most physically imposing person you'll ever see, with enormous biceps and a huge chest, his muscles actually bulging through almost any clothing he happens to wear, even heavy winter coats. He is not more than a few inches taller than Mr. Belton, but he appears to be at least twice the detective's size.

When Mr. Belton turns to face Uncle Luke, however, you'd think their ages and their relative size and strength might be the reverse of what I've just said. It is the older, smaller man who seems to want to threaten the younger, larger man. Mr. Belton picks up his heavy cane — which I happen to know is also a weapon — and taps my uncle on his chest with its curved handle.

"You listen here t' me, Mr. Big Shot Navy Hero," he says in his funny Brooklyn accent, "you and Jaakov, here, might need t' go t' bed and get some rest, because you're both namby-pamby mama's boys, but not me. I got intel in my head and in my boot camera that we need t' look at and talk about right now, tonight, without any foolin' around and restin' and sleepin' and doin' lazy things that'll put us behind in th' game we're playin', because th' game we're playin' is in full swing right now, and we gotta get ahead of these dirtbags and we gotta get goin' and wipe 'em out before they do any more mischief.

"Ya know what I'm sayin', Mr. Big Shot Navy Hero? Hm? Ya know what I mean?"

Uncle Luke breaks into uproarious laughter, as does Mr. Adelman, standing just behind him. And I smile happily, knowing that this is the way Mr. Belton usually speaks to people he likes and cares about.

Flurry and Max, hearing the laughter, relax still further. Max lies down and Flurry lies down beside him.

Mr. Belton next turns and limps — he always limps — into the dining room, where he sees there is a medium-sized table. He pulls out the chair at the head of the table and, slowly and painfully, sits down. Then he looks back into the kitchen at my uncle and Mr. Adelman.

"Well?" he says loudly. "We gotta get started here. We don't have time t' sit around starin' at the walls. Let's get goin'."

My uncle looks at me as he starts toward the dining room.

"Joanna?" he says, giving me a look that says, without any spoken words, *Can you help us, please?*

"Yes, sir," I say, and I get busy right away looking for refreshments in the tidy safe-house kitchen. It's good, I think to myself, to have a job to do, even if it's just finding and serving refreshments. And maybe I'll get to hear something about what Mr. Belton has learned, and about what kinds of things might be recorded in his "boot camera," whatever that may turn out to be.

4

The kitchen clock now reads 3:25 a.m. I've been sitting on a stool in the kitchen for an hour, listening to the men talk. Max and Flurry are both curled up and sleeping on the living-room rug just on the far side of the dining room. Neither of the boys has awakened, despite the fact that the men have not kept their voices particularly low.

I'm not sleepy, even though I only slept a few hours before Flurry nosed me awake when the garage door opened. I've been riveted to this conversation, which the men are allowing me to hear only because, I think, they have forgotten I'm here.

Mothers don't forget. But neither Mr. Belton nor my uncle nor Mr. Adelman has children. They easily forget that a 14-year-old is within earshot. So, once I had served the refreshments and taken a seat on my stool, just out of sight of the dining-room table where they were talking, I was completely out of their world. As a result, I've been treated to a treasure trove of things I might never have been told.

There *are* things that 14-year-olds should not overhear. I do know that. But, it seems to me, since I'm the visioner on whose reports this whole operation has been organized up to this point, I need to hear the outcomes of this rescue.

That's what I tell myself, anyway.

So, here is what I learned in the past hour.

First, the rescue of Mr. Belton went smoothly. The crossing of Buttermilk Channel in the inflatable was quick; the quarter-mile walk across the darkened island to Castle Williams was uneventful; and the long-unused, 200-year-old fortress itself was practically unsecured. A few snips with Uncle Luke's bolt cutters, and they were almost immediately in the only area in which a hostage could reasonably be held: a small cluster of meeting rooms near the center of the structure.

No guards were present.

At the start of this discussion, an hour ago, Mr. Belton explained to my uncle and Mr. Adelman that his kidnappers planned for him to be held in Castle Williams just last night and tonight. Early this morning he was to be moved far away from New York City. He did not know where. He just knew that his kidnappers did not put overnight guards and electronic protection devices in place because they expected to be gone from Castle Williams long before anyone would be able to formulate a guess as to where he might be held. They were complacent.

This last bit made me proud. If I had not been given my three prayer-dreams, and if I had not reported them right away, and if my uncle had not, because of my report, flown to the United States last night, and if we had not moved immediately to rescue Mr. Belton tonight, he would no longer have been at Castle Williams. He might have been taken anywhere in the whole world.

I am so thankful.

I also learn that, when Mr. Belton's captors left the castle last night, locking him in his room for what they thought would be just a few hours, he removed the tiny boot camera from the heel of one of his shoes and, once he had picked the lock and entered the main conference room, he had photographed a number of documents that had been left carelessly on a table.

"These dirtbags," he said to my uncle and Mr. Adelman, "weren't their first-string dirtbags, I can tell ya that. Th' only thing they did well was t' snatch me and get a blindfold on me. Other than that, they were not even varsity material. They didn't even go t' th' trouble of knockin' me out or puttin' earplugs on me, so not only could I hear their voices plain as day, but I could hear when we crossed th' East River into Brooklyn, prob'ly on the Brooklyn Bridge.

"It's easy t' know you're on a big bridge. Th' car noise sounds hollow or somethin'. And I knew we weren't crossin' the Hudson River — th' bridge we used wasn't that long — or th' Harlem River — th' bridge we used was a lot longer than that — and so, when we got into an inboard motor boat that night and went from a Brooklyn shore-point to a landing in less than a couple minutes, I knew just where we had t' be. We had t' be on Governors Island. Easy. Easy as eatin' a piece of cake.

"And these dingbats were unbelievably careless in their little chats with each other. It was like they were children; ya know, like they thought that, since I couldn't see because of my blindfold, I couldn't hear either! They actually talked about th'fact that I'd be there just two nights, and that 'th' boss' would be there before sunup the second night — that would be a couple hours from right now — and would take me so far away that nobody would ever know anything about my disappearance.

"And then, t' top off their stupidity, they put me in a room with just a regular lock on the door, like there is any regular lock I can't pick in about 15 seconds. So, last night, when they all left at about midnight, I just picked that pathetic little door lock and went right into their meeting room. I photographed everything they left on th'table, but haven't tried t' look at any of it yet.

"When I finished, I just went back into my room, put my blindfold back on, and planned t' get a little sleep before they came back this mornin'. Now, let's see what we got here in this little camera, gentlemen. Maybe some pretty good stuff."

Now, an hour later, I have stayed awake and I have listened quietly to their discussion of everything the photos showed. Several things stand out.

For one thing, there is a scripture verse that will be the public slogan for this whole plot. It's the lovely Old Testament verse in Micah, chapter 6, verse 8, which says, "What doth the Lord require of thee, but to do justly, and to love mercy, and to walk humbly with thy God?"

I hear that verse and I think of the second command from my last prayer-dream:

BAPTIZE THE SCRIPTURE

A second thing that stands out is something about a new kind of church, one called The Church of the New Century. There did not seem to be much in the document photographs that explained what this new church would be.

But when I hear this, I think right away of the third command from my last dream:

CLEANSE THE CHURCH

And then the three of them had a long, long discussion about the fact that there is nothing illegal about selecting a certain scripture verse for a slogan, or about starting a new church. There are, when you think about it, a million things people can try to do to hurt Christianity — to weaken it or distort it — that are not in the least against the law. But our enemies have always attempted to hurt the faith by any means they could, including doing many things that are very much against the law.

Among the clearly illegal things our enemies tend to do is, first, to try to kidnap or injure or even kill those of us who are visioners, because they know that God will lead us to place all sorts of roadblocks in their way, and, second, to break laws having to do with money. They break laws, for example, in the way they get money to produce the books or games or programs designed to corrupt the faith. They steal; they embezzle; they threaten families; they kidnap; they torture. They are willing to murder.

Mr. Belton and Uncle Luke and Mr. Adelman talk for a long time about the need to find out everything possible about the money that will finance these projects, these perfectly legal projects that Mum explained on the phone to Mr. Adelman when we got to his office just two days ago. She talked about our enemy's creating electronic games for children and young adults that will destroy their sense of right and wrong. She talked about their creating a series of graphic Bibles for young people, Bibles that will eliminate all references to God and the supernatural. She talked about these projects being better financed than the previous ones, being mostly electronically based, worldwide in scope, and multilingual. And now we have the completely new ingredient of launching a new church that will, it seems obvious, sponsor and sell the electronic games, and sponsor and sell the graphic Bibles.

All of that, and all perfectly legal.

At 3:45 a.m., while it is still dark, the men finish their session and get up from the dining-room table. After they have risen from their chairs, and are still collecting their materials, I move off my kitchen stool, tighten the belt on my new robe, and walk casually through the dining room. I head for the stairs to go up to bed, motioning for Flurry to come with me.

As I walk past them, the men look at me like I'm from another planet.

"Joanna!" Uncle Luke exclaims when he recovers from his astonishment. "What on earth! Have you been there in the kitchen all along?"

I smile back at him from the foot of the stairs. "No, sir, Uncle Luke," I say brightly.

"Ya heard everything we said, didn't ya, ya sneaky 14-year-old dirtbag kid?" says Mr. Belton, his lopsided grin giving away the playfulness of his gruff accusation.

I smile still more. "Why, no, Mr. Belton," I say sweetly. "I've been sound asleep, sitting on that stool in the kitchen. I haven't heard a single word you've said.

"Except," I add, still smiling and starting up the stairs with Flurry, "a few things about Micah 6:8 and The Church of the New Century and some interesting things about money … just a few things like that … nothing important.

"Good night, everybody," I say cheerily.

As Flurry and I continue up the stairs, I hear Mr. Belton say to my uncle, "Your sister is gonna kill ya, ya know, Luke. She's absolutely gonna kill ya."

"Yes," replies Uncle Luke miserably. "Yes, detective. Rebecca is *absolutely* going to kill me. It's just a matter of time."

Mr. Belton and Mr. Adelman laugh gleefully.

5

It's noon. We're just finishing a cold-sandwich lunch in our Brooklyn safe house. Reverend and Mrs. Morgan arrived just before lunch, driven over from the detectives' Manhattan office by the same policewoman who bought clothes for us yesterday. Mrs. Morgan, always so thoughtful, had asked the policewoman this morning to go by our Manhattan apartment and pack our own clothes in our suitcases. She did, and so when they arrived at the safe house, so did our luggage with most of our own clothes.

My morning prayers were pretty sleepy, since I went to bed — for the second time last night — after four o'clock and was awakened at six, not on purpose, by Mr. Belton, as he clumped around with his cane, getting ready to go to an early mass at the nearest Catholic church. He never misses, he says, because he's "no good" unless he starts his day in church.

I feel the same about my morning prayers, even though I say them in my bedroom before I even get dressed. I usually read something from our church's devotional material, then some scripture passages, then I give some thought to the people I want to pray for on that day, and some thought to the people and things I'm especially grateful for, and then I do my prayers.

Since I was so sleepy this morning, I didn't take very long with my prayers. If I'd kept my eyes closed any longer, I'd have been asleep, and I knew I needed to get up and let Flurry and Max out in the backyard.

One of the first things Mr. Belton did when he got back from church was to give all of us a set of prepaid disposable phones — burner phones — so that we can communicate with each other without our locations being traced by our enemies. He also gave two of them to Reverend and Mrs. Morgan, as soon as they arrived for lunch.

I find I'm surprised at how quickly I've gotten out of the habit of checking my mobile for messages. Usually I do that a dozen times a day, or even more. Suddenly, once Samuel smashed our mobiles and the things were just gone out of existence, I didn't seem to miss looking at mine. Some habits go away quickly, I suppose, especially when the choice is obliterated, the way Samuel obliterated ours.

Lunch is not quite over, and Uncle Luke and Mr. Belton are just completing, for the benefit of the Morgans and of Samuel and Gareth, their summary of last night's action and of the early-morning follow-up discussion that I listened to from my kitchen perch. They take pains to explain to the Morgans why law enforcement officials, on both sides of the Atlantic, tend to stand aside during these episodes that involve our family's visions. Whether individual police and detectives among them believe that our visions are God-Things or not, they have had enough experience over the years to know that we somehow have special connections with *Something,* and that that *Something* provides us with information that can't be found anywhere else or by any other method.

That, and the fact that Mr. Belton is so respected worldwide by law-enforcement people, lets us operate with the cooperation of police sometimes, but without their participation unless we ask for it. These burner phones and this safe house and the policewoman who bought our clothes and drove the Morgans to Brooklyn this morning, all those are examples. And the police *not* getting involved with the rescue of Mr. Belton from Castle Williams last night, because my uncle and Mr. Adelman were sure they could do it safer and better, is an example, too.

As my uncle and Mr. Belton and Mr. Adelman bring the Morgans and the boys up to date on events, I occasionally make a small contribution or even a small correction to my uncle's and the two detectives' report. I think that when a person is just sitting and listening, as I was, and not a part of the conversation, she may hear what is said more accurately and more completely than those who are part of the discussion. If you're part of the discussion, you're often thinking about what you're going to say next.

I wasn't. I just listened.

So, when Uncle Luke said that Mr. Belton never heard any reference to who, or what group, might be in charge of the enemy operation, and when Mr. Belton did not comment on that or correct that statement, I raised my hand, just like I would in school. My uncle stopped in midsentence.

"Joanna?" he said inquiringly, just like a good teacher probably would.

"Well," I say, a little embarrassed to be correcting my uncle in front of everyone, "Mr. Belton did mention that his kidnappers said that 'the boss' would be here — at Castle Williams — before sunup this morning, and that he, or she, I guess, would take him — Mr. Belton — so far away that nobody would ever know anything about his disappearance. I thought that might mean that 'the boss' is not a local person, and that 'the boss' might even be based somewhere other than in the U.S.

"Just a thought," I say, dropping my eyes and blushing, even more embarrassed to have suggested something about the location of the enemy leader's headquarters than I was simply to interrupt my uncle's presentation.

The group is silent for what seems a long time, deepening my discomfort. I think maybe they're thinking that my suggestion is ridiculous. I look up to see my uncle and the detectives looking at each other and nodding slowly, thoughtfully.

Finally, my uncle looks at me and says, "That's brilliant, Joanna!" And immediately most of the others turn and smile and nod their heads in my direction.

I, of course, just look down at the table and blush even more, hoping Uncle Luke will quickly continue his presentation and that everyone will turn their eyes back to him. After some time, when I think that, hopefully, no one is looking at me, I raise my eyes and find that no one is. Except Gareth. He nods his head at me and raises his eyebrows, as if to say, "Nice work, Joanna. Very impressive."

I smile again and drop my eyes. And I think to myself, *That's the kind of thing Samuel and I do so often. We just look at each other and know what the other is thinking or imagining or wanting to do. Are Gareth and I going to reach a point where we communicate, even without words, as well as my brother and I do?*

While I'm thinking about that, Uncle Luke, is, of course, finishing his presentation, and discussion begins. After just two or three comments,

Mrs. Morgan turns to me and says, "You know, Joanna, I'm just realizing that Cecil and I have not heard anything in detail about the third vision that Luke and our detectives have been making reference to. You told me everything about your first two dreams when we were still on the tour bus two days ago. But it sounds as if your third prayer-dream was in Grace Church, hours after we got off the tour bus. Should we not hear?"

My uncle is apologetic. "So sorry, Lily and Cecil. I had not realized.

"Joanna," he says, "would you mind?"

And so, I describe the third dream, and carefully state the three three-word commands that I was given. When I finish, I see Reverend and Mrs. Morgan look at each other, the kind of look couples give each other when they are, together, realizing that they have just heard something important that they, and maybe only they, completely understand.

"Joanna," says Reverend Morgan after a moment, "do you assume there may be a connection between those photographed documents' showing the Old Testament verse in Micah as our enemy's public slogan, and the second command in your prayer-dream: *Baptize the Scripture?*"

"Yes, sir," I say. "That was my first thought, in fact."

"Well," he replies, "as I think you all know, Lily and I have a ministry in the port village of Swansea, not far from our home in Carmarthen, Wales. We conduct services and lead Bible studies and literature studies for the employees of Mr. Jonathan Murphy's import-export business there. He employs nearly a thousand Welsh men and women, and we've had a thriving ministry there for years."

"Yes," I add quickly, "and that's the building complex where we found safety when Gareth was shot at by his uncle or his uncle's partner last month. Gareth made the guards understand that you, Reverend Morgan, were his father, and that Mr. Jonathan Murphy would be glad to receive us."

"Right," adds Samuel. "It was so great when Gareth had the guards call up the Morgans' church website on their computers, and had them look at Gareth's photo right there, a picture of him with one of the youth groups at the church. Gareth was *great.*"

Now it is Gareth's turn to look embarrassed, which he dutifully does. And I return the smile and nod he gave me earlier. I think we're getting better at this.

Reverend Morgan continues. "That scripture verse — Micah 6:8 — is the official Bible verse of Mr. Murphy's import-export business."

Silence immediately descends on the group. It continues for minutes.

We're all thinking the same thing. Is it remotely possible that our enemies' public slogan, from Micah, shown in the photographed documents, which happens to be the same core-value slogan used in Mr. Jonathan Murphy's import-export business in Wales, is connected to the command in my prayer-dream: *Baptize the Scripture?* Is it remotely possible that the suggestion I made minutes ago about Mr. Belton's overhearing his captors say that "the boss" was going to take him so far away that no one would ever find him, and the implication that that might mean that enemy headquarters are not in America, might actually connect to Mr. Murphy and his business in Wales, which happens to be the host site for one of the Morgans' ministries and which happens to be the refuge that was provided for us last month when we were being pursued by those murderous men?

All those connections! Is it possible, really possible, that they *all* intersect?

After the long, long silence, Mrs. Morgan clears her throat and then looks at us young people and asks sweetly, "Joanna, Samuel, Gareth? Would you like to take Max and Flurry out for a walk in the park?"

We know, of course, that this just means the adults want us out of the way so that they can talk about whatever they think they should, including speculation about our enemies, speculation that they think we should not hear. And I would guess that the Morgans are going to resist the idea that Mr. Murphy himself could be implicated in anything evil. They are very close to him.

Mrs. Morgan is probably right, though, that the next conversation should not include us. And, in any case, I'm glad to have a chance to get outside. New York City's July is hot, but much of Coffey Park is, we know, well shaded.

And Flurry and Max do need to get out.

Mr. Adelman rises from the table, saying, "I'll go with them."

We all know Mr. Adelman is armed. Without fail. That's why, outside his office, he wears a lightweight sport coat even in the midst of summer. The sport coat hides the shoulder holster and the powerful military handgun he carries.

We feel safe in Mr. Adelman's company. Maybe we shouldn't, but we do.

6

We've been here in Coffey Park for almost an hour now. The dogs have been exercised nicely, and now the two of them and the three of us are sitting or lying on the grass under one of the park's best shade-providing trees. Mr. Adelman is standing about 30 yards away, watching.

His eyes never stop roaming the park and the approaches to the park. I don't think a squirrel moves without his noticing. We know he is on guard for us, and we know he is staying far enough away so that he won't overhear us. He wants to respect our privacy without getting so far away that he can't move to protect us, if necessary. In his own way, he is just as thoughtful as Mrs. Morgan, always conscious of us and where we are, and always wanting us to be protected and comfortable and happy.

"What do you think, Gareth?" Samuel is saying. "You know Mr. Murphy pretty well, I think? Could he be our enemy? Is that possible?"

Gareth thinks for a moment, then says, "Yes, he could.

"I don't think it is *likely* that he is our enemy, but I remember what Detective Belton said about him last month in Wales, don't you?"

Samuel shakes his head no.

I nod my head yes.

"He said," Gareth continues, "that many powerful people are good when that suits their interests and bad when *that* suits their interests. Remember?"

"Oh, yes," Samuel replies, "actually, I do. That was when Mr. Belton showed up at Mr. Murphy's corporate headquarters in Swansea in the middle of the night with six or eight law enforcement officers, and whisked us away to Carmarthen."

Gareth nods. "Yes. And he also suggested that a lot of good people work for an employer who is all shades of good and bad, but the employees often have no idea whether the person at the top — the chief executive — is good, bad, or good in some ways and horrible in other ways."

"Yes," I add, "that was when we told Mr. Belton how good one of Mr. Murphy's assistants had been to us. She called herself our zookeeper. She was so thoughtful."

We then sit silent for a while, just thinking about all those connections that bubbled up at the end of our noontime conversation in the safe house. Finally, Samuel turns to me and asks, "You've never seen Mr. Murphy in any prayer-dream, right?"

"Right," I say. "The only person I've seen in my New York City prayer-dreams — the only person I've seen clearly enough to know who it is — is Dr. Cameron Stafford, not Mr. Murphy or anyone else I actually know. But there are, you know, quite a few people in the background of the first dream and in the foreground of the second dream. They're just shadowy figures, dark and blurry.

"They could be anybody. Anybody at all.

"And," I add after a moment's thought, "I've never even seen Mr. Murphy. Not even a photo of him."

We fall silent again, none of us quite comfortable with all these possible connections. None of us quite sure how to think about any of this.

I feel myself starting to get scared again. Not quite *seized by distress,* but on my way there. I look at Flurry, whose eyes are closed, as she lies on her side several feet away from me. I pat the grass next to me.

Flurry opens her eyes and immediately gets up, moves over next to me, and nestles close. After a moment, her eyes close again.

I put my hand gratefully on her furry head and close my eyes. My prayer starts automatically: *Father, hold us in Thy hands ... in Thy hands ...*

Chapter Four

1

It's nearly 11 o'clock on a moonless night. We're back at Coffey Park on a day that seems to have started a week ago, when Mr. Belton unintentionally woke me after I'd been asleep two hours, clumping around the safe house with his cane, getting ready for his early church service. Now, as with our early-afternoon visit to this park, it's the three of us, and Max and Flurry, and Mr. Adelman, and, this time, my uncle, too.

Since Mrs. Morgan was kind enough to bring our clothes to us when the policewoman brought her and Reverend Morgan at noon, we have changed clothes. The boys are wearing their jeans, and I started to wear mine, but when I realized late this afternoon that Mrs. Morgan was working to prepare a real dinner for us, I decided to wear the pretty blue dress I brought with me from London, to wear to church and for restaurant meals in New York.

It's simple and knee-length, sleeveless, a shade of light blue, but with a faint, darker blue vertical stripe that you can barely see. Mum thinks it makes me look even taller than I am, and I'm not sure that's a good thing, as skinny as I am, but she thinks I need to get accustomed to being tall. She wants me to be comfortable with my height.

I'm also wearing my nice sandals. They're dressy enough to be worn with my blue dress, but they're comfy, too.

When Gareth saw me as I came down the stairs for dinner, he stared. Then he blushed, of course. So did I. But he did manage to compliment me, and I did manage to accept the compliment without too much awkwardness.

Tonight, I thought about changing out of my dress to come with everyone to the park, but it seemed a lot of trouble, so I've kept it on. Now that we're here, I'm wishing I had changed into something else. We're running around with the dogs, and I'd be more comfortable in my gym shorts, even though they expose my much-too-skinny legs. My jeans would have been just right.

Coffey Park is roughly square. It might be about the length of a football field — that is, a soccer field — in each direction, but the part that we use with Max and Flurry is less than that, maybe as long as a playing field, but only half that wide. Our half has fewer trees, which is why we picked it for exercising Max and Flurry.

We've spread out around the edges of our section, which forms a rectangle. Mr. Adelman and my uncle are at each end of the rectangle, Samuel is on the side nearest the street, and Gareth and I are facing Samuel, on the opposite side, nearest the trees and the hard-surface oval that occupies the center of the park.

Using several orange-and-black road-marker rubber cones we found in the safe-house basement, we have laid out a course for the dogs to navigate, one that requires them to run in something other than straight lines to earn the healthy treats each of us is carrying for them. They learned the little course this afternoon in no time. German shepherds and border collies are just unbelievably intelligent.

But after almost 20 minutes of unceasingly racing from one of us to the other, dodging through and around the little cones, both dogs begin to get bored. These animals know the difference between actually working — herding or guarding, for example — and simply running for exercise. Seeing them losing interest, we set about adjusting the position of the cones so as to create a new set of challenges.

There are a number of street lamps placed at regular intervals throughout the park, so that, despite the absence of moonlight, we are never in complete darkness. And so, as I'm changing the position of one of the cones, I'm able to see that my uncle, 50 yards away from me, has stopped to look closely at a van that is moving slowly along the street near where Samuel is stationed.

Suddenly Uncle Luke shouts, "Samuel! Run to Jaakov!"

Without hesitation, without looking around to find the danger, my brother instantly begins a hard sprint toward Mr. Adelman, who, I see immediately, has drawn his gun from his shoulder holster. The weapon is pointed down, but Mr. Adelman is looking steadily at the van.

I look back at my uncle and see he is sprinting *toward* the van, which is still moving slowly along the street near Samuel. I feel Gareth grab my hand. He starts to pull me toward Mr. Adelman, who is 50 yards from us in the direction away from Uncle Luke. I grip Gareth's hand as hard as I can.

"Run, Joanna!" he says, but I already am.

Meanwhile, the dogs have started their own sprints, each in opposite directions. Max lives at the lodge in England with my mum's parents, Elisabeth and Jason Manguson. But Uncle Luke has done much of Max's combat training, and, in this situation, Max regards Uncle Luke as "his person." So, when my uncle shouts to my brother, Max turns and races to Uncle Luke, and now sprints beside him toward the van.

To Flurry, of course, I am "her person," more so even than my brother is. So, when my uncle shouts to Samuel, Flurry races to my side and now is running beside us toward Mr. Adelman.

I feel her beside us and so, for an instant, I am confused when I hear her sharp bark — her alarm bark — and see her spin around toward something behind us. I turn my head, still running with my hand in Gareth's, in time to see men in dark clothes running after us, overtaking us, and I see one of them in a hooded sweatshirt throw what looks to be a fishing net over Flurry, who is immediately entangled in the net.

I stop, pulling my hand away from Gareth's.

Before I can think, two of them seize me by each arm, while the one who threw the net over Flurry runs to me and tackles me, lifting me up onto one shoulder, then turning and starting to run back toward the trees. I hear Flurry barking and barking, but she is trapped, and everything is so confused I can hardly understand what else I am seeing other than the ground under my assailant's feet as he runs with me on his shoulder toward the trees on the other side of Coffey Park.

I am hanging upside down over my captor's back, my long hair falling down toward his legs. I realize after a moment that I have begun to punch feebly at the man's lower back, my skinny arms flailing away without having the slightest effect.

Suddenly I see a dark blur hurl itself through the air and fasten itself to my captor's leg. I hear the man scream, then feel him stagger and fall, throwing me to the ground as he does, and I realize Max has torn into him from behind, driving him to the ground. I also sense others are arriving, friend and foe alike: Uncle Luke, Mr. Adelman, Samuel, Gareth, the other two men I saw, and still others, probably those who were in the van. Everyone is fighting, punching, grappling. Max is a whirlwind, racing from one enemy to the next, snarling, snapping, biting.

I roll over in the grass, trying to breathe, holding my stomach where the man drove his shoulder into me. I push myself up painfully from the grass and just stand there, helpless, still holding my stomach, watching the incredible melee.

Suddenly, a gunshot.

It takes me a moment to realize Mr. Adelman has fired his weapon into the air. Everyone stops. Then I see that two of the enemy's combatants have drawn guns of their own, and have leveled them at Mr. Adelman. One of them then turns his gun toward me and, his gun pointed at my chest from 15 feet away, quietly orders Mr. Adelman to drop his weapon onto the grass.

He does. Immediately.

One of the others picks up Mr. Adelman's gun and, just as he does, we hear sirens in the near distance. With absolutely no hesitation, each of our adversaries turns and sprints as fast as he can toward safety, half of them toward the van, the others back into the trees behind me.

In just seconds the van is gone, so quickly that, when the police arrive, there is no sign of our adversaries. Suddenly our policewoman emerges from the trees, running, coming from the direction of our safe house, radiotelephone in her hand.

She stops a few feet from us and peers at each of us.

"Everybody okay?" she asks.

We all nod or murmur yes.

"Mr. Belton stationed me at the other end of the park, just in case," she explains. "I called in to the ready-response team as soon as I saw that van starting to cruise the other side of the park."

We all look closely at each other. My pretty blue dress is dirty, grass-stained and disheveled, and my sandals are gone, but I don't seem to be really injured. Samuel's nose is bleeding profusely, but he actually appears to be happy, as if he enjoyed the whole thing. My uncle and Mr. Adelman seem unharmed, as do Max and Flurry, who is just now arriving at my side, having been released by Samuel from the net that had ensnared her. And Gareth …

Gareth is gone. His disposable phone is on the ground near me, dislodged from his pocket when he was fighting to save me.

We look around the park, suddenly terrified. We listen for any sounds of him.

Nothing.

2

Half an hour later, in the living room of the safe house, Mrs. Morgan is screaming at me. She is screaming and sobbing at the same time, while Reverend Morgan, sitting next to her on the sofa, tries to hold her and comfort her.

"This is all *your* fault, Joanna Clark!" she shouts from just a few feet away from me, tears streaming down her face. "These visions of yours are responsible for all of it! It's *your* fault my brother tried to kill Gareth last month in Wales. It's *your* fault these people have taken him tonight.

"I wish we had never heard of you! I wish our family had never heard of your family! I wish …"

Mrs. Morgan collapses in her husband's arms, still sobbing. I sink slowly to the floor, onto my knees, my face in my hands, my hair falling down over my hands and down the front of my grass-stained blue dress. I am sobbing, too, uncontrollably, as I have, off and on, almost from the first moment we realized Gareth had been taken.

Flurry noses me from one side. Samuel kneels next to me on the other, his arm around my shoulder.

Neither Mrs. Morgan nor I can stop crying, nor can we speak. No one speaks. No one knows what to say. The silence is consumed only by the deep sobs from a mother whose son has been taken, and by the pitiful, high-pitched wails of a girl whose first boyfriend has been kidnapped. Kidnapped, as we all know, by enemies who really wanted to kidnap the visioner, but who settled for Gareth when Max and the others, including Gareth himself, came to my rescue.

Minutes pass before either Mrs. Morgan or I can regain control of ourselves. Our policewoman, the only person in the room other than members of the two families, Mr. Belton, and Mr. Adelman, brings tissue boxes to us both.

When someone finally speaks, it is Detective Belton, who has been leaning against his cane and listening for several minutes to Mr. Adelman's quietly delivered summary of what happened in the park. Mr. Belton clears his throat noisily and addresses his question to our policewoman.

"How many people at th' precinct office," he says tensely, "know we're here in th' safe house, ma'am?"

She shrugs.

"All of them, I think," she says quietly. "Maybe three dozen altogether."

"How many of 'em knew we'd be walking th' dogs tonight in th' park?"

"I don't know," she replies, "but anyone at our precinct who wanted to know that could easily have found out. This operation is not secret within our precinct, Detective Belton. Everybody there knows that your group is in danger, and that no one other than precinct personnel should be per-mitted to know anything about this, but everyone there knows about this operation, Mr. Belton. Everyone."

He nods thoughtfully, looking down unhappily at his cane. After sev-eral moments, the policewoman addresses Mr. Belton again.

"I'll resume my position in my patrol car, sir," she says to him. "And we'll set up a five- or six-officer perimeter for the rest of the night."

"Thank you, ma'am," Mr. Belton replies. "And thank you for gettin' th'response team t'th'park so fast. Those dirtbags had guns drawn, and they'd disarmed Detective Adelman. This outcome is bad — losin' th' kid — but it coulda been so much worse."

He looks at Mrs. Morgan.

"We've lost Gareth, Mrs. Morgan," he says, "but not fer long. I don't ever lose anybody fer long, ma'am."

As the policewoman turns to leave the room, Mr. Belton looks at Mr. Adelman and at my uncle, and the three of them, without a word to each other, move toward the front door.

"I'm gonna have a little talk with Jaakov and Luke," he says to us over his shoulder. "We'll be back in here with ya in five minutes."

As he clumps across the floor toward the porch door, being held open for him by my uncle, he again calls back over his shoulder in a voice that is nearly a shout, "Straighten up, people!"

And then, "We got work t' do tonight!"

The front door closes behind the three men at the same moment the back door closes behind our policewoman. Since Max has gone to the porch with the men, only the Morgans, Samuel, Flurry and I remain in the living room. The Morgans are still huddled on the sofa, Mrs. Morgan's face in her husband's chest, his arms around her. I am still kneeling on the floor facing them, my brother's arm around me and Flurry still nestled into my side.

I have wiped my face with the tissues, and, the instant Mr. Belton shouted over his shoulder to *straighten up,* I did straighten up. Now Samuel says quietly into my ear, "Joanna, do you want to go upstairs and change out of your dress?"

My brother doesn't usually think about things like that, but this time he does. I nod my head gratefully, and, with his help, I get to my feet. As the three of us approach the stairs, I hear Mrs. Morgan.

"Joanna," she says, no longer speaking hysterically or angrily, but not with her usual warmth and kindness, either, "I'm sorry to have spoken to you as I did. I was wrong. My words were wrong. My voice was wrong."

I nod, but am unsure what to say, partly because I feel she was right — that this really is my fault, the fault of my prayer-dreams — but also because she doesn't really *sound* sorry. I start up the stairs and I hear her again.

"Joanna," she adds, her voice now harsh, "I was wrong to speak to you that way, but I want you to know that, if we recover our son, we're going to take him back home, to Wales, and we intend for him never to see you or your family again. This is going to stop. Never again."

I'm so stunned by her words I can't put one foot in front of the other to move up the stairs. My brother puts his arm around me again, and helps me up the steps. Nothing else is said, either by Mrs. Morgan or by me. When we get to my bedroom, Samuel comes in with me and together we sit on the edge of the bed, with Flurry actually sitting on my feet, looking up at me.

After Mrs. Morgan's earlier, emotion-filled, shouted accusations, I had been overcome with sadness. Her accusations then seemed to infect me with tremendous guilt. She was so torn with fear and sorrow that her words had seemed heavy with truth. It seemed indeed to be my fault, just as she said. My dreams had ruined everything.

But then Mr. Belton's forceful command — *straighten up* — had seemed, by itself, somehow to expel most of the guilt and self-pity I was drowning in. I had instantly started to recover, had started to think like my mum thinks, had started to talk to myself the way my mum does: *Joanna, you're in God's hands; you've done your best with what was given you; you did not invite the prayer-dreams; you were chosen to receive them; your prayer-dreams have already saved Gareth's life once; you're almost certainly going to receive more of them; be ready now to help rescue Gareth; be ready now to do God's bidding; you have been chosen for this, and not just for the benefit of our families; for the whole world, Joanna; be ready, Joanna; you would not have been chosen if you were not strong enough to receive the dreams and to act on them.*

That's how Mum talks to me. That's how Mum talks to herself.

And so, just now, at the bottom of the stairs, the words Mrs. Morgan spoke to me had a completely different effect. This time, Mrs. Morgan just sounded mean. She sounded as though she *hated* me. As though she *hated* Mum and all of us. Her words didn't feel like an injection of guilt. They felt like an injection of hate. And this injection, I am finding, is not working.

I just feel sorry for her. I feel terrible *for* her. This time, I just want to help her. But I know that, if she meant what she said, she might not let me help her. She might not let me see her, or Gareth, ever again.

Samuel, still sitting beside me on the edge of the bed, finally speaks. He doesn't know what has been going on in my mind, and for once he guesses wrong.

"Joanna," he says tersely, "you need to do what Mr. Belton said. You need to *straighten up.* You've got work to do. *We've* got work to do."

I nod. "I know, Samuel. I know."

"I'll go out while you change clothes," he says. "Change your clothes fast, come on out, and we'll go downstairs together and wait for our orders from Mr. Belton. No time to wallow in self-pity, Joanna."

But I already know that. I take a deep breath and look down at myself.

"But my dress, Samuel," I say. "*Look* at my dress. It's ruined."

Then I turn my face up to him and smile, so he'll know I'm joking with him. So he'll know that I know that my ruined blue dress is probably the least important thing in the entire world right now. The very *least* important.

Samuel gets the joke after a moment, and he laughs his real laugh. The laugh he laughs when something really, truly strikes him as funny.

"Okay, Joanna," he says at the end of his laugh, now rolling his eyes at me, "that's what I want from my sister right now. Funny lines. Your dress is ruined. *That's* the big thing. *That's* the terrible thing right now. Very funny."

We smile our brother-sister smiles at each other, and he leaves the room, closing the door behind him. I hear his footsteps stop just outside my room. He's going to stay right there until I come out.

My brother loves me very much.

3

I've changed into my jeans, a pale pink blouse, and my dressy sandals, which we recovered from the park before walking back to the safe house. Samuel and Flurry and I reach the foot of the stairs just as the men and Max reenter the house from the front porch. Mr. Belton immediately barks orders at us.

"Kids," he says to my brother and me, "pack yer things and get ready t' go back t' Manhattan. There's at least one mole in the precinct office. We can't stay here any longer. Th' safe house is not a safe house if somebody at th' precinct is gonna report everything we're doin' t' th' dirtbags. We gotta get out. Now."

In 10 minutes we have packed our things and are sitting in my uncle's SUV with the dogs, headed back to the detectives' office. We'll all stay there from now on.

The Morgans, of course, had come over to Brooklyn just for the day, and had not intended to stay overnight at the safe house anyway. They are riding with the policewoman who brought them over at noon.

Mr. Belton and Mr. Adelman are riding with a different police officer. All three vehicles are traveling together in a line consisting of at least a half dozen police cars. At this time of night — it's now after midnight — there is little traffic, and we are across the Brooklyn Bridge and arriving at the detectives' office in no time at all.

Even though the detectives' Manhattan office was designed to serve as a modern-day fortress, I think the accommodations here are actually more comfortable than those at the safe house. The drawback is that exercising the dogs is not going to be something we can do ourselves. Arrangements are being made by our policewoman, whom we still trust, to have NYPD K-9 officers come by the office to pick up Flurry and Max twice a day, and to take them to Battery Park or other parks in lower Manhattan. The dogs can also use the tiny backyard on the ground floor of the office as many times a day as they want, but they'll need to be taken elsewhere for exercise.

The advantage of the Brooklyn safe house was supposed to be that no one except NYPD people knew of its existence, plus its nearness to Coffey Park. As it has turned out, there was nothing secret about its existence or its location, because, as Mr. Belton said, there is at least one "mole" in the precinct office, someone reporting everything to our enemies. With our now staying at the detectives' office, it won't matter if there is a mole at the precinct. None of us will be going out, and nothing can come in.

But the single reason we have moved so *fast* to the detectives' office is that we need to use its secure communications link to speak with Mum and Dad and my uncle's wife Kory right now. They need to know everything that's happened. And we are going to need them, too.

Within half an hour of our arrival at the office, all of us are assembled in the secure communications room, and Mr. Adelman is setting up the link. It's 1:00 a.m. here in New York, which means it's 6:00 a.m. at the lodge in England. Mum, Dad, and Aunt Kory are early risers. We'll probably be interrupting their morning devotions, but we certainly won't be waking them up.

The connection goes smoothly and fast, and I realize, watching Mr. Adelman work through the complicated set of passwords and relays, that he has been reporting to the lodge regularly, not just that first afternoon when I reported my prayer-dreams during our first secure communications session. I suppose I dimly knew he was talking to them every day, but I had not really thought about it until now. But naturally he wanted to report my uncle's and our dogs' safe arrival here, and our movement from here to Brooklyn, and Mr. Belton's successful rescue. After all, Aunt Kory and my mother are my uncle Luke's wife and his twin sister, so they've surely been holding their breaths throughout this whole thing.

What they, at the lodge, don't yet know at this moment, is especially crucial, and that's why we have moved so fast. They need to know of today's noontime discussion, when we became aware of so many possible connections, and they need to know what just happened tonight. So, Uncle Luke and, at times, Reverend Morgan and others of us explain the insights we came to at lunchtime today.

I'm interested to see that Reverend Morgan gets up promptly and moves closer to the speakerphone when the discussion moves in the direction of the Old Testament verse from Micah, and its use as Mr. Jonathan Murphy's company slogan and core value. And I realize, watching and listening to Reverend Morgan, that he does not necessarily connect any of this to Mr. Murphy personally, but rather to Mr. Murphy's *company*. And I realize, too, with a sense of thankfulness, that he has not at any point seemed angry with me or with my family. He has been focused on comforting his wife, not on being angry.

I start to think about this, but then make myself stop. I need to keep up with this conversation, and it is moving quickly.

At length, after many clarification questions from the lodge, the suggested intersections have been made clear to Mum, Dad, and Aunt Kory. To my surprise, it is Aunt Kory who asks to give a summary, "to see if I have all this straight," she says. Aunt Kory speaks in Dutch-tinted English. Her parents are Dutch, though she herself was born in England.

"The documents," she begins, reading, I think, from her notes, "that Detective Belton photographed made reference to Micah 6:8, the portion that reads 'what doth the Lord require of thee, but to do justly, and to love mercy, and to walk humbly with thy God?' and, as well, to something called The Church of the New Century."

"Right," grumbles Mr. Belton.

"Reverend Morgan," she continues without pausing, "has reminded us that Lily and he have an ongoing ministry with Mr. Jonathan Murphy's import-export operation in Swansea, on the south coast of Wales, and that posted everywhere in that company's hallways and work spaces is that exact Old Testament verse, that exact portion of the verse, and in that exact translation."

"Correct, Kory," calls out Reverend Morgan from his chair against the wall, where he has resumed his seat after speaking earlier into the speakerphone.

"Joanna," Aunt Kory continues, "took note of the fact that, in Mr. Belton's report of his capture and incarceration, he repeated his captors' statement that 'the boss' would arrive at Castle Williams at a time that would have been … let's see … not quite 24 hours ago now, and that 'the boss' would take Mr. Belton so far away from New York that no one would ever find him."

"Right," says Mr. Belton.

"And Joanna," she goes on, "then speculated that that could conceivably mean that 'the boss' was not an American, and might well have planned to transport you, Mr. Belton, to another country."

"Yep," says Mr. Belton. "I hadn't thought of that, but Joanna did."

Everyone looks at me again, nodding approvingly. I just look down. I don't know why. Gareth isn't even here, so I don't know why I still think I should be embarrassed at everything that comes in my direction.

"Finally," Aunt Kory continues, "Joanna's third dream, the one she received in Grace Church, featured three commands, the first having to do presumably with the rescue of you, Mr. Belton, from Castle Williams, but the other two forming the words, 'Baptize the Scripture' and 'Cleanse the Church,' and we note the possibility that baptizing the scripture may refer to Micah 6:8, and that cleansing the church may refer to The Church of the New Century."

"Good," says Uncle Luke to his wife on the other side of the Atlantic. "Good overview, Kory."

"And finally," she continues, barely pausing, "we note the possibility that all of this can be made to fit together, as follows: that Mr. Jonathan Murphy, or someone else on his senior staff, could, in fact, be 'the boss' who would have taken Mr. Belton away, and who could conceivably be at or near the head of the enemy organization; that Mr. Murphy or others in his company could, in fact, have been in league with Dr. Cameron Stafford in his efforts last month in Wales to eliminate the visioners and all who are connected with them, as a critical step in clearing the way for his efforts to produce electronic games and an electronic Bible, all designed to corrupt children and young people at various stages of development; and that Mr. Murphy or one of his staff could, in that process, be planning to start a new church which would focus equally on distorting Christianity, corrupting children and young persons, and profiting from the worldwide and multilingual sale of the electronic games and false Bibles."

There is a long silence while everyone thinks through everything Aunt Kory has just said. Then there are murmurs of assent from all around the table, with her husband finally saying, "I think you've summarized perfectly, Kory. That's the picture."

My uncle then pauses uncomfortably, leans forward toward the speakerphone, and says to his wife and sister and brother-in-law at the lodge, "Kory, Rebecca, Matt, I now have to report to you what just happened in Coffey Park, in Brooklyn, earlier tonight. We were attacked. The attackers tried to take Joanna. Thanks to Max, they failed. She's fine. But Gareth Morgan was taken instead."

Suddenly Mrs. Morgan is screaming again. She is screaming and crying as though someone flipped a switch and she instantly became the same devastated mother of a lost boy that she had been in Brooklyn earlier tonight.

"What are you DOING?" she shouts at us all and at the speakerphone, rising from her chair and yet starting to collapse as soon as she gets to her feet. "Gareth is GONE! Gareth has been TAKEN! My only child has been KIDNAPPED!

"Why are we not LOOKING for him? Why are we not talking about HIM? Why are we talking about ANYTHING other than my son?

"Tell me WHY?"

4

Now, 15 minutes have passed since Mrs. Morgan's second outburst of the night. Reverend Morgan has succeeded in quieting her and then escorting her tenderly from the conference room. The two of them have gone downstairs to their bedroom, located with the other sleeping rooms on the floor beneath the main office complex, here on the top floor of the detectives' building.

No one else has spoken a single word since her second heart-rending lament began. Everyone here and everyone listening at the lodge has seemed to understand that Mrs. Morgan needed to be attended to by her husband, and attended to before anything else could or should be discussed.

Although all of us, I think, agreed that the big picture needed to be reviewed, as my Aunt Kory has now done, before a plan could be put together to search for Gareth, we also understand how, to Mrs. Morgan, the long discussion of the problems and opportunities at hand must have seemed heartless to her. And interminable.

Mrs. Morgan's only child is missing. And we are not yet focused on that. We are not out looking for him. This is not something she should be expected to accept. And she clearly does not.

Yes, Gareth is my boyfriend. And, yes, I'm terrified to think where he might be and what he might be thinking. But I've been chosen as a visioner, and that means I have a confidence that others can't really be expected to have or understand. I'm — somehow — terrified and confident at the same time.

For now, the conference room still remains silent. We have listened to the elevator taking the Morgans down to the sleeping-room floor. And we have remained quiet, thinking, and, for many of us, praying.

Finally, my uncle speaks, both to us in the room and to his wife, sister, and brother-in-law in England. "I'm realizing," he says, "that I was wrong not to explain to the Morgans as soon as we began this session that we cannot realistically approach our search for Gareth without getting a grasp of the overall situation. As soon as we finish here, I'll go down and apologize to them face-to-face, and explain to them whatever decisions we will have reached here in the next few minutes."

My mum's voice comes over the speakerphone. "Yes, Luke," she says to her brother, "that was quite a bad thing. One of you should indeed have spoken to the Morgans about the process we'd need to follow. I feel horrible about this.

"In fact," she says sadly, "I should have asked the question of you at the start."

"And so should I," says Aunt Kory over the speakerphone. "I would never have launched into that long, long overview had I realized that the reasoning behind our process had not been explained to Lily and Cecil."

After several more moments of silence, Mr. Belton adds, "Well," he says gruffly, "that's what we get fer bein' so stupid as t' have no women in th' room other than Mrs. Morgan. If Eleanor had been here with us …"

His voice dies away, and a new and even sadder silence envelopes the room. Mr. Belton's beloved wife, Dr. Eleanor Chapel, passed away not so very long ago.

And Mr. Belton is right. Eleanor Chapel or Mum or Aunt Kory would have attended to the Morgans *first*. And I realize that this is a good lesson for me. I'm only 14, but there is no reason I could not have done something, said something, except that Mrs. Morgan is so angry at me, I don't know if she'd have listened.

And I know, too, that the men, or Samuel, could have thought about the Morgans' distress, and could have attended to them before doing anything else. But I also know they're not very good at that. These three men — Mr. Belton, Mr. Adelman, Uncle Luke — are not even parents. How could I have expected them to think of how this would look through the eyes of Gareth's mum and dad?

Suddenly Mr. Belton says loudly, "Let's go! Let's get to it!"

That shakes us out of our reverie. We all look to my uncle, expecting him now to lead a discussion of the next steps we should take. But Aunt Kory's voice comes over the speaker first.

"I've been on my military-grade computer," she tells us in her soft, high voice and interesting dialect, "since you, Luke, began your summary of events more than half an hour ago. I have found several interesting things about Mr. Murphy's import-export business and his current activities."

I should tell you that my uncle's wife Kory, though she was on active duty with the Royal Navy only two years, is still, like Uncle Luke, an active reservist, and has access to the latest technology. She knows more about technology than anyone I've ever known. And she is an incredible organizer. That's why she was the one to give us that long summary before Mrs. Morgan's second outburst.

Aunt Kory calls herself a geek. She says she loves data. She says she loves statistics. She says she loves technology. She says she loves looking things up.

"I find," she says now, "that Mr. Murphy's firm owns three airplanes, and that one of the fastest and longest ranged, a Gulfstream IV, logged out of the Swansea Airport — fewer than 10 miles west of his business location — late last week, bound for Teterboro Airport in New Jersey, just across the Hudson River from Manhattan. There is no date shown for the plane's expected return."

A stunned silence descends on our conference room. Mr. Belton nods his head after a moment and mutters, "Th' dirtbag. Th' rotten dirtbag."

"There's more," says Aunt Kory over the speakerphone. "One of his ships is shown as being docked right now on the east side of Staten Island, just south of Manhattan, and just a mile or so north of the Verrazano-Narrows Bridge that connects Brooklyn with Staten Island."

We look at each other, shaking our heads in wonder as the connections just keep multiplying and multiplying.

"There's still more," she continues. "Much of his importing and export-ing is with port cities you'd expect for the kind of business — Mr. Jonathan Murphy's business — that largely deals with automobiles and heavy ma-chinery, such as farm equipment. New York, of course. Philadelphia. Rio. Marseilles. Antwerp. Rotterdam. Major manufacturing import-export sites.

"But some of these port cities used by Mr. Murphy's ships look quite out of place to me, such as several of the Central American sites, or some of the South American ports like Caracas, or Paramaribo, or Montevideo. Some of these don't fit."

After a moment, Mr. Belton grumbles a single word.

"Drugs," he says.

"Right," says Mr. Adelman.

"That would conform to our enemies' standard business profile, wouldn't it?" says Aunt Kory from the lodge. "Mixing legal business with illicit business. Using dirty money to finance some of their biggest proj-ects, projects which are often perfectly legal in and of themselves, such as creating and manufacturing electronic games designed to destroy young peoples' sense of right and wrong."

"Or writing and manufacturing Bibles for children and young people," adds my dad, "designed to subtract everything supernatural from God's own reality, designed to reduce Our Lord to just another teacher."

After Aunt Kory reads to us the serial number and markings for Mr. Murphy's company's Gulfstream IV at the Teterboro Airport, and, after she reads to us all the available data about the company's ship that is docked at Staten Island, Samuel and I and Flurry are dismissed to go down to our sleeping rooms. We know why, of course. They are going to focus next on an extraction plan for Gareth, or, more likely, a number of extraction plans. And we know they are going to talk about levels of risk and levels of violence, and that's why they prefer that we not be present.

And that reminds me that Uncle Luke has not yet told my mother that he accidentally allowed me to sit in the kitchen of the safe house and listen to the men talk about everything just 24 hours ago. He's probably going to wait until he sees her when we get home. Then, as Mr. Belton said, she'll just kill him. And as my uncle agreed, she'll *absolutely* kill him.

This makes me smile. My mum loves her brother.

But she's going to be mad at him for letting me listen in to that conversation. I actually emit a little laugh, which Samuel notices, which means I have to tell him the whole story while we go to our sleeping rooms.

He laughs his real laugh.

"Mum is going to *kill* Uncle Luke," he says happily, imagining the scene.

5

I have just finished washing up and brushing my hair and getting my long nightshirt on when I hear the elevator's hum, and then I hear Uncle Luke tiptoeing from the elevator to the Morgans' room. I hear him knock quietly on their door, and I hear them invite him in. Then I hear muffled voices for several minutes, though, of course, not actual words.

I'm in bed and starting on one of my summer reading assignments in my e-reader when I hear my uncle come out of the Morgans' room and cross the common area. He taps lightly first on my door and then on my brother's door.

"Your mum wants to speak to the three of us privately," he says loudly enough for Samuel and me both to hear. Without any other comment, he turns and walks quickly to the elevator. I grab my robe, whisper to Flurry to come with me, and we and Samuel follow, me in my robe and Samuel in his tee shirt and running shorts.

On the way up to the office floor in the elevator, my uncle tells us that he and Mr. Adelman will be headed for Teterboro Airport in half an hour, with Max, in the SUV. Their plan is to disable the electrical system of the Gulfstream IV before sunup, so that its engines will not operate. They don't want the plane to crash. They just want to make it very hard for anyone to get that plane in condition to fly again.

He adds that Aunt Kory and Mum and Dad will be continuing their research, from the lodge, into Mr. Murphy's shipping business. They will next focus on the ship that is shown as being docked at Staten Island, here in New York Harbor. They will also focus on the buildings in the immediate area of that ship. They want to find out if any of those buildings are used specifically for Mr. Murphy's import-export business.

Obviously, they are thinking that Gareth could be held on that ship itself, or in one of the buildings used in Mr. Murphy's operation. I ask my uncle why he and Max and Mr. Adelman are not going first to that ship and those Staten Island buildings, rather than to the airport in New Jersey. He answers that our enemies could put Gareth on that airplane this morning and take him anywhere on earth. They want to eliminate that possibility right now, tonight.

The three of us and Flurry enter the conference room again. We see that Mr. Belton, Mr. Adelman, and Max have gone to the kitchen to wait for us to complete this family conversation with Mum. We sit down around the table. Flurry curls up at my feet.

Uncle Luke says, "We're here, Rebecca."

"Thank you, Luke," Mum says immediately.

"I know you're tired and sleepy, dear ones," she says, "but I want you to hear me say several things about the Morgans. First, I want you to keep in mind that Lily and Reverend Morgan were themselves kidnapped last month in Wales, and they were handled quite roughly throughout that experience. There is nothing in their backgrounds that would have prepared them for that. They were terrified then, and they are terrified now, doubly so, because they know their only child is being handled in the same way by some of the same people, or, at least, people in the same kind of organization. And they know Gareth is by himself.

"So, Lily feels accusatory toward us. Of course she does. Nothing like this was in their lives at all, until we entered their lives last month. And even though they and we all survived and were not seriously injured, they had been assuming that there would be no repeat of that kind of thing. Ever.

"You both know, Joanna and Samuel," she continues, "that that assumption is not a very good one, because evil persists, and we were long ago identified by these evildoers as people whom God has chosen to place in their way, to keep them from their goals. And yes, that means that these people do seem actually to believe in God, or else they wouldn't pay so much attention to getting rid of us. But, as I've told you both before, there are people who say to themselves, 'Yes, God exists, but I'm going to live as if He does not, and I'm going to get as much power and wealth as I can while I'm on the earth, no matter how I get it.'

"Yes?"

"Yes, Mum," Samuel and I say at the same time.

Uncle Luke just nods, knowing his sister can't see him do that, but knowing that what she really wants to hear is a yes from her children. And she has.

"I know Lily Morgan has said," Mum continues, "that she will take Gareth home to Wales as soon as he is rescued, and that she will permit no contact between our two families ever again. I know.

"And I feel certain that she means that right now, but that does not mean that she will mean that forever. She is a Christian woman and mother and wife. She may eventually decide that the connection between our two families is, in fact, one of the most important things in their lives. Or she may not.

"So, Joanna and Samuel, say your prayers. Be obedient to God. Let your obedience take you where it will. If God intends our families to be together again, then that will happen. If not, then it will not.

"And the Morgans know that, too, you know, though it may be hard for them to get their arms around that truth right now. After all, Gareth was taken just a few hours ago. The wound is fresh, still."

Mum pauses, thinking. Then she signs off for the night.

"All right, my children," she says, finishing our conversation. "Go to bed now. Wake up in the morning and do your prayers.

"We will do the same over here. We love you very much."

"Good night, Mum," we say together. "We love you."

"Good night, Rebecca and Matt," says my uncle.

And then he adds, as we and Flurry get up to leave, "Rebecca, could Kory and I have a little time together now?"

We smile again as we leave the conference room and head for the elevator.

Chapter Five

1

And so, *Heavenly Father,* I say, praying silently, alone in my sleeping room at the end of my morning devotions, *please comfort Gareth and his parents this day. Please be with Gareth, wherever he may be right now. Please stay at his side and help him to know Thy presence. Help him to feel our prayers for him, and help him to know that, with Thy help, we will come to him. Help him to know and feel the truth of Thy Son Jesus's words, "I will not leave you comfortless."*

And now, Heavenly Father, I ask that you "Stir up Thy strength, O Lord, and come and help us; for Thou givest not alway the battle to the strong, but canst save by many or by few." Be present, be present, Father, please, with each of us throughout this day, I pray in the name of Our Lord and Savior, Jesus Christ. Amen.

I open my eyes and think gratefully for several moments about my education, both at my Christian school and at our church, that education that has helped to place in my mind and heart so many wonderful phrases and passages from the Bible and from our church's prayer book. Such phrases and passages come to me so naturally in my prayer life. I am so thankful for my parents and for my teachers at school and at church. I have been richly blessed.

I have been awake now for almost an hour, washing up, brushing my hair, reading my Bible, and saying my prayers. It is nearly 10 now, and I am anxious to hear what happened on my uncle's trip into New Jersey to conduct his raid on Mr. Jonathan Murphy's private jet. If the whole thing happened as he and Mr. Adelman planned, they would have been back here at the office before sunrise.

I pull on my jeans and my everyday sandals, and a fresh, off-white blouse, and, with Flurry just behind me, take the elevator down to the ground floor, so that she can go out back for a minute or two. When she is finished and I have picked up after her, we take the elevator up to the office floor. As Flurry and I walk into the conference room, I see that the Morgans are not present, but everyone else is, including Samuel. They all look at me intently, asking with their eyes whether or not I have dreamed. I shake my head no, and sit down to ask about my uncle's trip to the New Jersey airport last night.

"Like clockwork, Joanna," says Uncle Luke. "That airport has surprisingly little security, given the kind of private planes it hosts: extremely expensive jets, for the most part, like Mr. Murphy's company's Gulfstream IV. We entered the main aircraft parking areas, with Max beside us, without much trouble. Jaakov and I both had military-issue infrared goggles, so we could locate security personnel from a distance.

"Kory actually unlocked Mr. Murphy's private aircraft electronically from her computer in England, if you can imagine. I don't really understand that, but somehow she hacked into the company's electronic systems deeply enough to disable that exact aircraft's onboard alarm and locking systems, and without doing anything else to other systems, aircraft related or otherwise. All we had to do, when she notified us on our mobiles, was operate the latch on the passenger-compartment door.

"Max acted as our sentinel, and we were in and out of the aircraft in about 10 minutes. They'll need to rewire the plane before they can use it again.

"We were over the George Washington Bridge in the SUV," he continues, "long before sunup, and then were here at the office by 5:30 a.m."

After a moment, my brother, rather bravely, I think, asks my uncle a question.

"Uncle Luke," he says tentatively, "were you and Mr. Adelman disappointed when you didn't have to fight anybody at the airport?"

Our uncle can be a little short with questions like that, but this time he answers my brother in a very gentle and kind way. "Yes, Samuel," he says, smiling at my brother, "I was just a bit disappointed.

"And that's a very good point you've made with that question. I think that, when some of us are truly prepared to fight, especially against an enemy who is likely to be good at fighting, it can be deflating to have nothing and no one to fight against.

"But, of course," he quickly adds, "that is always balanced by the relief of *not* having to fight and of *not* needing to hurt someone else, and of *not* getting in any way injured oneself."

Samuel beams at this expansive answer from our uncle.

"Thank you, Uncle Luke," he says gratefully. "I know what you mean."

"I would think you do," our uncle replies. "You've been in those situations yourself, haven't you, Samuel?"

Samuel nods, thankful to be complimented, and thankful to be treated as a fellow warrior by someone as accomplished as Uncle Luke. He smiles to himself, and I reach over and pat his hand. He gives me a look that says *Don't Do That.*

My brother doesn't always like it when I do that in front of other people. I'm just never sure when he is going to appreciate my little gestures and when he's not. But he's not actually mad. I can always tell when he's mad at me. And even when he is truly mad at me, he doesn't stay mad for long. Not at me. That's the best thing.

Detective Belton interrupts this little exchange in his usual manner.

"Let's get on point, people!" he barks from the other end of the conference table.

"Joanna," he says, looking at me with his black, deep-set eyes, "we already got a call this mornin', while you were still sleepin', from th' lodge. Not much good, though.

"Seems th' more yer Aunt Kory found with her computer about th' dirtbags' operation on Staten Island, th' worse it got. They got a bunch of leased spaces all over th' area, not just in th' area right next to that ship she found. If they've taken Gareth over there, he could be in any one of three dozen buildings. Or more.

"Or, of course," he adds unhappily, shaking his head, "he coulda been taken somewhere completely different than Staten Island. Know what I mean, kid? Hm?"

I nod. I feel I've disappointed him by not having a new dream to report. If Aunt Kory can't narrow the possibilities with her computer, I don't know how else we will know where to look for Gareth. An uncomfortable silence follows.

I think then of the Morgans, and, after a few moments, I ask, "Have the Morgans been upstairs today?"

"Yes, Joanna," says my uncle. "They were here in the conference room when Kory called earlier this morning with the information Mr. Belton just gave you. They were devastated to hear that from Kory, of course, although they were also gratified at our success in disabling Mr. Murphy's airplane.

"But after listening to Kory's report," he continues, "they went back down to their room, and without having breakfast. They didn't want anything to eat."

2

At noon, I listen from my chair at the conference-room table while Mr. Adelman talks into the intercom, and then buzzes into the building two NYPD K-9 police officers. I listen while he explains on the intercom, as he did with us just a few days ago, how to activate the movable wall on their right, so they can move into the elevator. When they arrive at the top floor of our building, they are escorted by Detective Belton, who knows them both, to the conference room. There, with me, Samuel, Mr. Adelman, and Uncle Luke, they are introduced to Max and Flurry.

The introduction goes well.

Both officers, a man and a woman, are obviously experienced in interactions with dogs who are new to them. They each drop to one knee, with their right hands extended toward the dogs, and with their palms up. They remain motionless while Max and Flurry then approach them and sniff to their hearts' content.

Only when each dog eventually sniffs out the "treat pocket" on each officer's uniform do the officers rise to their feet, so as to parcel out treats to their new canine acquaintances. They look each dog in the eye, and firmly speak the "sit" command before actually giving the reward. In just minutes, dogs and officers are friends — but clear on who is in charge — and ready to go to one of the lower-Manhattan city parks. We walk to the elevator with the four of them and send them off, satisfied that this will be an excellent substitute for what we expected to be our own daily walks with Max and Flurry in Brooklyn's Coffey Park.

Once Max and Flurry are gone, we return to the conference room and, as soon as I sit down and relax, I realize how exhausted I feel from these late nights and short sleeps. In fact, my eyelids start to droop while Mr. Belton is explaining something to us about how the NYPD K-9 corps was first developed.

He stops talking in midsentence.

"Joanna, honey," he says, more gently than usual, "yer fallin' asleep right in front of my eyes. No need fer you t' stay up. Go catch up on yer sleep. Y' haven't had much of that these last few days."

I know that Mr. Belton, and everybody else, would like me to go to sleep in hopes I'll be sent a prayer-dream that might help us think how to search for Gareth tonight. I don't really know if God-Things work in just that way, but I do know that when I prayed at Grace Church earlier this week, very much in need of a Divine Intrusion, one was sent to me almost as soon as I started to pray.

Anyway, I don't feel I have much choice. I can't stay awake. I'm just too tired to do anything other than go down to my sleeping room. Samuel gets up from his chair and comes with me, saying, "I'm pretty tired, too, Joanna. I'll do the same."

I don't know if my brother is really as tired as I am, or if he is just being considerate and making me feel less like a weakling. And I find I don't really care which thing it is. I'm glad to have his company on the way down to my sleeping room. But once I'm in my room with the door closed, I suddenly don't feel tired or sleepy anymore. This seems strange to me, but I lie down anyway, still in my off-white blouse and jeans.

I pick up my e-reader and think what I'd like to read, assuming I'll soon get sleepy again if I do. After a few moments, I decide to start with my e-reader's Bible, and to read first the story in the Second Gospel, fifth chapter, where Jesus is asked by one of the temple leaders to come to his home and save his 12-year-old daughter, who is near death. The story is familiar, of course, and I love reading it.

When I get to the part where Jesus takes the girl's hand and says, *Talitha Cumi* — "Little girl, arise" — I always get a chill down my spine, just imagining that scene, with her parents, distraught, watching the miraculous event from just a few feet away. This time, as I lie on my bed in my clothes, I realize, just at the instant I read the words, *Talitha Cumi*, that my mind is beginning to cloud over.

And I understand in a flash that it is happening again. My mind is being approached in exactly the way I have learned to recognize. A Divine Intrusion is arriving, just at the moment that we — and, especially, Gareth — are so desperately in need of God's help.

I shut the cover on my e-reader and close my eyes, concentrating hard. In just seconds the vision begins, forming itself into the image of something I can at first only dimly perceive. Gradually, though, the image becomes clearer, and I begin to understand that I am looking through a darkened, gray-colored corridor, one with exposed, unpainted tubes running along its ceiling and along the right side of its walls, and with small doors and wheels and valves showing at intervals, somehow in connection with regularly spaced openings all the way down the length of the corridor.

I can see that each of the openings would make a person step up and over what seems to be a 1-foot barrier coming up from the floor, and, at the same time, the person would need to duck her head so as to squeeze herself under the doorway's upper frame, which comes down perhaps 2 feet from the ceiling. This progression of small-sized openings, each with a hinged door and a wheel connected to the door, seems to continue for as far as I can see. And each portion of the corridor appears to have at least one ordinary door, each one of them closed, leading out of the corridor, each one of them on the right side.

And I know I am inside a ship. A large one.

I also gradually become aware that there is a steel ladder that drops down into the corridor, from the right, from the floor above, and that what little light exists within the corridor appears to come mostly from the light that shines down from the ladder's opening above me. Perhaps a full minute now passes before the image begins gradually to go away, but, before it disappears completely, I notice one more piece of the image that either had not been there before, or that I hadn't noticed until now.

That piece is a small, wheeled cart, halfway down the corridor, holding a pitcher, a cup, and an empty plate. The cart is just on the other side of the second hatch from the ladder. It seems to be nestled against one of the regular-sized closed doors, on the right side. And I think to myself, "That was someone's breakfast."

The vision fades. Suddenly I'm alone again on my bed. I open my eyes.

Quickly, before anything about the vision leaves my memory, I get up and slip my feet into my sandals. I open my sleeping-room door and run for the elevator. As I do, I call loudly for Samuel to come with me. I hear his feet hit the floor and in two seconds, he bursts from his room and runs to catch me at the elevator.

As the elevator door closes, we hear the Morgans' door open. They have heard me call Samuel. And they are coming to hear what I have to say.

And that frightens me. I'm scared of Mrs. Morgan. Gentle, sweet Lily Morgan has become a fearsome figure in my mind. Maybe the presence of an angry mum whose only child has been wronged will do that to any-body, not just me.

And, beyond that fear, the old fear returns. What if that was just a daydream? What if that was an ordinary daydream having nothing to do with anything in real life?

What if it's not a God-Thing at all? What if I'm all wrong?

Standing in the slowly moving elevator with my brother, I close my eyes and pray, *Please, Father, help me …*

We enter the conference room and I sit down while Samuel runs to collect the others. As everyone files into the room, the Morgans enter. My stomach tightens. I feel as if I may be sick.

3

A few minutes before midnight, I watch my uncle as he casts off from the Brooklyn Army Terminal, several miles south of Governors Island, and about three miles north of the Verrazano-Narrows Bridge that con-nects Brooklyn with Staten Island. I am sitting in the stern of our 25-foot inboard, a fast, powerful boat loaned to us by one of Mr. Belton's numer-ous well-to-do friends. He has helped so many people in New York during the course of his long career, first as an NYPD beat patrolman, then as an NYPD detective, finally as a private detective, that the list of well-placed New Yorkers who love him and who love to help him is long.

I am wearing my jeans, my light blue *I Love New York* tee shirt, and a black Gore-Tex jacket that my uncle purchased for me this evening before we left the detectives' office. I am wearing my everyday sandals now, but will change into better shoes once we get to the Staten Island pier.

Mr. Adelman sits next to me in the stern of the boat. He is the only passenger besides me, since Mr. Belton is too physically limited to be part of anything that demands agility, skill, and strength. And this rescue at-tempt will demand all three.

Why me, then? Because I saw what I saw.

Yes, it's true that, two days before the vision came to me at noon to-day, Aunt Kory had identified the ship docked at Staten Island through her electronic investigation into Mr. Jonathan Murphy's company records. But only my noontime vision today indicated, first, that Gareth is almost certainly held on that ship, rather than in any of the dozens of buildings that Mr. Murphy's company uses on Staten Island. And, second, only to-day's vision indicated a specific area within that ship in which we might search for Gareth: a specific corridor, on a specific deck, on a specific side of the ship, and at a specific place within that corridor.

Only I actually saw these things.

Despite that, there was much disagreement this afternoon among the grown-ups as to whether or not I should accompany Uncle Luke and Mr. Adelman on this rescue mission. Samuel and I, after my report of my noon vision, were not allowed to hear most of the debate, but we were brought back into the conference room after the adults had had more than an hour of discussion. And it was a strongly divided discussion.

At some point, they had decided that they actually wanted to hear my opinion on the basic questions that made up their debate. They wanted to know my thoughts. Did I think that I should be part of this dangerous and difficult rescue attempt? Did I think that I would be anything other than a hindrance and a burden to the two men? And, especially, given how detailed my report had been, did I think there was any need for me actu-ally to be present on that ship? Would not Uncle Luke and Mr. Adelman be perfectly able to identify the corridor and Gareth's location without me there?

As Samuel and I had sat down and listened to Mum and Detective Belton summarize the points in their debate, I could see how the debate had shaped up, with Mum, Dad, Aunt Kory, and Uncle Luke opposed to my going on the raid, and with Mr. Belton, Mr. Adelman, Mrs. Morgan, and Reverend Morgan in favor. My family on one side; Gareth's family and the two detectives on the other.

My family had argued that I, the visioner, would be exposed to cap-ture, the very thing our enemies wanted in the first place. Gareth had been taken from the park, they noted, only when the effort to capture me was defeated by Max and the others. Gareth was, in fact, now serving only as bait to get me into their hands. They also stressed that I was not physically strong or agile or quick or able to fight, and that all four qualities could prove essential in rescuing Gareth.

The detectives and the Morgans had acknowledged all of that, but had focused on several other considerations. That I, and only I, had been given today's vision. That I was the only one who had actually seen what had been sent in the vision, and that, once actually on board that ship, only I could be expected to recognize exactly which of a large ship's dozens of passageways was the right one. That there were, no doubt, small aspects of my vision that I had not been able to put into words, but that were in my memory, and that only I possessed those images and would be in position to recognize them. That I was, in fact, likely to be indispensable in the effort to locate Gareth. And that, if Gareth could not be located, he could not be rescued, no matter how capable my uncle and Mr. Adelman might be.

I'm sure that, if my parents had absolutely insisted that I not go on the rescue attempt, the others would have had to yield to them. They are, after all, my parents. But Mum and Dad were not certain that the others were not right, and that's why they had asked me back into the room, so they could hear my thoughts on the questions.

When it was finally my turn to speak, I spoke words that did not even seem to come from my brain. I heard myself saying the words, yet could hardly believe they were coming from me. I said that, yes, I was weak and unathletic and clumsy, and would certainly be a burden to my uncle and Mr. Adelman. But I said also that it was probably true to say that only I could recognize with any certainty the actual location that had been pinpointed in my vision. Only I could be *sure*.

I said also that, in the words of Mr. C. S. Lewis, words our family repeats to itself and to others so often, *"Courage is … the form of every virtue at the testing point. …"* I said that, if the virtues demanded of me tonight could be said to be love and caring and responsibility, then I should be able, with God's help, to convert those virtues into courage.

I said all of that and said it well and with confidence. I don't know how.

When I finished, silence dropped on the room like a blanket. There was no sound from anyone in the room, nor from the lodge, over the speakerphone. And I was so silent I nearly forgot to breathe. I could not believe I had said those things to these wise, experienced adults whom God had blessed and guided during all their battles with these enemies, over the all these years.

How had that happened?

4

Now, many hours later, our sleek inboard cuts through the waters of New York Harbor like a knife, its throaty engine noise seeming to me to announce to the entire world that we are on our way to rescue Gareth. But I know that my uncle and Mr. Adelman have thought through the details of this raid with their usual care.

For example, they have brought along the same inflatable raft the two of them used to cross Buttermilk Channel in their rescue of Mr. Belton from Castle Williams two nights ago. The raft is lashed onto the deck of our boat, near the bow. From my stern seat, the raft just appears as a black, shapeless nothing.

The men have planned to tie our noisy 25-foot inboard to a pier about 200 yards away from the ship. They then plan to approach the freighter either on foot, walking along the pier, or in the inflatable raft, using its tiny electric outboard motor, a motor that hardly makes any noise at all.

We swiftly cover 2 miles on a southerly course, hugging the Brooklyn shoreline, the looming, dimly lighted shape of the Verrazano-Narrows Bridge growing larger, dead ahead of us, with every passing minute. Then we turn sharply right and cross the harbor narrows to Staten Island. Moonlight is intermittent, sometimes allowing us to see and be seen, but at other times enclosing us in complete darkness.

Uncle Luke, a skilled boat handler from his years in the Royal Navy, nestles our inboard under a pier, as planned, 200 yards north of Mr. Jonathan Murphy's freighter. The ship appears to me, even from this distance, the largest non-military ship I have ever seen. It is riding high in the water, apparently having been unloaded earlier, but not yet having been loaded with new cargo for its return trip across the Atlantic.

Seeing the freighter riding so high, my uncle decides to use the inflatable, so that he can tie the raft to the ship's exposed rudder shaft at its stern. He expects sentries to be guarding the bow and the starboard side of the ship, since those are accessible from the dock. The guards will, he thinks, assume that intruders would come only from those directions, rather than using a water approach from the stern.

Now we make our final preparations before launching the inflatable raft. As practiced back in the detectives' Manhattan office, we cover each other's faces with black shoe polish. We don leather gloves designed to help us climb from the raft to the ship's deck. We lace on rubber-soled shoes designed to help us climb, and to allow us to walk silently through the ship. The men carefully place their military-issue infrared goggles on their faces, loop the goggles' headbands around their necks, then allow the goggles to drop down onto their chests until they are needed.

Next, Uncle Luke puts on his custom-made shoulder holster with its array of knives, ropes, wire cutters, bolt cutters, and other tools that may be needed. As always, my uncle does not carry a firearm.

Mr. Adelman does, however. He has replaced the handgun he lost during the fight in Coffey Park with what appears to be an even larger one. He checks his replacement handgun and confirms that the weapon is loaded and ready. He straps on his shoulder holster and places several additional ammunition clips in a trouser pocket.

I double my ponytail to shorten its fall down my back and secure it with an extra set of rubber bands. I check the weapon that my uncle and the two detectives have prepared me to use if necessary.

The weapon is a police-grade TASER. It can fire two probes up to 15 feet away from an adversary. It does not depend upon pain to incapacitate the enemy. Its action is neuromuscular. It is compact and not even shaped like a gun. And it has a built-in LED flashlight for illuminating dark areas like the ones we are going into tonight.

I was given two hours of training this afternoon after the decision was made to include me on the rescue mission. Two floors below the conference-room floor, the detectives have installed a fully equipped gym. The three men, and Samuel, spent the available time giving me practice and instruction, yet at the same time trying not to tire me too much. They knew, of course, that they could not make me stronger and more agile and less clumsy in one afternoon, but they also knew they could give me practice in doing the things that I might be called upon to do tonight.

I practiced with the TASER, of course. I practiced climbing a rope of the sort I will have to climb from the inflatable raft to the stern of the ship. I practiced helping my uncle or Mr. Adelman fight against enemies without getting in their way. This last thing really means using the TASER's contact feature, rather than its 15-foot shooting range, and using its contact feature carefully, such as on the heel of an enemy without touching Uncle Luke or Mr. Adelman with it.

They tried to teach me to use a short club as a means of helping them fight, but I was so completely inept with that, they quickly gave up on the idea, as they did with several other ideas that would have required more strength and agility than I actually have. In the end, they were satisfied that, with the few things I *could* do, I had been prepared as well as could be expected.

However, psychologically and emotionally, I am an absolute wreck. I seem torn between, at times, forgetting to breathe entirely, and, at other times, breathing so deeply and desperately that I get light-headed. In the hour before we left the detectives' office building, I prayed in my room for most of that hour, asking for God's help in doing my part in rescuing Gareth. Even though, at times, I was trembling and crying while I prayed, I eventually felt there was at least some chance that I might get through this.

Flurry was with me for that hour. She is always quiet and still when I pray. She seems to know that her role is just to be present with me. And that's enough.

I comforted myself at times this afternoon by thinking about the similarities between what I was going to try to do in this rescue mission, and in things I do in ordinary life. Like playing my violin in public, or reading the scripture lesson at the 11 o'clock service, or giving an oral book report in class. I get nervous before all those things, but if I feel reasonably well prepared, I get calmer, more confident.

Samuel was the most help there, talking with me in my room about how he prepares for soccer matches, and how important it is for him to mentally rehearse doing things right. And, once the action starts, to focus only on the very next thing, not on the whole match, especially if it begins to look like things may not turn out well.

Just do the next thing well. And then the next thing after that. Until the end.

So it is now that, having prepared back at the office as much as possible, and having prepared here in the boat as much as possible, I begin to feel a settled, prayerful calm. And I am pleased when my uncle asks me to pray for Gareth's rescue.

We three kneel together in the stern of the boat, and, in a small circle, we hold hands and I say aloud, in my best strong voice, one of our church's centuries-old prayers, the one that I often pray to myself, and the one that I know Uncle Luke has in mind. "Almighty Father," I say, "we pray that Thou wouldst take our cause into Thine own hands, and judge between us and our enemies. Stir up thy strength, O Lord, and come and help us, for Thou givest not alway the battle to the strong, but canst save by many or by few. Help us, Father, to find Gareth, our lost one, and to bring him safely to his mother and father. Be with us at every moment, please, and bring us all safe home. And Father, if it can be done, please help us do this with no one's being badly hurt, neither us nor our enemies.

"Please, Father … Amen."

Each of them adds his own *Amen,* and we rise.

It's time.

5

Uncle Luke holds the padded grappling hook in one hand, looking up at the stern of the enormous ship, some 25 feet above our tiny inflatable raft. After several swings of the hook, he launches the four-pronged implement 30 feet straight up, then, with a subtle movement of his wrist, causes the rope to ripple just enough for two prongs of the grappling hook to clamp onto the edge of the deck high above us. He tugs downward, hard, to force the hooks to bite into the planking. Then, without a second's hesitation, my uncle goes up the rope hand-over-hand without the use of his legs.

Incredible.

As he reaches the deck, he grabs one of the stern rails with one hand and pulls himself over the railing and onto the deck. After checking his surroundings for a moment, he looks over the edge and gestures for Mr. Adelman to follow. Mr. Adelman does, but he ascends the way I will, coiling the rope around his knees and ankles in such a way that he supports his weight with his legs, while raising himself one arm's length at a time, using his arms and gloved hands.

He takes twice as long to reach the deck as my uncle did, but he succeeds easily and, as Uncle Luke pulls Mr. Adelman onto the deck, both of them look down to me and wave me up. I am so scared that my strength seems doubled, and, using the same technique Mr. Adelman used, just as I practiced this afternoon, I move up the rope quicker than I had imagined I would. In just seconds I am being pulled over the stern railing by the men, who, I see immediately, have removed their weapons from their shoulder holsters — a large knife, Uncle Luke; the enormous handgun, Mr. Adelman — and appear ready for anything.

Visibility is good enough for us to see that the afterdeck is clear. Aside from a trace of moonlight coming through partial overcast, there is a spotlight mounted on the ship's superstructure that illuminates much of the stern deck area.

We know from my noontime vision that the passageway we need is on the port side of the ship, since all of the doorways shown me in the envisioned corridor were on the right, leading to the interior of the ship. The absence of doorways on the left meant that the passageway that I saw was next to the hull of the ship, on its port side.

I remove my TASER from my Gore-Tex jacket pocket, and follow the men around to the left side of the ship's superstructure. There are no sentries in sight, and I think to myself that Uncle Luke must have been right, that the guards are posted on the starboard side of the ship, at the gangplanks, and at the bow, next to the pier.

We come almost immediately to a steel ladder leading down into the portside passageways. Without stopping, we start down in single file, my uncle going first. We stop at the base of the ladder and look down the long, dimly lit passageway that runs forward from stern to bow. It seems that, at least here on the second deck, the infrared goggles will not be needed. The passageway lighting is dim, but good enough.

We see hatch after hatch — small doorways with hinged doors and wheels attached to each, designed to be shut and made watertight with the turn of the locking wheel — going frame after frame as far as we can see. I peer down the length of the corridor. The men wait for me to decide whether or not this is the envisioned passageway. After several seconds, I shake my head no.

They do not ask me why. And I appreciate their unquestioning acceptance of my judgment that this is not the correct level, because I would not be able to say why it is not. It appears to be consistent with the description I gave everyone at noon, but there is something about *this* passageway that does not fit what I saw in my noon vision.

And the difference is not merely that there is no rolling cart to be seen. We have all agreed that the cart might not be present in Gareth's passageway at midnight, since it stands to reason that it had been used for his breakfast or lunch. At this time of night, the cart might or might not be present. It is not the cart's absence that tells me this is not the right level. It is something else, and I can't put that "something else" into words. It's just that the image in front of me does not match the image in the vision.

We immediately start down the next ladder to the third deck. And there we repeat the same sequence. I look carefully down the third-deck passageway. And I decide the match is not perfect. And I shake my head no. And we move down to the fourth deck. And from there to the fifth deck below the main deck.

There, I look again down the passageway and, after several moments, I sense that, this time, there is a match with my noontime vision. And now that I sense the match, I realize what there is about this fifth-deck passageway that is different from those we just examined on the second, third, and fourth decks.

The difference has to do with the curvature of the hull. As we have descended further and further down to, and, probably by now, well below, the ship's waterline, the hull — the left-hand wall of the passageway — has begun to curve inward as it moves down toward the ship's keel, thereby making the passageway narrower at floor level than at ceiling level. But the difference is not so dramatic that I could have put words to the change. Not until now.

I nod to the men. "Yes," I whisper.

We move swiftly through one of the open watertight hatches, then, after 30 feet of travel, through a second hatch. This brings us to a closed door on the right side of the passageway. The door is padlocked.

The men look at me again. And again, I nod my head. "Yes," I say.

My uncle sheathes his knife, pulls his infrared goggles up and onto his face and raps lightly on the doorway. He whispers Gareth's name. There is no response. Uncle Luke removes the bolt cutters from his shoulder holster, fastens the cutting blades to the padlock, and, with his immense strength, pops the padlock shaft cleanly in two. He sheathes the tool, removes the padlock with his gloved hands, and gently turns the door handle, pushing as he does. The door yields.

When the doorway's opening is sufficiently wide, he peers inside. After a moment, finding the lighting from the passageway into the small space adequate, he drops the goggles down again, and pushes the doorway all the way open. He then stands aside so that Mr. Adelman and I can see.

I see Gareth in the dim light, lying on the deck, facing the opposite wall of what appears to be a storage closet for cleaning equipment. Uncle Luke and I move to him and together kneel beside him. My uncle places his hand on Gareth's shoulder and he startles into wakefulness, turning his head to us in alarm, then quickly moving into a sitting position. I am for a moment confused that he seems frightened at the sight of us.

But then I remember how we look. We have blackened faces and black clothing, and we would appear to him merely as silhouettes, since what little light there is comes into the room from the passageway behind us. He sits up fully and cowers against the bulkhead behind him, his eyes wide.

"Gareth," I say.

He makes no response, continuing to look fearfully from one of us to the other. He draws his knees up against his chest, and then covers his face with his hands.

Uncle Luke puts his hand on my shoulder and indicates that I should move out of the way. I do.

Uncle Luke then looks up at Mr. Adelman and gestures for him to come forward. The two of them lift Gareth from the floor, their hands under each of his arms. My uncle, who, despite his immense strength, is several inches shorter than Gareth, turns his face up and whispers, "Gareth, I'm Joanna's uncle. That's Mr. Adelman on your other side."

My uncle then looks at me and nods in my direction. "And that's Joanna."

Gareth turns his face and his eyes slowly to me, as if he is waking from a trance, and our eyes meet. Seconds pass. And then his shy smile slowly appears, just a trace, and, just as slowly, the smile disappears.

"Joanna," he says softly.

And I rush to him and embrace him thankfully. And I realize as I do that the men are truly holding him up. I sense that he is so weak he cannot stand without their help.

I hear him say in my ear, his voice shaky, "It's really you, isn't it?"

And I whisper to him, "Yes, it's really me."

Uncle Luke, much more focused on the task at hand than I am, at that moment, speaks to him again, still holding him up. "Gareth, can you walk unassisted?"

Gareth nods. "I think so."

The men partially release him, and he immediately sags to his knees. We see that he will not be able even to walk the length of the passageway, much less to climb the ladders and then descend by rope to our inflatable.

Uncle Luke looks at Mr. Adelman and says in his command voice, "I'll use the one-man fireman's carry, Jaakov. Take Joanna's TASER and lead up the ladders to the stern deck. I'll follow with Gareth. Joanna, stay close behind me."

My uncle and Mr. Adelman quickly lift Gareth to his feet. Then, more quickly than I can quite follow, and with only a little assistance from Mr. Adelman, Uncle Luke lifts Gareth and drapes him over one shoulder, preparing to carry him, as Detective Belton would enjoy saying, "like he was a half-full sack of potatoes."

I pull the TASER from my waist pack and hand it to Mr. Adelman, who immediately flips it to its "on" position. He then turns to the door, leans out into the passageway just far enough to see, and, TASER in hand, moves fast back toward the ship's stern ladder system. My uncle follows with Gareth, just as fast. And I fall in behind them, moving as fast as I can without actually running.

As we reach each deck — the fourth, then the third, then the second — Mr. Adelman pauses before actually stepping from the top of the ladder into each corridor, looking intently down the length of the passageway toward the bow before exposing himself to view. At the second deck, he does this, shrinks back, and then turns to my uncle and me, looking down at us and holding up, first, two fingers, then his index finger, then thumb and index finger curled into each other, twice, in sequence, to indicate two men in the second-deck passageway, roughly 100 feet away.

He turns back to the passageway, waits until the men have their backs turned, and moves swiftly to the final ladder and on up toward the main deck. My uncle, with Gareth still draped across his shoulder, does the same. When it is my turn, I look down the long passageway and see both security men looking directly at me.

I freeze. For long seconds, I can't seem to move.

But when both men start to move toward me at a run, I finally stumble up the last step to the second deck, turn to the final ladder, and, still stumbling, start up to the main deck. As I do, I hear one of the men shout, "Hey! Stop! Stop there!"

I scramble to the top of the ladder and, at the opening to the main deck, I see Uncle Luke already moving swiftly toward the stern. Crouched next to me as I step off the ladder onto the main deck, I see Mr. Adelman right there next to me, TASER in one hand, gun in the other.

"Go!" he says quietly to me. And I do.

I run as fast as I can to the stern where Uncle Luke is already hoisting himself over the rail, somehow without dislodging Gareth from his shoulder. As I arrive at the rail, I hear in the distance behind me an electrical buzzing sound from the direction of the portside ladders, and I know that Mr. Adelman has fired the TASER. Two seconds later, I hear a second buzzing noise, this one longer and different in tone from the first, and I know that he has used the contact feature of the TASER on the second sentry.

By then I am over the rail myself. I begin the process of wrapping my legs around the rope, preparing to begin the 25-foot descent to the raft, where Uncle Luke is already placing Gareth into one of the cubbies in the raft. The cubbies have been designed to hold supplies or equipment, but, in this case, one cubby will hold a 15-year-old boy who seems barely conscious. Before I start my descent, I look back across the ship's afterdeck and see Mr. Adelman, now on the starboard side of the freighter, looking forward toward the bow on the side next to the pier. Apparently satisfied with what he sees, he turns and runs toward me, motioning for me to go. And I do.

In seconds we are all in the raft and my uncle is expertly flipping the end of the grappling hook rope, causing a ripple to move up the rope to the hook. This, in turn, dislodges the hook so that it plummets from the main deck directly into his hands. As he coils the rope and tosses it into an empty cubby, Mr. Adelman is already starting the tiny electric motor of the raft and motioning for me to cast off from the ship's rudder shaft, which we have used as a hitching post of sorts.

I do. And swiftly, silently, we are gone, disappearing into the vast darkness of the New York Harbor at midnight. No sound of alarm pursues us.

I crawl over to Gareth, reach for his hand, and hold it tight.

Chapter Six

1

Once again, I am awake in the middle of the night. Uncle Luke, Mr. Adelman, and I are seated in the detectives' Manhattan office conference room. We reached the office less than half an hour ago, and found everyone awake and waiting for us.

Gareth and his parents went downstairs to their room as soon as we arrived, and, I noticed, without speaking to me. But the rest of us are assembled at the conference table. Mum, Dad, and Aunt Kory are on the speakerphone. They, at the lodge in England, have been awake all night.

My mum began to cry softly as soon as she heard my voice. Mum doesn't cry often, but we understand exactly why she is. Her tears bring tears to my eyes, too, but I'm smiling all the while. So, we know, is my mum.

Flurry and Max are curled under the table. Both appear to be sleeping, but I'm not sure German shepherds and border collies are ever deeply asleep. I think they are always a little bit awake. The working breeds are *always* at work.

After the three of us report on the details of the rescue of Gareth, and after my family acknowledges that the others had been right — Uncle Luke and Mr. Adelman could *not* have found Gareth without me there on the ship with them — the discussion moves to next steps. Given the Morgans' determination to take Gareth home as soon as he was rescued, Uncle Luke and Detective Belton have arranged for a long-range NYPD helicopter to fly the Morgans to Dover Air Force Base at noon today. That will be in time for them to board the same Royal Air Force transport aircraft that brought Uncle Luke and the dogs across the ocean earlier this week. Gareth and his parents will be home in Wales, even with the time difference, not long after midnight tonight.

I listen to this with less sadness than you might think. Gareth did not at any point during our transit of New York Harbor, or during our drive in the SUV from the Brooklyn Army Terminal to the Manhattan office, show that he even knew who we were. The only time he seemed himself was just for that moment after I hugged him on the ship and he responded by saying, "It's really you, isn't it?"

I don't know exactly what's wrong, but I'm convinced he needs to get home and see his family doctors more than he needs anything else. And so, my main feelings are wrapped up in this enormous worry that he has somehow been damaged, either by the kidnappers or just by the experience of being taken and imprisoned for 24 hours.

I don't feel sad that he's not going to be here with me. Instead, I feel terrible that he got taken and that he got thrown in that miserable little room for so long. I feel terrible for the awful fear that must have filled him up for every minute of that time. And yes, I feel guilty about it all, and for the same reasons Mrs. Morgan spoke when she was so hysterical the other night, when she said it was all my fault. I know there is more to it than that, and I know that I could not really have done anything other than what I've done, and that I didn't ask to be sent any visions, and that my last vision is what made it possible for us to rescue him.

But I still feel terrible. And I still feel guilty.

Flurry licks at my ankle. How does she know? Really, how?

I try to attend to the discussion, and find that I am amazed at what I hear. Aunt Kory, through her ceaseless electronic investigations, has found that several different organizations are involved in planning for a "stupendous" — that's the organizers' word — event to be held in Madison Square Garden soon. It is going to be staged as a *flash* event, as something that will appear to be unplanned, something prompted by an overwhelming public demand for it.

She has found that this "Stupendous Flash Event" is expected to serve as the launch point for The Church of the New Century. That is the same church mentioned in the documents Mr. Belton photographed while he was held at Castle Williams.

And everywhere Aunt Kory finds these Madison Square Garden Stupendous Flash Event references, she also finds references to the scripture from Micah 6:8. The two things are found together nearly every time, she says.

She goes on to explain that some of the funding for the flash event appears to be coming from what we suspect is illegal drug traffic from Central and South America, drugs transported on Mr. Murphy's freighters and container ships. And she reminds us that my third vision, the one with nine words, emphasized BAPTIZE THE SCRIPTURE and CLEANSE THE CHURCH just as much as ATTACK THE CASTLE, which we were able to do immediately to get Mr. Belton back with us.

My aunt goes on to say that systems are already in place that allow people from all over the world to send their money to The Church of the New Century, just by using their mobile-phone apps for that purpose. And, of course, there will be thousands of people actually present in Madison Square Garden for the flash event.

Everyone, both those to be present for the event and those to be watching and listening on their devices, will not only be invited to give their money to the church itself, but to purchase the new electronic games and the new "non-religious" Bibles for young people. She says the games and the Bibles appear not yet to be in production, but that people will be invited to send their money on the promise that their games and Bibles will be sent as soon as manufacturing gets underway.

"This is," Aunt Kory continues, "surely one of the most powerful plans ever cooked up for corrupting Christ's work on earth. Think about it. It is designed to poison the minds of young children, teens, their parents — even some pastors who may get caught up in the excitement — using every form of electronic communication and electronic money-transfer method and device. And combining illegal activity and legal activity as smoothly and perfectly as anything I can imagine."

"Right," adds Mr. Belton quickly. "And, ya know, millions of dollars that are gonna be pumped into this thing are gonna go right back t' th' drug kings and th' drug dealers everywhere, all over th' world, but with just enough money goin' t' good causes t' make it look like th' dirtbag leaders are payin' fer *good* things everywhere. So, they can show that *some* people are really bein' helped by their dirtbag schemes."

We smile. We love to hear Mr. Belton talk. There is no one like him.

"And," adds my mum, "don't forget the multiple-language feature of all of this. The electronic games, the electronic Bibles, the church services — all of this — will be sent and broadcast in dozens of languages all over the world."

After a silence while we try to think through what our choices and chances might be, Aunt Kory gives us one more piece of information. "Oh," she says, "I nearly forgot. I do need to tell you this puzzling thing. I can't find a single piece of concrete evidence that Mr. Jonathan Murphy is personally involved in any of this. I *assume* he is.

"But," she continues, "it is his chief financial officer, an economist named Dr. Judith Hannerty, whose name is connected with much of what I can uncover so far. And she has been logged out of the Swansea import-export office for just as many days as Mr. Murphy has. In fact, she and he may both be there, together, in New York City. I can't be certain."

After a moment, Mr. Belton adds, "Well, when I heard 'em talk about 'th' boss' when they were holdin' me over there in Castle Williams, I guess it coulda just as easily been this Dr. Judith Hannerty woman as it coulda been Mr. Jonathan Murphy. One's as good as th' other, seems t' me.

"Or as bad."

2

It's midmorning now. Once again, I have gone to bed late and have "slept short," as Mr. Belton likes to say. And we are again seated at the conference-room table, having finished a late breakfast and cleared everything away. Mum, Dad, and our aunt are present on our secure link to England. For them, it is mid-afternoon.

I'm wearing my everyday sandals and my other pair of jeans — the pair I did not wear last night on our rescue mission — and a different short-sleeved off-white blouse. My hair is down, and looks nice, since I took time to brush it after finishing my morning devotions, and since it hasn't had time to get messy and tangled.

For what seems like the dozenth time this week, I find that I am completely amazed by what I am hearing. Detective Belton is explaining that, two hours ago, just after he got back from early mass at his Catholic church, he was asked by Reverend Morgan to come downstairs. There was something that he and Mrs. Morgan wanted to discuss with him immediately, and in private.

"Reverend Morgan told me," Mr. Belton has been saying to us, "that Mr. Jonathan Murphy called 'im on his mobile early this mornin', about seven. Said that his assistant in Wales had notified 'im that th' Morgans were here in New York. Said that he, Mr. Murphy, would like t' take th' Morgans, all three of 'em, t' breakfast.

"And when Reverend Morgan told Mr. Murphy that he and Lily and Gareth were plannin' t' leave at noon today t' get an afternoon military flight from Dover Air Force Base back home t' Wales, Mr. Murphy said no, don't do that. Said he had somethin' to propose to Reverend Morgan that oughta change his mind about goin' home so fast.

"And," continued the detective, "th' Morgans talked it over and said okay. They got on th' elevator, all three of 'em, and left t' meet Mr. Murphy as soon as they finished talkin' t' me about it.

"And that's where they are right now. Still there. Still havin' breakfast with Mr. Jonathan Murphy! They've been gone close t' two hours now."

At Mr. Belton's explaining that "all three of 'em" have gone to meet Mr. Murphy for breakfast, my heart does a flip-flop. It sounds like Gareth is better. But if he's better, I think, why didn't he wait here to see me when I got up?

Then I remember. His mother has made clear that she does not want him to have anything to do with me or with our family again. Ever.

Mr. Belton is speaking again. I try to pay attention.

"Ya see, Jaakov," he is saying to his detective partner, "Reverend Morgan has been sorta th' unofficial pastor t' Mr. Murphy's import-export business fer a long time now. And Lily and Gareth, too, have been part of that ministry all along. It's been a family thing from th' start. Th' family is very close t' Mr. Murphy. That's why th' three kids — includin' Joanna, here, and Samuel — were sheltered at th' import-export place last month when th' *other* dirtbags were chasin' 'em all over Wales.

"And that's why it's been hard for th' Morgans t' get their arms around th' idea that Mr. Murphy himself is really a bad guy.

"Know what I mean, Jaakov? Hm?"

"So," Mr. Adelman replies after a moment's reflection, "this invitation to breakfast from Mr. Murphy could be just the sort of courtesy you'd expect, once his assistant let him know the family was here in New York City?"

"Well, yeah," says Mr. Belton, "except fer Mr. Murphy's tellin' Reverend Morgan on th'phone that he didn't want 'im t' leave fer home today. Wanted to tell 'im somethin' that he thought would change his mind about that. *That* sounds like more than just an everyday courtesy.

"Know what I mean, Jaakov? Hm?"

At that moment we hear the buzzer from the street-level entrance to the building. Mr. Adelman gets up from the conference table and goes over to the front-door intercom-and-camera console. On the monitor, he sees the Morgans waving up at him, and says, "Please come up" to them through the intercom. He waits for them to enter the vestibule, helps them operate the sliding wall system, and then, once the elevator is in motion, he returns to the conference table.

I am surprised when the Morgan family comes into the conference room. I had thought they would just go directly to their room on the floor below us, to finish packing for their noon departure. When we see that they are going to join us in the conference room, there is a general shuffling of chairs and people to get Reverend and Mrs. Morgan seated at the table. I look at Mrs. Morgan several times, and at Gareth once, but neither of them makes eye contact with me. They seem not to want to see me, not to want to acknowledge that I'm in the world at all.

Samuel and I move from the table to two of the chairs along the wall. Flurry comes with us and curls up on the floor between Samuel's chair and mine. We both reach down and scratch behind her ears. She then puts her head down on her front paws, gives a big sigh, and closes her eyes. Max has not moved. He remains near the hallway door, lying down, but with his head up and his eyes and ears alert.

Gareth takes the chair next to me, on the other side from Samuel, because that is the only empty chair left in the conference room. Once he is seated, I look at him and smile. He does not look back at me. He averts his eyes and stares straight ahead. He does not smile. I then turn my head away from him, my heart falling into a deep well of sadness. Tears form in my eyes. I can't help it. I am just suddenly so very sad.

Since my face is turned slightly toward my brother, he sees what just happened. Samuel can be very alert when he wants to be. And out of the corner of my eye, I see him shift forward slightly in his chair, just a little movement, but enough for me to look him in the eye, through my welling tears. I am horrified to see my brother's face.

He is furious. Anger, *towering* anger, flashes across his face and he fastens Gareth with a look that says plainly, *if you are going to be mean to my sister, you are going to have me to deal with, Gareth Morgan.*

Suddenly there is a deafening CRASH from the other side of the conference table. Everyone in the room jumps in her or his seat, eyes wide and staring up at the looming figure of Lieutenant Luke Manguson, Royal Navy officer, who has smashed his fist into the table with such force that I am surprised the table remains in one piece.

Uncle Luke fixes Reverend and Mrs. Morgan, whose backs are to me, with a gaze of such ferocity that the gaze in itself causes them both to shrink down in their chairs. He speaks in a low, steely voice in the absolute silence of our conference room.

My mind flashes momentarily across the ocean. I picture my mum, who has spent her entire life around her twin brother. The thought occurs to me that my mother knows exactly what is about to happen here in this room.

"Cecil and Lily," Uncle Luke says, "I have just watched you two, and your son, continue to refuse to acknowledge my niece's existence. I see the tears starting down her face, and I want you to know that *I will have no more of this*.

"Lily, I tolerated your outburst at Joanna and our family the other night, because your only child had just been taken, and you were terrified. I understood. I let it go.

"But now Gareth is back with you, and he is back with you *only* because my sister's 14-year-old daughter had enough courage to volunteer to accompany Jaakov and me on one of the more dangerous missions I have been on in recent years. I can assure you that, had Joanna not been with us on that ship, we would never have found your son. *She risked her life for him.* And now he is here with you, present, safe.

"If your decision remains as it was earlier, never again to allow Gareth and Joanna to see each other again, that is certainly your right. But I will tolerate no more abuse of her. She did not ask to be sent visions. They are *sent* to her. What would you have her do? Would you have her cut herself off from God? Is that what you want?

"Her last vision led us to your son. Until that vision, we did not even know with any confidence that he was on board ship, to say nothing of his precise location on a very, very large vessel.

"If it is your intent to maintain what appears to me to be actual *hatred* for my niece — and that's the correct word, insofar as I can see — then I am telling you now to leave this place. Leave our family. Go downstairs, pack your things, and Detective Belton will arrange for our policewoman to have her car in front of the building in 15 minutes. She will take you to the NYPD heliport, and you can be on your way to Dover Air Force Base. And then home to England.

"Decide now. Joanna is a *chosen* girl. My patience has ended."

Uncle Luke remains standing, his stare no less intense than when he slammed his fist into the table. Samuel takes my hand. Flurry rises and nuzzles my leg. My embarrassment is complete. I just want to be somewhere else.

Over the speakerphone, I begin to hear a sound that I do not at first recognize. Then I do. It is clapping, slow clapping from the other side of the Atlantic Ocean. And it gradually dawns on me that my mother is giving her view of the matter. Without saying a word, she is giving us her comment on her brother's speech.

Lengthy applause for my uncle, from his sister, my mother.

3

"And so," Gareth is saying to me, half an hour after my uncle's explosion in the conference room, "I was so humiliated by my own cowardice that I couldn't stand to face you, Joanna. Or even look at you. I just wanted to do what my mum said. I just wanted to go away from you and your family and crawl into a hole somewhere.

"You deserve someone better, Joanna," he concludes with immense sadness in his voice and on his face.

It turns out that Gareth was not exactly kidnapped from Coffey Park. Not in the way we all thought. No, it turns out that he ran away from the fighting, into the trees nearby, and was then caught by two of our assailants as they ran to their vehicle. They decided on the spot to drag him to their vehicle. Only at that point did it turn into a kidnapping, but it was a complete accident, in the eyes of the kidnappers, that the victim was Gareth. They had wanted me, the visioner, not him.

And that's what he means by his cowardice. He is telling me that he ran away from the fighting and that he has been too ashamed to face me or to say anything to me at all. He is telling me that he felt his mum's decision, as she explained it to him last night when we got back to the office from our rescue mission, was the best one for *me*. That the best thing for *me* was for him to go away and never see me again.

We're sitting together in the detectives' gym, alone except for Flurry. The gym is really the only place we can be alone other than in one of the sleeping rooms. So, after my uncle's tirade in the conference room, when the adults then asked us to leave, Mr. Belton thoughtfully suggested that we go to the gym to talk. He meant Samuel, too, but, in the elevator, Samuel said he would just go to his sleeping room so that Gareth and I could have a talk by ourselves. I wasn't sure that was a good idea, and neither was Gareth, but Samuel gave me a look that said *Go Talk To Him*.

So, I took a deep breath and nodded to Samuel, assuring him that I would. He got off the elevator on the sleeping-room floor, and Gareth and I went down one more, to the gym level. Now I am sitting on a rolled-up exercise mat in one corner of the gym. Gareth is sitting on a bench used for weight lifting.

He sits facing me, about six feet away. Close, but not very.

He seems finished with his explanation of why he has not wanted to talk to me, and why he accepted his mum's decision that he should just fly home with his parents and never see me or our family again. We have been silent for several minutes now, while I think about what he has said and try to decide what to say back to him. He waits patiently for me, something I think he learned from us last month in Wales.

Most people are uncomfortable with silence. Our family is not.

Finally, I look up at him from my seat on the rolled-up mat and say, "I understand part of this, Gareth. I certainly understand your running away from all the fighting. Uncle Luke and Mr. Adelman and Max are trained fighters, and Samuel seems just naturally to love fighting, at least when there is something important to fight for. And Flurry would have fought, if she hadn't been caught in that net. She would protect me from an army.

"But, Gareth," I say, "this is no different from your running from those people that tried to kidnap me at Penn Station the other day. Samuel grabbed my arm and ran, because he has certain gifts and habits. You don't have those gifts and habits. I don't either. And it's okay that we don't.

You know what the Apostle wrote about gifts. We all have different gifts. None of us has every gift that a person could have.

"Don't even think any more about running away from those people at Penn Station or at Coffey Park. Really. It's okay."

"But, Joanna," he says, "look at what you did for me last night. You were brave enough to help rescue me from that ship. You had the courage to go with your uncle and Mr. Adelman, and to find me and bring me back here. You risked your life for me. *You* were brave."

I shake my head no.

"That," I say, "was the result of a God-Thing, Gareth, and of a lot of serious discussion and debate and preparation. That was not an instinctive reaction to danger. My instinctive reaction to danger, surely, is to run from it.

"And besides," I add, with a little smile, "I was terrified throughout the thing."

He smiles back at me. Just a little hint of a smile.

"But, Gareth," I continue, looking at him with my most serious face and shaking my head a little at him, "this thing about not speaking to me or my family for the rest of our lives. That's different. That's completely different. And that's not okay at all.

"I think all of us understood what your mum said to me just after you were taken from the park. She was distraught. I would be, too, in her shoes. Anybody would.

"But she was thinking about protecting *you*. She was thinking that, if you never had anything to do with us again, you would be safe."

I nod my head. *"That's* understandable."

"But *you* were going to accept her judgment, not for that reason, but because you wanted to protect *me* from *you*.

"I'm sorry," I say firmly, *"that* is just wrong. I get to decide — not you — whether or not it is good for me to be with you, for me to be your girlfriend."

I think this is the first time I have said that word to him. But I don't blush.

"You're saying that, because you ran away from the fighting, you're not worthy of being my boyfriend, that you're not worthy of me. Well, that's something I get to decide, Gareth Morgan. And I have decided."

I look at him fiercely. Or my version of fiercely.

"Don't *ever* do that again. Don't *ever* turn away from me and not look at me and pretend I don't exist. Never, never, *never* do that again."

4

A few minutes after our talk in the gym is finished, Gareth, Flurry, and I stop on the sleeping-room floor and I knock on Samuel's door. I am feeling so happy that when my brother opens his door, I jump into his arms and give him my biggest hug.

"They're not leaving!" I say. "They're staying with us!"

When I release Samuel from my bear hug, he looks questioningly at Gareth, who says, "Right. At breakfast this morning, Mr. Murphy talked my mum and dad into staying here in New York at least through next Monday night, and maybe longer than that. Monday is the night for this thing we seem to be calling the "Stupendous Flash Event" at Madison Square Garden. It's not really a flash event, technically, because it is being very carefully planned, but it will *seem* like a flash event to many people. And Mr. Murphy wants my dad to help him lead the event.

"And," he adds, "given your uncle's, um 'warning speech' that he gave us earlier in the conference room, I don't think Mum or Dad is going to say *anything* about our families not being together.

"In fact," he adds, looking at me, "Mum got up this morning feeling horrible about things she said, Joanna. I think you were going to get a nice apology from Mum, even without your uncle's, um, explosion."

"If she will just change her mind," I say, "I'll be happy. No apology needed."

I turn to Samuel. "I think," I say to my brother, "that we should all go upstairs right now, so we can hear details and be part of the conversation."

Samuel looks at me skeptically. I know what he is thinking. That they won't want us to be there. Not yet.

"We need to insist, Samuel," I say. "We three are fully engaged in this thing. We need to be part of the conversation.

"We just need to insist."

Samuel shrugs and looks at Gareth as if to say, *Well, looks like she's decided to be in charge. You know how she can be. There's no use arguing. We might as well go along with her.*

The boys smile at me, and we head for the elevator.

As soon as we exit the elevator and enter the conference room, the conversation stops and everyone looks at us. After a moment, my uncle speaks to me, since I'm standing in front of the boys.

"Need something, Joanna?" he says.

I note that Uncle Luke's demeanor has changed completely from the furious version of him we saw before we left the conference room earlier. He seems relaxed and even energized and happy now.

"We need to be part of the discussion, Uncle Luke," I say to him with a surprising, to me, absence of self-consciousness. Sometimes my own presence in front of other people defies my understanding. Sometimes I seem poised; at other times, the opposite. This seems to be one of the poised times.

My uncle just raises his eyebrows, expecting more. So, I provide more.

"The three of us are just as immersed in this as all of you are. And, so far, I'm the only visioner. And we're not children any more. We think we can help."

My uncle smiles broadly and looks first at Mr. Belton, then at Mr. Adelman, then at the Morgans. They each smile and nod at him, and so he addresses the other three over the speakerphone. "Rebecca, Matt, Kory?" he asks.

"Fine, Luke," says my dad, speaking for the three.

"But you're still a little rotter, Joanna Clark," says Detective Belton, smiling in his impish way. "And I'm gonna tell yer mother right now, in front of everybody, how ya sat in th' kitchen at th' Brooklyn safe house th' other night, listenin' t' everything we said, and knowin' we'd forgot ya were there. An' then ya came traipsin' through th' kitchen like you'd done nothin', smilin' at us and pretendin' you'd heard nothin'.

"And I said to yer uncle right then an' there, ya little rotter, that yer Mom was gonna *kill* yer uncle Luke when she could get her hands on 'im, fer lettin' ya sit in that kitchen an' listen t' us all that time, and at three in th' mornin', too.

"Yer a little rotter, Joanna Clark. I'd call ya a dirtbag, except yer mother is listenin', and, if I call ya that, then she'd kill *me*, next time she sees me."

There is laughter all around the conference room, then a silence. My uncle wags his finger at Mr. Belton, pretending to threaten him, and then sits with his head in his hands, shaking his head. Everyone is waiting to hear what will come over the speakerphone from the lodge. Finally, my mum's voice comes from across the ocean.

"Luke," she says quietly, "I am going to break my best tennis racket over your head, and then I'm going to make you cook Kory's dinner for the next month.

"No, wait," she adds, reconsidering, "that would be punishing *Kory.*"

In the happy laughter that follows this exchange, we three, pleased that we've been accepted so easily, take our seats against the wall, using the same chairs we occupied during my uncle's speech to the Morgans. Flurry comes with us, and, this time, so does Max. The two dogs curl up next to each other in front of our chairs. We settle, and I reach down to pat both dogs.

Mr. Belton clears his throat, signaling he is about to resume the discussion. But before he can actually begin, Mrs. Morgan suddenly pushes her chair back from the table, rises, and turns toward me. She steps past Max and Flurry so that she is standing right in front of me, and, despite having on the cream-colored dinner-and-church dress she brought from home, she drops to both knees and places her hands on my knees. She lets her face fall slowly into her hands, as they rest on my knees.

"Joanna," she says, her voice choked with emotion.

"Joanna," she says again, but as she tries to say something to me, she begins to cry. In just seconds, her small body is wracked with sobs, uncontrollable anguish pouring from her. And no words other than my name.

Reverend Morgan, himself dressed in a light-colored summer suit, gets up from the table and quickly steps around the dogs to kneel beside his wife, holding her shaking shoulders in his hands, trying to comfort her as well as he can. He looks up at me, asking forgiveness on her behalf with his eyes. I lean down and put my face in her soft brown hair, whispering in her ear, "It's all right, Mrs. Morgan. I understand. I really do understand."

And so, the three of us remain, just that way, for what seems a very long time, without more words being spoken, just holding each other. At some point I realize that Gareth is also kneeling beside his mum, and that his hands are also on her.

Finally, her tears begin to subside, and slowly she lifts her face to mine. Hers is a face filled with remorse, a face devastated with shame. I put my hands on her face and I say softly, "Your son was lost, Mrs. Morgan. I understand. We all understand."

She shakes her head. "I said horrible things to you, Joanna. I couldn't sleep last night, just thinking about what I said. Please, please forgive me.

"I have no excuse, Joanna. None at all."

I lean forward and kiss her forehead.

"I just wanted him back," I say. "And he's here."

5

Now it's the evening of the same day, a Friday. All the discussing and planning was finished by late afternoon, in time for Mr. Adelman to begin his observance of the Jewish Sabbath at sundown. The K-9 officers came by during the meeting and took the dogs again. Our policewoman brought a nice catered meal up to the kitchen somewhat later, placing everything in the refrigerator, so we could decide individually when to have the evening meal.

Now it's bedtime for Samuel and me, our regular bedtime, and Mum has again asked to have a private session with my uncle, my brother, and me, even though, for her, it is two in the morning. Dad and Aunt Kory are with her on our secure link to the lodge. We've just taken our places in the conference room, and Flurry and Max have both settled themselves comfortably under the table.

"My dears," Mum begins, "let's review everything before you go off to bed. We've gained quite a bit of clarity today, and I want to be sure that our family is settled on the main questions and the main answers, so far as we have them at this point.

"And Joanna," she adds, "you or I may dream at any point. If we do, we need to be clear on how to think about whatever we are sent. Yes?"

"Yes, Mum," I say.

"First," she continues, "we are in agreement that Mr. Murphy's financial officer, an economist named Dr. Judith Hannerty, is the force behind everything that is happening right now. We think that Mr. Murphy runs his company loosely, trusting his senior staff to manage his day-to-day operation. We think he himself is exactly the person Reverend Morgan and Lily Morgan have always understood him to be: a man who wants his company to be a good place to work, a good place for families, a good place for people of faith, a good place for people to spend their entire working lives, a good place for young people to enter the business world."

"Yes, Mum," my brother and I say at the same time.

"Detective Belton," she continues, "with his worldwide connections and his worldwide respect in law enforcement communities, has quietly engaged some of his friends in the FBI, there in the United States, and in MI5, here in the United Kingdom, to help us confront the threats. These government agencies cannot, of course, help us directly with any threats specifically to Christianity. The faith can be legally threatened in both countries and anywhere else on earth.

"But Dr. Hannerty appears to have involved Mr. Murphy's company in worldwide drug shipments resulting in people being murdered, people being drawn into addiction, people being drawn into forced prostitution, politicians being bribed, church leaders being corrupted, and more. Anything that can be bought or sold, when enough money is offered, is being bought or sold."

I reach for a pad of paper and pen, so that I can make a few notes as Mum talks. My uncle shakes his head at me and, at the same time, my brother reaches out and grabs my wrist gently. "Oh, right," I say.

We have been taught never to write anything down when our family is in crisis like this. There should never be a written record, on paper or electronic, that someone else might uncover. We are to remember everything without that kind of assistance. I'm such a compulsive notetaker that it's hard for me to remember that.

"The flash-event launch for The Church of the New Century," continues Mum after a moment, "is scheduled for Monday next, there in New York. This 'church' is being set up to attract money from Christian believers all over the earth. That money will be used for all the purposes I just mentioned, but also to promote the kind of 'church' that will manufacture electronic games and Bibles for children and young people, games and Bibles designed to destroy all sense of right and wrong in growing children.

"We expect Reverend Morgan," she adds, "to have a role in the flash event, though that bit of information may not be given in advance to Dr. Hannerty and her people. And that means that two agendas — incompatible with each other — are being prepared for the flash event: one by Mr. Murphy, Reverend Morgan, and others, and another by Dr. Hannerty and her accomplices both inside and outside the import-export company.

"Cecil's role is going to be worked out with Mr. Murphy and a small group of NYPD, FBI, and MI5 people. None of this means that the danger is over, as you can imagine. The enemy is powerful, resourceful, and well funded."

Mum sighs, thinks for a moment, and then says in conclusion, "Kory will continue to work through every technological avenue she can develop. And you and I, daughter, will be ready to see and hear whatever we may be sent.

"Yes, children? Yes, Luke? Yes to all of that?"

"Got it, Rebecca," says Uncle Luke, speaking for himself and for us.

"Right, then," says Mum, "say your prayers and try to get a real sleep. We love you, every one, including those two who are no doubt curled up at your feet."

Good-nights are said all round, and Samuel and Flurry and I go to the elevator. Max stays with Uncle Luke in the conference room. We assume our uncle wants to do more thinking before he goes to his sleeping room, which is between Samuel's and Gareth's rooms, and across the common area from Reverend and Mrs. Morgan.

Samuel and Flurry and I get off the elevator on the sleeping-room floor and walk together to the door of my room. Samuel and I say good night to each other, and Flurry and I go in. I start to close my door and then think better of it. I step back into the common area just as Samuel disappears into his room.

"Samuel?" I say.

He steps back. He looks at me, eyebrows lifted.

I look down, embarrassed. "Samuel?" I say again.

"What is it, Joanna?"

"Would you mind sleeping with Flurry and me tonight, on the fold-out sofa in my room?" I say uncomfortably. "I'm, um, a little scared."

Samuel doesn't hesitate, or ask me what I'm scared of. He just says, "Sure," and goes into his room to brush his teeth and to pick up his e-reader. In about three minutes I hear his door close and he stops at my door and knocks lightly.

"You ready?" he whispers through the door.

"Ready," I say, having undressed and put on my long nightshirt.

Samuel comes in, wearing his warm-weather sleeping outfit: a tee shirt and running shorts. He picks up the lightweight blanket from the back of the sofa, and lies down without even pulling the sofa bed out. He spreads the blanket over himself and says good night again.

He will be asleep in minutes.

Knowing that, I motion for Flurry to jump up to her place at the foot of my bed and I turn off the lamp on my nightstand. I would normally check my mobile for any messages before I do anything else, but with these disposable prepaid phones, there isn't anything to check anymore.

They're just emergency communication devices, and we all understand that.

So, I pick up my e-reader and open it to the Bible, but I don't start to read. I want to think first about why I am scared tonight, why I wanted my brother to sleep in my room with me and Flurry. It's not something I gave any thought to when I asked him to do it. It was just a spur-of-the-moment thing.

Nothing comes to me, though, and so I decide I was just having a leftover case of nerves from the rescue mission for Gareth. That was only last night, although it seems much longer ago than that. And I certainly *was* scared by that — before, during, and even after it. Just a delayed response, I decide.

That's all.

I'm so sleepy that I only read one passage — the account of the young Jesus staying behind when his parents leave Jerusalem after Passover — before closing up my e-reader and shutting my eyes. I start my nighttime prayers, but, as often happens when I'm tired and sleepy, I fall asleep while praying so that, when the prayer-dream arrives, as it does immediately, I'm not sure afterward when the prayer stopped and the dream began. I only know that the dream was not a normal dream. Normal dreams don't happen in this way. I'm getting good at knowing the difference.

This dream is short, but it has an urgency about it that, I think, leads the dream itself to wake me up. My eyes open and I think for several minutes, doing my usual checking to make sure that it couldn't have been a regular dream or even a daydream. Satisfied that it couldn't have been either of those, because nothing actually happened in this dream and yet an urgency was somehow sent to my sleeping mind, I lean over and turn on the lamp.

Samuel is already sleeping. I can tell by his breathing.

I slip out of bed and walk barefoot over to the sofa. I place my hand on his shoulder and he is instantly awake. He sits up, rubs his eyes, and looks at me.

"Samuel," I say, "We need to get Uncle Luke."

As soon as I explain why, I grab my robe from the door hook and we motion for Flurry to come. Samuel doesn't bother to put on anything other than the tee shirt and running shorts he is already wearing, and we go to the elevator without getting dressed and without even putting on shoes. When we pad barefoot into the conference room, with Flurry's toenails clicking behind us, we find our uncle and Max have been joined by Mr. Belton since we left the room half an hour ago. They look up in surprise.

"Joanna dreamed," says Samuel.

I describe the prayer-dream quickly to the two men, explaining how this vision was brief, and seemed to be about the office building itself. All I was shown, I say, was the building, from overhead, as if from a helicopter. The vision was static; nothing moved. But the sense I was given was that we were not safe here, that there were threats to us, right here in this office fortress.

That the threats were right now.

"Samuel," says Mr. Belton, "go get Jaakov, quick."

Seeing my brother hesitate, he adds, "Yes, it's his Sabbath, but he's allowed t' engage an enemy when there's a threat. He can fight on defense, if he has to.

"Go."

When Samuel and Mr. Adelman return, Mr. Belton summarizes my prayer-dream nicely and then goes on to note that the moving wall in the building's ground-floor vestibule can be operated only by the retinal scanner, which is set only for the two detectives' eyes, and by the buzzer on the console in the conference room. And he notes that the interior fire stairway opens onto the small, fenced backyard, and does not have a handle or keying device on the outside.

It can be opened only from the interior stairwell.

"And that," says Mr. Adelman, nodding his head, "leaves the roof."

We are silent while the men think about the building's vulnerability from the roof. They quickly conclude that the roof could be accessed from the building on the west side, since its roof is at the same level, and since the two structures are separated only by a six-foot-wide alley. They discuss how intruders could gain access to that neighboring building, get onto its roof, place a ladder across the gap between that building and ours, and be right on top of us in minutes.

Without wasting another minute, Uncle Luke and Mr. Adelman snatch their shoulder holsters from the locked gun closet in the hallway. And Mr. Adelman brings a third shoulder holster and weapon to Mr. Belton.

Mr. Belton straps on the shoulder holster and says, "Kids, I'm gonna go down t' th' sleepin' room floor and set up shop in th' common area. Yer uncle and Jaakov will go t' th' roof with Max.

"You two stay here with Flurry," he says. "Ya can pull out a couple of th' sleepin' bags from th' coat closet and lie down here or in th' lounge area, if ya want."

And suddenly the men are gone. We get the sleeping bags and take them into the small lounge area next to the conference room. The lounge area has sofas and several upholstered chairs.

We roll out the sleeping bags on two of the sofas.

Flurry climbs onto my sofa and curls up at my feet. The floor lamp in the corner, which stays on much of the time, is still on, but we don't care. It's dark enough.

Samuel and I say our good-nights again, and I pick up my e-reader. I decide to read a bit from one of C. S. Lewis's Narnia stories. I've always felt the Narnia books were written with quite young children in mind, because of the talking animals. But, even if Mr. Lewis had in mind children much younger than I am, I still like reading them.

I open my e-reader to *The Last Battle,* and go right to the final chapters. I want to read about Aslan welcoming everyone into Heaven after the fighting is over.

I need to think about Aslan tonight.

Chapter Seven

1

It's Sunday evening after dinner. Two whole days have passed without anything big happening. At least, nothing that Samuel, Gareth, or I have been told about.

Friday night was eventful, though. After I told my prayer-dream to my uncle and Mr. Belton, they and Mr. Adelman and Max quickly prepared for trouble. And when the trouble arrived, Uncle Luke and Mr. Adelman and Max were on the roof and ready. In fact, they were not even on *our* building's roof by then. Leaving Max in position on our own roof, they laid a ladder across the rooftop from our building to the next one. Then they crossed over to that roof. Once there, they prepared for visitors.

They didn't have long to wait, leading us all to realize why my prayer-dream had had such urgency attached to it somehow. Soon after Uncle Luke and Mr. Adelman were in position, three intruders emerged onto the neighboring building's roof, expecting no opposition, and, as my uncle puts it, found themselves immediately "incapacitated" by him and Mr. Adelman. I don't think they used a gun — although they may have used that TASER — but they didn't seem to want to report to us young people any of the details. They just told us that they incapacitated the three, bound and gagged them with the tools and equipment Uncle Luke carries in his shoulder holster, and left them there for NYPD officers to collect Saturday morning.

During the day Saturday, the detectives arranged for their security company to spend time on our roof, setting in place something that sounds to me like some enormous TASER that can incapacitate — that word again — anyone who tries to gain access to our building from our roof. Whatever it actually is, it has a timer. It turns itself on at sundown, and off at sunrise.

Saturday night in our family's private session on the secure link with Mum, Dad, and Aunt Kory, I talked to my mother about the strange thing that happened Friday night, when I asked Samuel to sleep in Flurry's and my room because I felt scared. I explained to her that my prayer-dream had come right away, warning the men to prepare quickly for trouble on our building's roof. It's the first time, I said to Mum, that I'd ever been forewarned, so to speak, while fully awake, that there might be danger coming. And, I said, it was a vague warning. A feeling, not a vision. Nothing concrete. Just enough for me to ask my brother to stay in my room with me.

"Mum," I asked, "have you ever had that happen to you? A sort of warning that is so vague that you can't say for sure that it really *is* a warning?"

My mother was thoughtful for quite a while, then she said, "I don't think so, Joanna. I've had wide-awake *visions* before. And I've certainly had many anxious moments since my first vision long ago, but I think they were all in connection with some danger we knew we were about to face. Like how you felt on your rescue mission to save Gareth the other night.

"But, no," she continued, "I don't remember ever feeling what you felt. And I think that's extraordinary, that you would experience something of this sort — merely a *feeling* — that would come to you before an actual vision. A sort of minor-key Divine Intrusion that unsettled you enough for you to ask Samuel to stay with you.

"I think this is a wonderful thing," she continued, "and something I'm going to remember for myself, in case I ever have that same kind of forewarning. I think you've taught us all something important, dear. Thank you.

"And, Samuel," she added, "thank *you* for not questioning your sister's anxiety the other night, and for just going ahead and moving onto her sofa as soon as she asked you to. I can't tell you how much your dad and I appreciate how you two are with each other when the visions come to our family.

"We're very, very grateful."

That conversation was last night and, overnight, while we slept, both my mother and I received vision-dreams. The two vision-dreams were very different, and I only know a little about Mum's.

Hers was reported to us late this morning, after Reverend Morgan led us in a worship service in the lounge area next to the conference room, where Samuel and Flurry and I slept Friday night. He used the parable of the sheep and the goats from Matthew 25 for his text, and delivered a wonderful message to our little group. We had moved the speakerphone into the lounge, so that Mum, Dad, and Aunt Kory could listen and be part of the service.

After the worship service, Mum and I reported our dreams to everyone. Mum explained that her dream was entirely for Aunt Kory's benefit, and that it focused on electronic code words and passwords that Aunt Kory would be able to use to dig further into Dr. Hannerty's plans for Monday night's Madison Square Garden flash event. I think we're going to be amazed at what Aunt Kory will accomplish with this kind of vision-dream help from my mother.

As for my vision-dream, it arrived early this morning and, like the Friday night prayer-dream, it somehow woke me up when it ended. I quickly put on my robe and knocked quietly on my brother's and then on my uncle's doors, so I could report right away. I wanted to be sure they would be able to help me remember everything for later, when everyone would be listening.

After worship today, Mum reported first, and then it was my turn. I looked occasionally to my brother and my uncle, while I gave my report, to make sure I was remembering everything and being clear in my explanation.

"This morning's vision-dream," I began, "seemed very long compared to my others. Minutes, it seemed, not just seconds. The whole thing took place in what I'm certain must be the interior of Madison Square Garden. And it presented itself to me like a movie, like a movie preview of Monday night's flash event.

"My viewpoint was from one end of the arena, from just above floor level, behind the stage. The first specific thing I noticed was the enormous scoreboard that's suspended from the roof of the arena. It's the biggest electronic thing I've ever seen.

It's four-sided, of course, so people can read it from any seat in the building. I only saw it for a few seconds, I suppose because it was blank during my vision-dream. Nothing ever appeared on it.

"The arena seemed almost completely filled to me, but I might be wrong. It may have been that there were so many people visible in my vision that I just *thought* the arena was filled. I don't know. But I know that thousands of people were in the arena seats, and maybe another two thousand more were on the folding chairs that covered much of the floor where, I suppose, they must play basketball.

"But after I was given this general view of the Garden — its scoreboard, its seating, and the enormous stage — my attention was mostly drawn to people who seemed to be coming toward the stage from behind it, through a tunnel, on my left. It was a tunnel that, I think, must lead from the dressing rooms to the arena, and must, on some occasions, bring players or musicians or speakers out onto the arena floor. And, with the stage set like it was, this tunnel was bringing people to a small set of stairs going up onto the stage itself, from behind."

"Joanna," interrupted Uncle Luke, "don't forget what you told your brother and me earlier this morning. I mean the part about the catwalk leading up to, and above, the scoreboard, which, by the way, everyone, will be an info-board Monday night, rather than a scoreboard."

"Oh, yes!" I said. "Before my attention was drawn to the tunnel coming in from the left, behind the stage, I was focused for a few seconds on a black metal catwalk leading from the right side of the area — the right side, that is, from my vision-dream's viewpoint — up and *over* the top of the scoreboard, hundreds of feet above the floor. I suppose its purpose is to allow workers to reach the scoreboard itself — the info-board, that is — for maintenance or repairs or something. But the fact that my attention was drawn to that catwalk may be important. I've found that, when a dream makes me focus specifically on something, it usually turns out to matter."

"Yes, it does," I hear my mother murmur over the speakerphone.

"Next," I continue, looking at my uncle and my brother for confirmation, "was this bright green golf-cart thing that moved back and forth from the depths of the tunnel to the rear of the stage and back again, several times. And the last time it stopped behind the stage, two men got out of the cart and opened a long silver box mounted on the back of the golf cart. As I watched in my vision-dream, the two men — I couldn't see their faces — started pulling weapons from the box. Rifles. Pistols. Things that looked to me like hand grenades.

"I think I may have cried out in my dream at this point. Samuel didn't hear anything from his room, but I think I cried out some kind of warning, and I think that may be what woke me up.

"In any case, that was the end," I said. "There was no tidy ending. The vision-dream just stopped when I cried out. It just stopped with the men and the rifles and pistols and hand grenades still there, right in the center of my vision. I knew that I needed to tell Samuel and Uncle Luke everything, before I forgot anything, so I did."

I stopped. I looked again at Uncle Luke and Samuel. They nodded.

Uncle Luke said, "That's it, Joanna. That's what you gave us this morning."

2

As I said before, it's now Sunday evening after dinner. And even though nothing big has happened since Friday night's excitement on the roof, that doesn't mean that we haven't been busy.

Since Mum's Saturday night vision-dream, Aunt Kory has been focused on using clues from that dream to probe further and further into the electronic trails that connect to Mr. Murphy's financial officer, Dr. Hannerty. And here in the detectives' office, Gareth and Mr. Adelman have been able to use other clues from my mother's vision-dream to investigate some of the electronic systems in Madison Square Garden, including those that control that enormous info-board hanging from the roof over the arena. I think all three of them will be up all night, each working on a separate piece of the puzzle.

We need control of the info-board Monday night. Whatever appears on the info-board will also be appearing on individual screens on electronic devices all over the country and the world. We can't let our adversaries determine what shows there.

And Samuel and I, although we are not as good as our aunt, or Mr. Adelman, or Gareth, have enough understanding of how to investigate things electronically to go deep into Madison Square Garden's blueprints, on file electronically at New York's City Hall. We are beginning to get a picture of how people can get weapons into the building, and then right up to the stage where the leaders of The Church of the New Century's flash event will be assembling Monday evening. We see how they might get close, but we don't know why they would.

Surely, we keep saying to each other, there are easier ways to hurt or even kill a few people than to shoot them or throw a grenade at them in front of 15,000 people and millions more, maybe, watching on TV. So, we're not sure what pieces of information or what elements of electronic control will actually matter when the time comes. We'd like to know more than we do, but we know we can't know everything.

And we agree, Samuel and I, that there are moments when we feel confident that we — our family, the Morgan family, the detectives — will succeed. We will figure it all out — or figure it out *enough* — by Monday evening, and will prevent whatever damage is being planned, damage to people, damage to the faith, damage to everything. But there are moments when we feel overwhelmed, helpless to understand exactly what is being planned, or exactly who is doing the planning, or even why they want to do their evil.

But maybe, we say to each other, a certain level of evil is always impossible to understand, even if you're the one doing the evil. Maybe evil is not supposed to make sense. Maybe it's just what evil does. It's just what evil is.

Just as Samuel and I are saying these things to each other, Gareth steps out of the elevator and into the common area on the sleeping-room floor, where my brother and I set up two of the detectives' computers earlier this afternoon. Seeing us in quiet conversation, he hesitates.

"Should I go back upstairs?" he says to us uncertainly, "so that you two can keep working in those electronic archives? I don't want to interrupt."

Samuel stretches and says, "I'm ready for a break. You, Joanna?"

"I'd *love* to rest my brain for a while," I say.

There is an awkward silence while we all try to think of what to say next. It is Samuel who rescues us.

Sort of.

"I know," he says brightly, "you two should have a date!"

Gareth and I glance at each other, smiling uncomfortably. Then we look back helplessly at Samuel, hoping he will somehow take away the discomfort.

He rolls his eyes at me.

"You know," he says, beginning to get irritated at us, "a date! A boy-girl thing. A boyfriend-girlfriend thing. A date. What's so hard about a date, Joanna? Just go somewhere with Gareth and *talk* to him. A DATE!"

Tears of embarrassment form in my eyes. I can't help it.

Samuel, his face close to mine, sees them coming. His face changes from irritation to embarrassment — of a different sort from mine — in a flash. He reaches out and pulls me to him, hugging me hard.

"I'm sorry," he whispers in my ear after a moment. "I'm so sorry."

I nod against his shoulder and press my face down into his shoulder, hoping to dry my eyes against his shirt. It seems to work.

Gareth, still standing, and several feet away, does not see the tears or hear my brother's whispered words. He stands confused by what he sees from us, and when he speaks, it is in response to Samuel's suggestion of a "date."

"Well," he says finally, "I'd like that, Samuel, but where?"

"Tell you what," says my brother, releasing me and trying to restore some order to the disjointed conversation, "let's go down a floor to the fitness center. I'll go over to the corner that has all the free weights and the cardio equipment. I'll work out for an hour or so, and you two can sit in the opposite corner where that little lounge area is, with its sofa and free soft drinks. You can talk while I do my workout.

"That's a date, you know," he says with such satisfied finality that he and I both close our computers without another word, get up from our chairs, and start for the elevator, Gareth trailing behind us. Two minutes later we are each in our assigned positions, with Samuel in the far corner of the fitness room, starting his workout, and with Gareth and me in the opposite corner, sitting on the little worn sofa with our soft drinks, ready to begin what, for us, is the hardest thing: just talking.

I decide to start.

"How is your work going with Mr. Adelman?" I ask, taking the coward's way out by asking Gareth a business question.

He responds in kind. "Good, I think. I'm a little better than he is with moving around in the software programs, but he knows so much more about the kind of thing we should be looking for. I think we're pretty good together.

"And," he adds, "whenever your Aunt Kory sends us something, that allows us to leapfrog dozens of steps we might have had to take otherwise."

Silence falls on us. We listen to the whir of the elliptical machine on the other side of the room, and look idly at Samuel. He is, as always, the picture of athleticism, graceful and strong, effortlessly working the machine.

"Your brother is such an impressive athlete," Gareth says. "I'd like to be more like him, but I know you're going to say I should just appreciate the things I can do well.

"Aren't you?" he adds, looking at me and smiling his lips-closed, no-teeth-showing smile, the one I've gotten so accustomed to.

"Yes," I say, and realize this is my chance to talk about us, about boyfriend-girlfriend things, as Samuel so forthrightly pointed out a few minutes ago.

3

I decide to plunge in.

"Gareth, I've never told you that, after anything *big* happens in my life or my brother's, our parents hold what they call a debriefing when it's all finished. I think that term is leftover from my dad's days as a U.S. Naval officer, or maybe from Uncle Luke's days as a Royal Navy officer, but, either way, it's our term."

Gareth nods expectantly.

"Last month," I continue, "when everything was over and the danger went away — at least, went away for a while — Dad debriefed with Samuel, and Mum debriefed with me, right there in your church in Carmarthen. Mum and I were in one of the Sunday school rooms, and Dad and Samuel were right across the hall from us, in another one."

"I remember when that happened," Gareth says. "My parents and I knew you four were in the church, just next door to our house, having discussions that morning. And I was pretty sure I knew what kind of discussions you were having. We didn't exactly do that sort of thing, but we did talk about what happened, and what might happen from then on, just not all at once, not all at one sitting."

I think to myself, *maybe this is going to work … maybe we'll be able to have a boyfriend-girlfriend talk … maybe we'll be able to talk about how we feel toward each other … maybe we'll feel even closer when we finish our talk … maybe it will be easier for us to be together, and easier for us to talk to each other.*

Then I realize Gareth has said something that I didn't hear at all, and that he appears to be waiting for me to say something back. He is looking at me and smiling his little smile. *Such a great little smile,* I think to myself, *but I like the bigger smile, too, when his teeth actually show.*

"Joanna? Are you there?" asks Gareth.

I immediately blush. I cover my face with my hands.

"Oh, my goodness," I say through my hands. "I'm so sorry, Gareth."

He laughs.

There! There's his big smile. Such nice teeth, too.

There is another short silence, but this time I recover myself without prompting from Gareth. I take a sip of my soft drink and try to remember where I was about to go with this conversation. And I do.

Now looking vaguely across the fitness room at my brother, somehow feeling that the sight of Samuel exercising will make this easier, I begin.

"Mum talked to me about what it means for someone to have a close relationship with a visioner. She talked about what our dad had to sort out, to work through, when he realized that the person he was, well, falling in love with … was a visioner."

At this phrase — *falling in love with* — my worst blush ever runs right up to my face and again my hands seem involuntarily to come up to try to hide this horrible change in color. But as soon as my hands arrive at my face, I feel Gareth's hand on my wrist — the wrist nearest him — pulling that wrist gently away from my face and down into my lap.

I manage to turn my head and look at him. He is not smiling now.

"It's okay, Joanna," he says quietly. "Go on. We need to do this. Really. We just need to do this. What else did your mum say that day?"

Encouraged by his obvious willingness to be this serious, I take a deep breath. I look toward Samuel again, trying to take my mind back to that session with Mum.

"Mum told me that you had, in a way, become part of our family during those terrible days last month. She said that, no matter what happened in your future and mine, there would always be a special relationship between us, because you were a part of everything that happened then. You saw what my visions did. You saw that my visions saved your life.

"But you also saw," I continue quickly, "that my visions — and the plain fact that you were always with me — were what put your life in danger in the first place. She said that anyone who chooses a life with a visioner is choosing a life of danger, a life in which evil will always be searching for the visioner and for anyone close to her.

"And when I said to Mum," and here I actually turn my face away from Gareth, because I know the words are going to be too hard, "that it sounded to me as though she were suggesting that you and I would eventually *marry* each other, she said no, not necessarily, but that regardless of how your life goes, and how my life goes, this episode and this *rare* relationship between a visioner-girl and a boy-whose-life-was-changed-by-the-visioner-girl will make our other relationships different from what they otherwise might have been, always and forever, no matter what else happens.

"And," I continue, now turning my face back toward Gareth, "she said that you and your parents would need to face those facts, and would need to decide whether or not any sort of relationship with us was a good idea.

"So, when you were kidnapped from the park in Brooklyn and taken to the ship, and your mum was so angry, and when she said to me that, once we had gotten you back, she wanted to take you to Wales and she wanted to be sure that you and I never saw each other again . . . that made perfectly good sense to me, Gareth.

"I felt terrible, of course. Absolutely terrible, but I understood. And you can see why."

"Yes, I can," he says immediately, still not smiling, still completely serious, "and the truth is that I have spent quite a lot of time over the past few weeks thinking about that exact thing. I did not talk to my parents about it, and, if I had, maybe my mum would not have blown up that way when I was taken. Maybe she wouldn't have been so angry with you and your family. Maybe she would have been prepared.

"But," he continues, "whether or not, I absolutely do understand what your mum meant. And — if you can imagine, Joanna — the thought mostly just makes me excited about my future, and the possibility that it might even be *our* future, and that, whether it is yours or mine separately or together, this means that you and I have something to look forward to, something terribly exciting and terribly important — *terribly important* — that nobody else does! Think of it!"

Without meaning to, I reach for Gareth's hands and suddenly we are holding hands — all four hands entwined — and looking into each other's eyes in a way we have not done, up until now. And I think to myself, *this is how boyfriend-girlfriend love feels … this is it exactly. This is what leads people to say "I love you" to each other …*

But I don't.

Prompted by something that feels leftover from my early-morning prayers today, something that feels continued from my morning devotions, I say something better. And it comes to me in a glorious flash.

"At the end of my long talk with Mum last month," I say, now smiling at him and conscious of the warmth of our hands together, "we agreed that my responsibility as a Christian girl was obvious. My responsibility was, and is, to say my prayers every day, and to read my Bible every day, and to try to follow God's leading every day, and to try to live the life of a good Christian person every day, and … if that means that you and I are together for any longer than we already have been, then we will be together for however long that might be … and if it means that we go separate ways at some point, then we will go separate ways at some point. It's really quite simple, isn't it?"

Gareth smiles — his small smile — and nods his head, adding, after a very long and very thoughtful moment, "Yes, it is. But Joanna, let's do try to make it the first thing. Not he second thing.

"Please?"

And we laugh aloud at this, joyous at the clear simplicity of the thought.

And then he slowly leans toward me. And my heart starts beating faster than it really should. And I think …

Oh, my goodness! He's going to …

And suddenly I hear my brother, calling to us from the elliptical machine on the other side of the fitness room, "Oh, for goodness' sake, Gareth," he says, smiling his teasing smile, but shaking his head vigorously from side to side while continuing to work the machine, "you're *not* going to try to kiss my sister right here in front of her brother, are you? I said you two should have a date and TALK to each other.

"For *goodness'* sake, Gareth!"

4

Monday is here. Until it came, I had not realized how I have been dreading its arrival. I woke up nervous, did my devotional readings nervous, said my prayers nervous, got dressed nervous.

We've scheduled our final conference-room meeting for noon our time — late afternoon for Mum, Dad, and Aunt Kory — and the K-9 officers have just taken Flurry and Max for their daily outing. I'm sitting on a bench with my brother and Gareth in the common area outside the bedrooms, waiting to take the elevator up to the conference room when the time comes. We have about 30 minutes.

"So, Joanna," Gareth is saying, "last night is the first time you've had a dream that was simply a repeat of an earlier one? And that's never happened before in the family's experience?"

"Oh, I don't know about the whole family," I say, "because that goes back such a long time. It's not just Mum, you know. It's her mother *and* her father, it's our dad's mum, and it may go further back than that. So, it's three of our four grandparents, Gareth, and then who knows how deep into our ancestry.

"But," I continue, "it's certainly *my* first repeat. The vision took me inside Madison Square Garden again, with all the same pieces that I was given early Sunday morning, when that vision woke me up, and when I woke my brother and my uncle, so I could quickly tell them the details.

"But I didn't wake them this morning. Everything was the same."

The boys are quiet for a moment, then Gareth says to us both, "Do you think they're going to want us to be at the Garden tonight?"

"They're going to want Joanna there," my brother says with finality. "No question. Probably not you or me, Gareth."

I look a question at Samuel.

"Same thing as with the ship rescue," he says. "There may be pieces — maybe really small pieces — in your repeat vision that you won't remember until you're right in the middle of things. That happened on the ship. It could happen again.

"In fact," Samuel adds, "that may be why this vision got repeated in the first place. Because there may be small ingredients in it that won't be called out to your conscious mind until you are right in the middle of the fight."

"The fight?" says Gareth, looking at Samuel.

Samuel sighs — a little impolitely, I think to myself — and says, "Gareth, you don't think this is going to be a piece of cake, right? You don't think we're going to sail through this thing without being attacked, and attacked *hard,* by the people organizing this flash event, right? You *know* this thing could blow up in our faces. Right?"

"Well," Gareth replies after a moment's reflection, a little sheepishly, "I admit I had allowed myself to *hope* that the event would go smoothly, from our standpoint. Maybe I was just being naïve."

"I'd say so!" says Samuel, this time with obvious rudeness.

"Samuel," I say to him softly, looking him in the eye, not smiling.

He looks down for a moment, then looks up at Gareth. "Sorry, Gareth," he says quietly, but meaning it.

He then looks at me. "Sorry, Joanna," he says, also meaning it.

"I think I'm just wound up tight right now," he says, trying to help us understand his momentary rudeness to Gareth. "I *want* to be there, in Madison Square Garden, tonight. I *want* to be there and ready to fight. I want them to let me be in charge of Max, so he and I can charge those people on the stage and tear everything up and ..."

"Samuel!" I say. *"Don't."*

He looks at me, trying not to get angry.

"You know Uncle Luke doesn't think like that," I say, reminding him of how our uncle has taught us to think about fighting. "He prepares himself for anything and everything, but what he *wants* is for everything to go completely smoothly. He *wants* to be there, to be able to protect our family, to be able to do what is needed, but he prepares himself in prayer, in prayer to be given the wisdom to do right and the courage to do whatever is needed.

"He never *wants* to 'charge into people and tear everything up,' because he never *wants* violence to be needed. You know that."

Samuel looks glum. But he nods his head after a moment, and says, "Yes. I know. I know how I need to be.

"But I'm going to be really disappointed," he adds, "if they don't let me go to the Garden tonight. I want to be near you, Joanna."

He gives me a look that says more than any words could.

My brother loves me. I've told you. He just does.

5

The noon conference starts on time, called to order by Detective Belton. "Everybody doin' okay over there?" he says in the direction of the speakerphone, addressing our parents and Aunt Kory at the lodge in England.

"Yes!" comes the three-person chorus over the secure line.

Satisfied, Mr. Belton convenes the meeting, which is to be our final preparation for tonight's Madison Square Garden launch of The Church of the New Century. He asks the visioners to report first.

Mum and I provide identical reports, identical in the sense that overnight we each experienced a repeat of our most recent visions, hers focused on electronic passwords and codes for Aunt Kory, and mine on the interior of the arena. Aunt Kory then goes into some detail about her progress within the systems feeding Mr. Murphy's worldwide financial linkages and, as well, feeding Dr. Hannerty's electronic connections to New York City: the Garden, the shipping, the Gulfstream IV aircraft, The Church of the New Century and its money-transfer systems, ingoing and outgoing.

I lose track of Aunt Kory's mystifying report early on, but Mr. Adelman and Gareth not only seem to stay abreast of the details, but even understand the details well enough to ask questions. I gather, in the end, that everybody is satisfied with the technological preparations, but are all concerned about unforeseen and unforeseeable electronic and other countermeasures.

Like those weapons that were suggested in my last visions. The ones I think were held in the box on the rear of the green golf cart.

From this unsettling discussion of countermeasures, we move to tonight's assignments. I am surprised to learn that Reverend Morgan and Mrs. Morgan will be on the dais this evening with the leadership of The Church of the New Century. Reverend Morgan explains — with a bit of embarrassment, at first, it seems to me — that he was in private conversation much of Sunday afternoon with Mr. Murphy, at Mr. Murphy's request. He goes on to say that Mr. Murphy has invited him to give the opening remarks this evening, and he has accepted.

"It was obvious to me," he says, "that our friend Jonathan was motivated to offer me this role in part because he feels so guilty about Gareth's kidnapping. He assured me over and over that he knew nothing about the thing, and that he was astonished and horrified to learn that Gareth was taken to one of his own freighters.

"He said," Reverend Morgan continues, "that he has his chief financial officer, Dr. Hannerty, working to find out exactly what happened and to discover who, either within the company or within the New Church, might have been responsible. Jonathan promised me that he would bring in UK or U.S. law enforcement, or both, as soon as Judith has developed the trail enough to identify the culprits."

"*WHAT!?*" comes a voice over the secure line.

"*WHAT!?*" says the same voice again, without pause.

It's our aunt Kory, of course. And I admit that I feel like making that kind of exclamation myself. *Dr. Hannerty? Really?*

"Jonathan Murphy," Aunt Kory then says, "is having *Judith Hannerty* investigate Gareth's kidnapping? Reverend Morgan, can you be *serious!?* Can there be a better example of having the fox investigate the henhouse? She is the *source* of much of the evil that we are facing right now. She is behind much, or all, of the very developments we are trying to forestall!

"Sir, what is he *thinking!?* And what are *you,* Reverend Morgan, thinking!?"

There is a long pause. We are all looking at Reverend Morgan. He is looking down at his hands, folded in front of his chest on the tabletop. Mrs. Morgan places her hand on top of her husband's.

When Reverend Morgan looks up, he fastens his eyes on his son, then on me, sitting beside Gareth. "Joanna," he says gravely, "I have taken your nine-word vision from last week into my heart, from the time you first reported it until this moment.

"I think we all agree that the first command was immediately accomplished: ATTACK THE CASTLE. And Detective Belton is here with us precisely for that reason."

"Yes, sir," says Mr. Belton in his deep, rumbly voice.

"But," Reverend Morgan continues, "the commands to BAPTIZE THE SCRIPTURE and CLEANSE THE CHURCH are, in my mind, Joanna, commands delivered explicitly to me, the ordained minister in our group. And so, when Jonathan asked to meet with me yesterday afternoon, I did. And when he apologized for any role his company or the New Church might have had in our son's kidnapping, I accepted the apology. And when he said he had instructed his finance officer to investigate, I simply thanked him for that action.

"And I did all that," he says, just as solemnly as when he began, "because I wanted the chance to BAPTIZE THE SCRIPTURE and CLEANSE THE CHURCH. And so, yesterday afternoon, I gradually turned the conversation with Jonathan in the direction of the purposes and strategies of The Church of the New Century. And by the time our meeting was over, I had in writing an agreement from Jonathan on two things.

"Those are, first, that a second scripture will henceforth be displayed alongside Micah 6:8 everywhere that verse has been, and will be, shown, all around the world. That will include Jonathan's corporate offices in Wales, in his shipping offices around the globe, on the ships themselves, and in all communications associated with The Church of the New Century."

"John 14:6!" blurts Gareth excitedly, smiling broadly.

His father returns his son's smile.

He nods proudly at Gareth, and says "Exactly, son. Exactly."

Father and son share a long look. It is a moving moment for us all, partly because we see this profound appreciation of father for son, and of son for father.

But, even more so because we realize that everywhere on earth the shipping firm's original core value — "what doth the Lord require of thee, but to do justly, and to love mercy, and to walk humbly with thy God" — is seen, an accompanying verse will now also be seen. It is Jesus's response to Thomas's question, "How can we know the way," with our Lord's answer being, "I am the way, the truth, and the life."

We see that it's the Covenant of Love baptizing the Covenant of the Law.

The New Testament baptizing the Old.

After a lengthy silence, Reverend Morgan resumes. "And, Joanna," he says, looking at me again, "that third command in your vision of last week — CLEANSE THE CHURCH — is clearly something I had an opportunity to begin to do yesterday in my meeting with Jonathan. And so I spoke with him about some of what Kory has uncovered in her electronic pursuit of the church's financial irregularities: the lack of transparency in the money trails, the apparent connections with drug operations and other un-Christian and even anti-Christian organizations. And the apparent role of his chief financial officer in all of that.

"And he again expressed his dismay that these kinds of things could be associated with his company or with the New Church, and he urged me to give assurances tonight to all present in the Garden and to all watching and listening electronically that every cent of every contribution will go to the New Church's primary charity: Christ-centered education all over the world.

"That, in turn, means two things: first, the New Church will, in fact, not be a church at all, but an endowment fund to which churches and Christ-centered schools will be invited to apply for funds; second, that his assignment of Dr. Hannerty to investigate Gareth's kidnapping is simply a means of keeping her attention focused in the wrong direction.

"I prepared my remarks last night and finalized them this morning," he concludes. "Jonathan has approved them all. I cannot tell you how gratified I feel to have been chosen to deliver such a message. I thank you all, on both sides of the Atlantic."

Silence falls on the group, both those in this conference room and at the lodge. Finally, it is Detective Belton who speaks.

"Reverend Morgan," he says, leaning his small, worn body into the conference table, his gnarled hands clutching one of the NYPD-issued prepaid phones, "yer thinkin' is that Murphy is gonna let ya give th' openin' fer this thing, and that Murphy's whole operation — his shippin' business and his New Church — is just gonna fall in line with whatever ya say tonight? Ya think it's as simple as all that?"

"I think it might be, Mr. Belton, or it might not be," Reverend Morgan replies. "But I think that my job will be to supply opening remarks that will assure all listeners — those present in the arena and those in their homes around the world — that this is truly God's work. That the "New" piece of The Church of the New Century is as "Old" as the Christian church's beginnings, as recorded in the Gospels and the Acts of the Apostles. I am confident that Jonathan himself endorses every word I have prepared. Whether or not those in critical positions under him — in his company and in what we have called his New Church — will follow along, I can't say."

"Ya don't think, sir," Mr. Belton persists, "that this Hannerty woman and her people are gonna throw a monkey wrench in th'whole thing?"

"I think, sir," replies Reverend Morgan quietly, "that our group, on both sides of the ocean, is going to prove better than her people, and that God has demonstrated His engagement in opposition to this threat from the start. We saw His hand in the outcomes last month in Wales, and we'll see His hand in the outcomes tonight.

"I have confidence, sir, that God is with us."

At that moment, Mr. Adelman rises from his chair to respond to the street-level indicator, and buzzes our two K-9 officers into the building. Moments later, Flurry is curled up at my feet, her white-tipped tail thumping on the floor while my hands stroke her furry head. Meanwhile, Max sits down next to Uncle Luke.

His ears are up, his eyes bright. Max is ready.

So, I hope, are we.

Chapter Eight

1

I'm wearing my newly dry-cleaned blue dress, the one that I wore when we were attacked in the Brooklyn park. The one that was, I thought, ruined forever when Max tackled the man who was running with me draped over his shoulder, and when I tumbled head over heels into the park grass.

But the dress was only dirty and grass-stained, not torn, and everything came out nicely at a dry cleaners used regularly by the NYPD, one specializing in hard-to-remove spots and splotches. Our policewoman asked for special attention to my dress, and she appears to have gotten it.

And not just that. Our policewoman actually stopped at one of the clothing stores and bought me a little matching purse to go with my dress. I think she probably used her own money, though she said she didn't. She has been *so* thoughtful.

So I'm happy with how I look for this huge event. Not only is my dress pretty, and not only do I have a little matching purse, but Mrs. Morgan has given me a wonderful little ponytail fastener, one that has a small white flower attached to the band that actually does the fastening. She says she has had it for many years, going back to the time when she wore her hair much longer than now, when she sometimes chose a long ponytail for special occasions.

She then spent part of the afternoon working to get my hair brushed and put up into a tight ponytail. The little flower-fastener is perfect, as are my dressy sandals. I feel as though I have been dressed like the queen of the town: a pretty dress, matching purse, flowery ponytail fastener, dressy sandals.

So, here I am, looking as nice as I can, sitting behind the stage in Madison Square Garden in New York City, midway up the bleachers, on about the 15th row. Samuel had been right this morning in the fitness room when he insisted that the adults would want me here for the event. And for the reason he gave: that some details from my inside-the-arena visions might not open themselves to my conscious mind until the thing was underway.

In fact, all of us, including the boys, to their mild surprise, are here except for Detective Belton, whose physical limitations make him the obvious choice to stay at the detectives' office in communication with Mum and Dad and Aunt Kory at the lodge. There was quite a lot of debate in the noon conference about whether or not the boys and the dogs should come. In the end, it was decided that, equipped with their burner phones, the boys could help be extra eyes and ears for Uncle Luke, Mr. Adelman, and the additional NYPD security people that Mr. Belton had helped to arrange for the event.

The same for the dogs. They, too, are here to provide extra eyes and ears and, in the case of Max, extra muscle and extra intimidation. When a trained German shepherd has his eyes fixed on someone who is doing something the shepherd's handler does not like, then that someone usually wants to be somewhere else.

Anywhere else.

Madison Square Garden can seat about 20,000 people, depending on how the arena is configured. This is a flash event, meaning that publicity only started about 48 hours ago, and so the arena won't be filled.

The event organizers — Dr. Hannerty and her team — wanted to give the impression that The Church of the New Century is being born as the result of huge, spontaneous popular demand. And they know that the really significant attendance will be via electronic means. People don't need a lot of advance notice to turn on their devices at home, wherever they may be.

Gareth is seated about 10 rows above me, and off to my right. Samuel is also about 10 rows above me, but off to my left. Samuel has been given one of the TASERs, since he is the strongest and most athletic of us young people. Flurry is sitting on the concrete floor at my feet. No one is sitting anywhere near us, since we are behind the stage and these are the least desirable seats in the arena for this kind of event, one in which there is a stage at one end of the Garden.

Max is with Uncle Luke. The two of them are at floor level, over to my right. Mr. Adelman is also at floor level, to my left, just in front of the tunnel that my last two visions have emphasized, the tunnel through which the golf cart needs to travel to get to the rear of the stage.

Uncle Luke and Mr. Adelman also have NYPD TASERs.

Reverend and Mrs. Morgan are just arriving at the back of the stage. They are climbing the steps to stage level, and being welcomed by Mr. Murphy, whose photo I have seen many times by now; Dr. Hannerty, whose photo I have also seen several times; and others whom I don't know.

There are half a dozen other men and women. I don't know if they are part of law enforcement, leaders in the New Church, officers in Mr. Murphy's shipping company, or just what. None is wearing a uniform, but that doesn't mean that some of them couldn't be detectives or FBI or MI5 or something else.

They all take their seats on the dais. It's about five minutes until starting time for the event. The arena is buzzing with anticipation.

I'm very nervous.

Suddenly, about a dozen uniformed NYPD officers emerge from the tunnel on my left, each one carrying some official-looking document. Each of them walks up to one of the dozen or so NYPD officers who are already stationed near the stage. They show the document to those already in position, and, one by one, each of those officers moves toward the far end of the arena, leaving the new group in position near the stage.

No one else — Uncle Luke, Mr. Adelman, Samuel, Gareth, those on the dais — seems to think this might mean something. But I do.

I hit the speed dial on my burner mobile, which connects me to everybody, and I say, "Mr. Belton, about a dozen uniformed NYPD officers just showed a document to the dozen officers who were already here in the stage area, and those original officers just turned and walked away, toward the other end of the arena. The new officers are the only ones near the stage now. That seems wrong to me.

"Did you expect that, Mr. Belton?"

"No," he says.

Just that one word.

We five who are seated behind the stage all look at each other. This has to be wrong, but there doesn't seem to be anything we can do about it. Then I notice Dr. Hannerty appearing to exchange glances with one of the new uniformed officers. He nods his head at her, then at some of the others who just arrived with him.

At this point, my attention goes to the colossal four-sided info-board suspended from the Garden roof as it comes to life. Until now, it has simply displayed the Old Testament verse from Micah 6:8. But now those words fade from the screen and are replaced by a view of the stage, and, a moment later, a focus on Reverend Morgan as he rises from his chair and moves toward the pulpit.

Once he is there, the visual tightens on his face.

Meanwhile, my attention is caught by something just above the info-board. I catch a glimpse of movement. There is someone, or more than one someone, moving about *on top of the info-board.*

My eyes move to the spidery catwalk, the one I saw in my prayer-dream, that leads from a ladder against the arena wall and then seemingly across thin air, high above the arena, to the info-board itself. Someone has used that catwalk to position themselves hundreds of feet above the floor.

I hit my burner's speed dial again. I report this to Mr. Belton.

"Sir," I say, "just like my vision suggested, there are people up on top of the info-board. They must have used the catwalk to get there.

"Just wanted you to know, sir."

"Got it, Joanna," he says.

That's all.

I turn my attention again to the info-board's display. I'm fascinated by the enormous screen image of Reverend Morgan, his face seemingly 30 feet long and nearly that wide. Even the color of his dark brown eyes is perfectly discernable from this distance. He closes those eyes and bows his head in prayer, saying in his rich, medium-pitch voice, "Our Father in Heaven, may the words of my mouth and the meditations of all of our hearts and minds be acceptable in Thy sight, O Lord our strength and our Redeemer. Amen."

2

Reverend Morgan then welcomes the thousands who are present here with us in Madison Square Garden, and the hundreds of thousands who are watching from their own homes around the world. He explains why this launch of The Church of the New Century is being held as a flash event.

He talks briefly about what that means, emphasizing the importance in today's technology-driven world of getting people's attention and then almost immediately beginning the thing without the long delays necessary in the days of slower communication. And he talks about the fact that perhaps 50 times as many people are viewing the event from their homes as are physically present in the Garden.

Reverend Morgan then acknowledges Mr. Jonathan Murphy, asking him to stand in recognition of his exemplary and pioneering role as the CEO of a worldwide shipping business, one that features a Bible verse — Micah 6:8 — as its now universally known "core value." Mr. Murphy stands to acknowledge the applause, and his face is briefly featured on the screens suspended high above our heads.

Mr. Murphy resumes his seat, and Reverend Morgan then turns back to the cameras and the assembled thousands. He introduces Dr. Judith Hannerty.

He identifies her as the chief financial officer both of Mr. Murphy's company and of The Church of the New Century. Then he stands aside while she rises and takes her place at the pulpit.

The cameras tighten on her face, as they did on Reverend Morgan's. She has strong features: a prominent nose and chin, and a mouth that somehow seems severe until she begins to speak. And then its severity is softened, because she is able to smile while she talks. It's an engaging smile, seemingly genuine.

Dr. Hannerty's hair is shoulder length, and is a dull red in color, what some might call rusty. Her glasses have heavy black rims, and add to the forcefulness of her appearance. Although the cameras are focused now only on her face, I see from behind her that she is tall, about the same height as Reverend Morgan. This I could see when he stepped aside and waited for her to get to the pulpit before walking back to his seat.

I also see from my vantage point behind the stage that she is wearing a dark suit — skirt and jacket — and medium-high heels. The jewelry that I am able to see on the screen is small and gold: loopy earrings and a small cross on a delicate necklace.

I am able to notice all this about her appearance because she does not begin to speak as soon as she arrives at the pulpit. She seems purposely to take her time arranging her notes, then even more time to look out over the assembled congregation and, finally, into the camera.

Very effective, I think to myself. *She is very much in control, and wants us to be sure to notice that she is. And we do.*

Her remarks focus first on what she calls the "old church" — the church of the previous century, and of all the centuries before — implying that the "old church" has failed to adapt its ways to the modern situation. She talks about the world's needs: hunger, poverty, disaster relief. All the things we see on the news reports.

At no point does she mention Jesus Christ. That gets *my* attention.

And then she says this: "As Reverend Cecil Morgan told you in his introduction, I serve as the chief financial officer both for Mr. Jonathan Murphy's shipping company and, as well, for The Church of the New Century. So, if you'll indulge me for just a moment, I want to talk to you about money — yours and ours — before Reverend Morgan returns to the pulpit to complete his remarks.

"As most of you have read in our announcements," she says, "you can transfer money from your own checking and savings accounts *with your mobile phone or from any device you have at your disposal*, just by following the steps you'll see on the screen in just a moment. We have made this as simple as possible, so that no one needs to be a high-tech person in order to support our church's causes."

She smiles engagingly at this. Reassuringly.

She goes on to list some of the groups that will benefit from everyone's contributions. The screens — both here in the arena and on people's devices everywhere — show needy children and adults who, she says, will benefit "from every penny you send from your mobile, or other device, to this digital address, the address you were given earlier, and which you will see now, again, on your screen, both here in Madison Square Garden and on the device you have in front of you at home."

At this point, Dr. Hannerty gestures dramatically upward, toward the info-board suspended from the arena roof. With all eyes in the arena focused upward toward the gigantic info-board, and with hundreds of thousands of eyes around the world staring intently at their small screens, Dr. Judith Hannerty presses a button on the console mounted on her pulpit.

And the display instantly changes. Dr. Hannerty's image on the screen is replaced by words written in bright red script:

JESUS SAITH …
I AM THE WAY, THE TRUTH, AND THE LIFE.

I think to myself excitedly, *Aunt Kory and her helpers — Mr. Adelman and Gareth — have done it! They've got control of the info-board and of all the screens in front of everybody watching this, from anywhere.*

And I am instantly even *more* nervous than I was already.

Then my eyes return to Dr. Hannerty, her back to me at the pulpit. I watch as she looks down at her console and begins to press keys in desperate confusion. She presses keys, looks up at the info-board, looks down again, presses more keys. Then it seems to me she may have succeeded, because the giant screens go black.

But only for a few seconds. The momentary digital blackness is then replaced by a block-letter announcement, also in red:

An announcement from

Mr. Jonathan Murphy, chief executive officer of

Murphy International Shipping Company,

and president of The Church of the New Century.

As Dr. Hannerty watches the info-board helplessly, the announcement explains to the world, both in the arena and beyond, that, while a small percent of any funds sent to the digital address previously provided by Judith Hannerty has indeed gone to people in need, most of the money has been used to pay for illicit activities worldwide: drugs, weapons, extortion. After this stunning information has been displayed and read by all, many of those illicit activities and the organizations sponsoring them are listed on the screen by name, chief executive, city, and country.

This portion of the announcement — *written,* I think proudly to myself, *by Aunt Kory and Mum and Dad, and inserted into the display by remote override of Dr. Hannerty's program, helped, no doubt, by whatever Mr. Adelman and Gareth have been doing from this end* — concludes by stating that the digital site established by Dr. Hannerty and her people has been disabled. It has been replaced by another digital site, and the address for the new site appears separately and stays on the screen for more than 30 seconds, giving people time to record it and to link to it.

3

While Dr. Hannerty continues to fight helplessly with her console, now banging her fists on the sides of the pulpit, a fresh announcement scrolls down the screen. This one states that The Church of the New Century is immediately defunded and disenfranchised on Mr. Murphy's authority, to be replaced instantaneously by *The Endowment for Christian Education Worldwide.*

Once the endowment is fully funded, the announcement explains, Christ-centered schools and sponsoring churches around the world may apply for funding on an annual basis, with an international, interdenominational panel making decisions on the applications. This portion of the announcement concludes with a stunning message:

There is no "new church."
There is only the traditional church of Jesus Christ.
Commit yourself to the Christ you have come to know,
and to your own church in your own community.

Give generously of your time, money, and talent to your own church.
And, if you can, contribute as well to
the *Endowment for Christian Education Worldwide*
by using the following address or link.

At this moment my burner buzzes and I lift the phone to my ear. I hear Detective Belton's rumbling voice. "I got th' NYPD SWAT people comin', folks. Keep yer heads down. Some of 'em will be comin' up the tunnel. Some of 'em will be goin' up that catwalk. They're comin' in *hot*, folks.

"Watch yerselves."

Flurry suddenly stands in front of me and, listening and looking intently down the tunnel to our left, she starts her alarm bark, a sharp, short series of barks designed to alert me and Samuel to something dangerous that is coming toward us.

I press the speed dial on my phone and quickly say, "Flurry is doing her alarm bark, everybody. Something is coming up the tunnel.

"Oh," I say almost at once, "it's the green golf cart from my visions."

The cart speeds silently through the tunnel toward the back of the stage. It stops at the steps leading up to the rear of the stage. Four large men climb out. They move quickly to the back of the golf cart and unlatch the cover of the long silver box that I was given to understand in my visions would be filled with weapons.

But Flurry's bark and my phone warning may have come in time, because I see that Samuel, Mr. Adelman, Uncle Luke, and Max are already on the move. As the men begin to reach into the box, each one starting to extricate a fearsome-looking long gun, Samuel and Mr. Adelman arrive and tackle two of the men from behind, then quickly apply their contact TASERs to the exposed skin on each man's neck.

The response of each is frightening. The two men pitch forward violently, staggering and falling. Shuddering, uncontrolled, seizure-like movements. Now they are prone on the concrete floor. Both of them completely helpless.

But in less than two seconds, the other two men swing the heavy stocks of their rifles into my brother and Mr. Adelman, one striking Samuel squarely in the face, and the other striking Mr. Adelman in the throat. Both of them fall to the floor, their heads seeming to hit so hard they bounce off the concrete.

One of the men then spins around and aims his rifle at the info-board high above the arena floor. He fires a stream of automatic rifle bullets right into the nearest screen. The screen goes black, shards plummeting down toward the arena floor. And in that split second I glimpse several figures, high atop the info-board, diving down out of sight, trying to avoid what they must assume is automatic weapons fire directed at them.

The other man raises his rifle, holding it by the barrel like a club. He prepares to strike Mr. Adelman as he lies, possibly unconscious, on the floor.

At that second, Max arrives and rips into the man's right bicep, tearing the rifle from his grip and riding him to the floor. A fraction of a second later, Uncle Luke arrives and discharges his contact TASER into the side of the other man's face, the man who had just fired at the info-board.

He falls as if shot, collapsing on one of his partners and reproducing the same, seizure-like movements as the other two. Uncle Luke then turns to the man attacked by Max, says something to Max, and, as Max pulls away, Uncle Luke squeezes the man's neck with both hands, pressing with his thumbs in a way that appears to make the man go unconscious in just seconds. The man collapses, joining his three mates on the floor.

Meanwhile, the arena has gone crazy. The gunfire into the info-board not only terrified the thousands of people present in the Garden, but glass shards from the screen have come crashing to the floor, appearing to miss one of the sections where people were sitting on folding chairs, but frightening all those nearby into a stampede toward the nearest exits.

At nearly the same time, the uniformed NYPD officers who showed documents to the officers originally in place around the stage, have reacted to all this by moving to attack or arrest Uncle Luke and, to my horror, more than one of them has pulled his handgun, possibly to use on Max. But Max is a blur of ferocity, lunging from one of them to the next, so thoroughly immersed in the sea of officers that none of them could fire his weapon without hitting his mates.

Suddenly, without my seeing where they have come from, the SWAT officers summoned by Detective Belton are here. They race into the fray in their black body armor, clubs, and automatic weapons and, in a flash, magically restore order around the stage. And I see other SWAT officers, coming from a different direction, have begun to scale the ladder leading to the catwalk, thereby gaining access to those of our adversaries who are positioned on top of the info-board and who appeared to dive for cover when the bullets flew into the screen just below them.

The rest of the arena is a confused mass of people fleeing in all directions. I see that Reverend Morgan and Mr. Murphy went to the pulpit, pushed Dr. Hannerty aside, and are trying to address the throng.

And suddenly I remember that the adults insisted on my being here tonight because sometimes details of my visions do not fully come to life until I am living the event. And I find that is happening to me right now.

I remember that, in my last visions, something comes at me from behind — from directly behind — with a purpose that is focused on me, not on the stage. The realization comes to me too late.

They are upon me.

As they lift me off my feet to carry me away, I see one of them throw a net over Flurry, just like at the park last week, and I see Gareth flying to my rescue, pushing one of the men aside but almost immediately being smashed in the face by the fist of another of my attackers.

The last thing I see is Flurry trying frantically to get herself out of the net, Gareth falling face down over two rows of seats, and, in the distance, Uncle Luke and Max fighting their way through the false officers, helped by the SWAT officers, all of them trying to reach the stage.

Someone pulls a hood over my head. Blackness falls over me.

4

After my abduction from the arena, the silent, hooded ride in a van — judging from the sound of the sliding door that opens for me and closes behind me — lasts only a few minutes before we park in what sounds like an underground garage. No one speaks to me or touches me during the ride. The sliding door opens, someone helps me out, and, minutes later, after an elevator ride, I am seated in a folding chair.

Someone removes my hood and leaves the room. A man is seated in another folding chair, facing me.

"Joanna," the man says to me, "do you feel better?"

My eyes try to adjust to the light in the small room.

"Joanna," he says again, "are you feeling all right?"

I try to think what my answer is.

"No," I say finally.

"What can we do to help?" says the man courteously.

I try to focus on him. He is seated in front of me, wearing a nice, light-colored business suit. The room seems to have no windows, and just one small lamp, over in one corner. No one else seems to be present.

"You could," I say slowly, "let me go to my family and my border collie."

"Oh," he says quickly, "we will, Joanna. And quite soon."

The man appears to be Mr. Belton's age. Over sixty. But not "old."

His hair is graying. He has a salt-and-pepper beard. The beard is trimmed close, and, in fact, is barely noticeable. It's his eyes that are noticeable. They are gray, a little like my mother's, but not so striking as hers. A bit dull.

Since he does not add to his comment about letting me go to my family and my border collie "quite soon," I ask, "How soon?"

And then, without waiting, I add, "Why am I here? Why did you take me?"

He smiles and nods. "Yes," he says not unkindly, "you'd be wondering that, wouldn't you? I'll explain after we've brought you something to eat, Joanna.

"What would you like? We have sandwiches, fruit, sweets. And to drink?"

The man is British, judging from the dialect. Maybe Scottish.

I shake my head no.

"Please answer my questions," I say, trying not to whine.

I sit up straighter in my folding chair. I don't want to *look* whiny, either.

"All right," he says. "You're a visioner, of course, and you are, therefore, useful to your family, and others, when you are available to them. Here with us, you're not available to your family, and, even if you dream, you can't report your dreams to anyone. To anyone but us, that is.

"Not that we expect you to talk to us about your dreams, of course, but we wouldn't mind at all if you did."

He says this last thing with a little chuckle, trying to be funny.

I don't smile.

"As for how soon we'll take you back to your family and to your border collie," he continues, "that depends on how things go, Joanna. When we reach the point where it no longer matters to us whether or not you have your visions, then we'll return you to your family. Until then, I'm afraid you'll need to be here, with us.

"We don't think the wait will be long," he concludes, "and you'll be comfortable here, I can assure you."

I look down at my blue dress. It still looks nice, even though they handled me roughly when they lifted me off my feet and carried me from

Madison Square Garden. Then I realize I don't know how long ago that was.

"What time is it?" I ask stupidly, as if that mattered.

He looks at his watch. "It's a little after nine, Joanna. Are you tired? Is it your bedtime? It must be … what … about two o'clock in the morning in London?"

I decide to say yes. Maybe he'll leave me alone if I say yes.

I nod my head. "Well," I say, "do I have a place to sleep?"

"Oh, of course," he replies. "This building was once a small hotel. You'll have a nice room, with a private bathroom. As I said, you'll be comfortable."

"Will my room have a Bible?"

"Yes, of course. We're Christians here, Joanna."

I look him in the eye at this remark.

He smiles again. "You're thinking that Christians wouldn't snatch you away from your family and your border collie, aren't you, Joanna?"

I don't answer this. I just keep looking at him, unsmiling. My face feels heavy, frozen. I don't think I'd be able to smile, even if I wanted to.

"Christians have to do some difficult things at times, don't you think, Joanna?" he says. "Your uncle Luke, for example, handled some of our people pretty roughly last month in Wales, and I'd say he and your brother and Detective Adelman were making things hard for our people earlier tonight in the Garden, too.

"And that German shepherd of yours! My goodness, Joanna, Christians can be pretty hard when they have to, don't you think?"

I look down again. I don't want to try to argue with this person.

I give a big sigh. A real one.

"I really am tired," I say truthfully. "A bedroom would be nice right now."

5

My interviewer and another man — the one, I think, who removed my hood — escort me down a long hallway and into my room. My interviewer shows me that there is a bathrobe hanging in the closet and toiletries in the bathroom. He notes a small refrigerator, opens it, and shows me an array of juices. Finally, he points to a shelf just above the refrigerator containing a variety of snacks.

"Rest well, Joanna," he says with what sounds like genuine kindness in his voice. "We'll send a breakfast up for you about eight o'clock in the morning.

"Good night," he says, and starts to close the door behind him and his mate.

"Sir," I say quickly, before the door closes, "may I have the little purse I had with me at the arena?"

He turns to face me. His smile is gone. His face is like stone.

"What purse?" he says.

And I see who he is.

The door closes.

And I know that I will be without my burner phone, my passport, and what little money I had. I have only what I'm wearing.

I stand for long minutes in the middle of the room, not moving, just thinking. Then I go to my refrigerator, get a small tomato juice, and then pick up the King James Bible that rests on my night table. I carry my juice and the Bible to the only armchair in the room. Seated comfortably, and strangely refreshed after just a few swallows of cold tomato juice, I decide to ask myself some questions.

What happened in the Garden, after I was carried away? I know that Samuel, Mr. Adelman, and Gareth were all struck hard in the face, and fell just as hard or harder onto hard surfaces. Flurry was caught again in one of those nets. Uncle Luke and Max were terribly outnumbered by their enemies. Reverend and Mrs. Morgan were surrounded on the stage.

What happened? I can't know, I say to myself. *I can only hope that the SWAT officers and the "real" NYPD officers, who were probably racing back to the stage, where they were originally posted, will win out.*

What happened? I can't know.

Then I think of my own situation.

I've been kidnapped, I say to myself. *Why am I not terrified?*

I think about this for several seconds, and find my answer unsettling.

I'm not terrified, I answer myself, *because no one has hurt me, no one has threatened to hurt me, my questioner has been courteous and thoughtful with me, and I'm in one of the nicest rooms I've been in since I left home.*

I think about *this* — my answer to myself — for several seconds, which is how long it takes for me to understand how ridiculous I'm being. I'm not terrified, then, because people are being *nice* to me? People who have forcibly taken me from my family? People who want to keep me from my family until the conflict — the *war*, Uncle Luke would say — has been won by them?

People who have been planning to create electronic games for children and young people, games designed to crush their sense of right and wrong? People who have been planning to create graphic Bibles for differing ages of children and young people, Bibles that will eliminate all reference to God and that will treat Our Lord Jesus as just another really good *teacher*, not the Person who died and rose and lives to change the world eternally?

Those people are being *nice* to me, and so I'm feeling *comfortable* in my very nice room, having been treated with kindness by this very nice man? This man who will no doubt be back tomorrow morning to continue to question me, and who will possibly not be so very kind and thoughtful as the hours and days go by?

Seriously? I say to myself at the end of this thinking.

This thinking does not, of course, make me feel better. In fact, it makes me feel worse. But it also makes me feel that I need to grow up.

It makes me understand that I need to consider the fact that these are some of the worst people in the world, and that they have plans that must be defeated, and that these people regard me — and my family — as among their very biggest obstacles. It makes me understand that these are the people who have tried, at one time or another, if we go back into the past, to kill nearly every one of us who have struggled against them. Maybe not these exact people in every case, but the same evil that has brought them to our doorstep. The very same evil. Right here.

So, I think to myself, *let's have done, Joanna, with sitting here drinking tomato juice and relaxing with the "niceness" of it all. You're alone now. Grow up. Read. Pray. Prepare for what's coming.*

And so, I do. I take a deep breath, and I pick up the Bible.

As I often do, I use the ending of the eighth chapter of St. Paul's letter to the church in Rome to move into my evening prayers: "For I am persuaded, that neither death, nor life … shall be able to separate us from the love of God, which is in Christ Jesus our Lord."

I rise from the chair, stand, turn to face the chair, place the open Bible on the seat on which I sat, and, pulling the hem of my dress up just enough so that I do not kneel on the dress, I sink to my knees on the soft rug, facing the open Bible. My prayer goes first to thanksgiving: for the protection that God has always offered our family, for the guidance He has always provided for us, for the comfort — *I will not leave you comfortless* — that He has always brought to us.

I then ask God for His forgiveness for my failures, especially my failures during this very day: my failure to be quick enough to warn everyone when the false NYPD officers showed some kind of documents to the actual officers, and replaced them all around the stage; my failure to alert everyone quickly enough that the golf cart was coming up the tunnel; my failure to understand what was happening behind me, and to get Flurry and Gareth and myself out of the way of the kidnappers. My failure to fight hard enough against those who took me from my family, Flurry, and Gareth. And the failure that allowed me to be at ease with the man who talked to me here in this building, the man who so easily, by being so courteous, led me to relax and to be pleasant to him. My failure to let him know that I understood who he was, and what he wanted, and what he and his people seek to do.

And finally, I pray for us: for our family, for the Morgans, for Flurry and Max, for Mr. Jonathan Murphy, and for those thousands of Christian people who had come to Madison Square Garden in hopes of experiencing something holy, and for those hundreds of thousands of Christian people who were watching and listening on their devices, around the world, hoping for a worshipful experience and for the chance to help the faithful everywhere. I pray for God's help for all of us, and for His strength for me, tonight and tomorrow. For guidance. For mercy.

When I finish my prayers, I rise from my knees and go to the window. Until now, I've been aware that my room *has* a window, but I've been too focused on this whirlwind that has beset us this evening to go to the window to see if its view gives any hints as to where I am.

I look down from the window and find that my room appears to be on about the fifth floor of this building. Across the street is a much taller building, and, as I look to my right and then to my left, I can see nothing that could serve me as a landmark. In fact, this could be a view from a window in a building in any large city on earth.

I consider what Uncle Luke would do in my situation. Or, more realistically, what my brother would do. This leads me to test the window, to see if it can be opened.

No. It is sealed. Maybe Uncle Luke would actually break the window and use one of those ropes he carries with him to descend somehow. Not a helpful idea for me.

I return to my chair.

Not willing quite yet to give up entirely on doing something daring, I give some thought to what might happen if I simply opened the door into the hallway, walked the hallway to the nearest Exit sign, went down the steps to street level, opened a door — probably one marked "Alarm Will Sound" — and sought help from someone. This seems impossible, since surely there is a sentry in the hallway, or a camera monitoring the hallway, but why should I not try?

Since the only reason not to try is fear, and since, I say to myself, *courage is the form of every virtue at its testing point*, I rise again from my chair, walk to the door, place my hand on the doorknob, and pull the door open. My eyes immediately encounter those of a man, one I haven't seen tonight, standing across the hallway and obviously prepared to prevent any escape attempt I might make.

"May I help you?" he says without smiling.

"No, thank you," I say, feeling foolish.

I close the door and, knowing it won't prevent anyone's coming in, I engage the lock on my door. They all have key cards, of course, so it's just one of those gestures I make sometimes to make myself feel a bit better.

Suddenly I am truly exhausted. And, acknowledging that, I am almost instantly overwhelmed with loneliness. I want Flurry. I want my brother.

Above all, I want my mother.

The tears come, and, crying softly, I get ready for bed.

6

Sleep comes fast. Lying in bed in the bathrobe that is my only available sleepwear, I'm too sleepy to read or think or add to my earlier prayers. I pull the sheet up to my chin. I glance at the clock on my nightstand. It reads 10:45 p.m.

The next time my eyes open to look at the clock, it reads 4:45 a.m. *Six hours' sleep,* I think to myself. *That's pretty good. I should feel refreshed.*

But I don't. I quickly realize that I'm not better than I was when I gave up and went to bed. I'm still afraid. I'm still terribly lonely.

There are more than three hours to go before the time I was told a breakfast would be brought to me. Sadness pushes hard at my mind. I don't feel grown up now. I feel more like a small child with every passing minute. Helplessness covers me.

But at some point, I am, once more, sleeping. And during this second descent of sleep into my mind, a new dream begins to form. As before, my dreaming mind is now quick to recognize what is coming. And also, as before, my dreaming mind focuses eagerly, fully intent on what is about to be given to it.

The vision arrives immediately. In my mind's eye, I look out of a small window, thousands of feet above an ocean, billowing white clouds reaching up toward an early morning sky. I am in a jet plane, crossing an ocean, the sun rising somewhere behind us. I look away from the window and down at the small tray table in front of me. A leather-bound Bible rests on the table, its front cover open. Stamped into the inside cover I read the words: *Property of Jonathan Murphy Shipping Import and Export.*

I look up from the book. Stenciled onto the leather seat back in front of me I read: *Gulfstream IV.* This is, then, not a commercial jet; this is a private jet. This is one of Mr. Jonathan Murphy's private jets.

At that moment a flight attendant — the only person I see in this small passenger compartment, although I realize others may be on board — hands me a little oval mirror. I hold the mirror up to my face and my eyes widen.

I am my mother.

I stare into the image of my mother's face, the elegant, high cheekbones, the vicious, V-shaped scar along the right cheek, the penetrating gray eyes. Then her eyes close and I am given to understand that she, my mother, is being sent a dream of her own. And my own vision then reveals the nature of my mother's vision: her vision is of her only daughter.

Her vision is of me.

I turn my visioning eyes away from the mirror. I look again out my window, and down at the vast ocean below me. And now I see emerging in the distance, as the sun continues to brighten this enormous panorama, a familiar coastline.

I am my mother. And I, as my mother, begin to sense my daughter's desperate presence, ever closer in the lessening distance ahead.

Chapter Nine

1

It's a little after eight o'clock Tuesday morning. I've finished my breakfast. I'm wearing my blue dress and my nice sandals, the only things I have. I have done my best to recreate the beautiful ponytail Mrs. Morgan fixed for me yesterday.

I didn't want to try to sleep with my hair pulled tight by its floral fastener, and so I had to start over this morning, first with nearly 10 minutes of brushing, using the too-small brush that was part of the toiletries kit in the bathroom, then with my best effort at pulling my very thick, very long hair into the confines of my new fastener.

My Bible reading and prayers were hopeful, as you can imagine, after the early-morning dream that was given to me. The dream meant to me that my mum is fully engaged now in an attempt to rescue me. My vision might or might not mean that she is actually on one of Mr. Murphy's private jets, flying overnight to New York.

But it seems to me that, at the very least, my dream means that Mum is fully occupied with saving me from this new danger. And it means, too, I think, that she has been given her own vision regarding how to get to me, whether the actual rescue is going to be attempted by Mum, or Dad, or Uncle Luke, or Mr. Adelman, or Mr. Belton, or the NYPD, or whoever. One way or another, my mum is being driven every moment toward my rescue.

I have no doubt, really. None.

Oh, and I did the math. With the time change between England and the United States, Mum could indeed have left in one of Mr. Murphy's jets before sunup in Wales, and yet have arrived in New York not long after sunup here. If she is herself actually coming, she could be right here in the city already. It's a thrilling thought.

But my morning prayers focused more on what I will face in a few minutes. I expect my questioner to come and get me, and to take me to the room he and I were in last night. I expect him not to be quite so nice this morning. And I have tried to prepare for this, both during my prayers and in my planning time, after my prayers were over.

Nevertheless, when the knock on my door comes, I'm startled, even though I've been expecting it. I go to the door and open it. It is the same man.

"Good morning, Joanna," he says, smiling, his tone friendly and warm.

"Will you tell me your name, sir?" I say.

This is the start of my plan. Part of my plan is to try to engage this man on more of an equal level, even though I'm just a girl and he is older than my parents. He uses my name regularly. I plan to use his.

At my question, his face changes. The smile disappears. A stone face.

"I will not tell you my name," he says.

"Furthermore," he continues after a moment, "it is I who will ask the questions this morning. It is you who will answer them. Do you understand?"

His look is hate filled. I begin to understand that this man hates me. Hates us.

I do not reply. The reality of this man's hatred slaps me into something that I didn't quite plan to be. My face has frozen. A heavy face.

I can't help it.

I didn't plan to be like this. But suddenly I am.

I simply stare back at him. I don't even know why. I feel I am in God's hands, and that I must just be what I am in my heart: a Christian girl who has been taken from her family by people who hate. This man is not my friend. This man is the enemy.

He stands aside and motions for me to walk in front of him down the hallway. I do. The hallway is longer than I remember it.

We enter the same room we were in last night. I sit in the same chair.

He sits in front of me, as before. He is dressed much like he was last night, in a summer suit and tie. He looks the same, but he is not. He is no longer making an effort to make me feel comfortable. He wants me uncomfortable this morning.

He looks at me sternly. "Did you dream last night, Joanna?"

I'd like simply to return his gaze, but I can't. I avert my eyes. I turn my head and look away. And I am reminded that this room has no windows.

It's a cell.

"I see from your non-response, Joanna Clark, that you indeed did dream," he says. "What did you see in your dream?"

I return my eyes to his.

"I'm not going to talk to you, sir," I say. "I'd like to go back to my room, please."

He looks at me and smirks.

"You're not going back to your room," he says, "until you answer my questions."

I look away again. I'm not strong enough just to stare back at someone who hates me. I can't do it.

"Joanna Clark," he says now, leaning toward me and seeming to relish using my last name, "we have your dog."

The color drains from my face. My eyes grow very wide and I look at him horrified. *"What?"* I say, stricken.

"We have your border collie," he says. "Oh, we've treated her well. For *now.*"

I stare at him, disbelieving.

Pleased that he has shocked me, he leans still closer to me.

"We have treated her well, I say, *up till now,*" he adds, "but that will change, Joanna Clark, unless you begin to behave yourself like you should. My questions, after all, are quite simple. You need to answer them.

"If you do not … " He leaves the sentence unfinished.

My mind is racing. *Is he telling the truth?* I ask myself. *Is it possible that they kidnapped Flurry, and not just me, last night?*

Suddenly, the Lord seems to tap me on the shoulder, and, His presence seemingly near to me now, I remember my resolve: to behave like an adult, to conduct myself as an equal to this man. By bringing up the creature — my Flurry — whom I love and for whom I am responsible and for whom I would die willingly and on whose behalf I am fearless, this man has perhaps done something he did not anticipate.

He has raised up in me something that is perhaps the opposite of what he hoped and expected. He has raised up love.

And I think to myself, *This man has raised up in me love for this member of our family, this border collie, but it is love transformed into something else: courage … the form of every virtue at its testing point.*

"If you do not …" he says again, "if you do not answer my questions, then your dog, your beloved border collie …"

"Where is she?" I say, my voice strong, interrupting the man in mid-sentence. "Why did I not hear her in the van last night? Why have I not heard her while I have been in this building? What did you feed her last night? What kind of food did you give her? How much food did you give her for her dinner? What kind of bed did you provide for her? Where did you take her for her walk, so she could go to the bathroom last night? Where did you take her this morning for her walk? What did she have for breakfast? How much water did you put in her bowl?

"You realize," I continue without pause, speaking as rapidly as I ever speak, and increasingly angry as I do, "that she has a chip imbedded under the skin of her neck? You realize that she can be tracked precisely to this building by any veterinarian who has the equipment to do that? You realize that my family can find me in minutes just by dropping by an animal hospital this morning?"

"Silence!" he shouts at me from close range. Raising his fist as he does.

I stand up quickly and look down at him as he continues to sit on his chair, too surprised to rise, his fist still raised. "You *don't* have Flurry!" I say emphatically.

"You don't even know what I'm talking about," I add, as the man rises from his seat and stands in front of me, so that I am now looking up at him. "You know nothing about caring for an animal, and you know nothing about locator chips. You're just trying to scare me into talking to you, and I will *not*.

"And," I continue, unable to stop, "it's perfectly obvious to me that you are lying about Flurry. She is not here. You know nothing about her. You've told me this lie to try to get me to talk to you. And so I say to you again, I will *not*."

He raises his fist again. Fury is on his face.

I actually step toward him, so that we are only inches apart. I can feel his breath on my face.

"You're going to hit a 14-year-old girl now?" I say to him. "*That's* what you're going to do? You're going to prove how brave you are by beating up a skinny teenage girl? Really? *That's* what you're going to do, sir?"

The upraised fist crashes into my cheek, full force, spinning me around. As I fall to the floor, blackness covers me like a shroud.

2

My head hurts. Pretty badly, too.

I'm in the bed in my room, lying on top of the sheets. I don't know how I got here, or who brought me. I try to sit up, but that hurts my head more, so I let my head drop back to my pillow.

Gradually I realize that I can't see well out of my left eye. I reach to my face with my left hand and feel a swollen mass of flesh covering that whole side of my face and forcing my eye nearly closed. I also slowly realize that my left nostril seems obstructed. Exploring that area with my fingertips, I find caked blood in that nostril and, in fact, covering much of the left side of my face.

I force my mind to move elsewhere on my body, just to get a sense of whether or not there are other injuries. I then feel the soreness along my rib cage, on the right side, where I apparently hit something as I fell to the floor.

I gingerly press my ribs with my hand. The pain does not seem severe, so, I think, there may not be broken ribs.

I raise my head, despite the pain, just enough to look down at myself. I see my dress seems to have survived yet another crash landing without being torn, though it is, of course, thoroughly wrinkled. I also see that I am barefoot. Maybe my pretty sandals are lost, or maybe someone brought them to the room. Maybe they're on the floor beside the bed.

I hope so. I liked my dressy sandals.

I turn my head to look at my bedside clock. It reads 11:15 a.m. *My goodness,* I say to myself, *that's more than two hours after my session with my interviewer, almost three hours. Have I really been unconscious for such a long time?*

But thinking hurts my head. And I find I don't even want to think hard, about my injuries or about anything else. I'm just tired, somehow, though I really haven't done anything strenuous. And I'm actually sleepy, it seems, even though I slept plenty of hours last night.

Maybe this is what concussions are, I say to myself. *Maybe when you're hit hard in the face by a fist, and you fall hard to the floor, your brain just doesn't work very well for a while, and it just wants to rest, and maybe even to go back to sleep.*

Groggy as I am, I make myself sit up — pain now shooting through my head and my ribs — and push the sheet down, pulling my feet up and sliding them down under the covers, not caring that my dress is going to be impossibly wrinkled when I get out of bed. I just want to sleep.

I put my head back on the pillow and pull the sheet up to my chin. I place my fingertips on my face. The swelling on my left cheek and around my left eye is, if anything, worsening. My left eye can see almost nothing now.

I sense that sleep is coming on me. *Maybe I'll dream,* I think to myself. *Maybe my mum and dad will come while I'm asleep and take me away.*

Maybe I'll wake up somewhere else.

Maybe.

3

I awake with a start. At first, I can't think where I am, or why.

But slowly my memory begins to work. I remember.

I turn my head to look at my bedside clock. That's when I realize I can see nothing at all out of my left eye. I see with my good eye that the clock reads 9:35 p.m.

My mind struggles with this. *You mean I have slept more than 10 hours? Is that possible? Then it must be dark outside,* I think to myself.

I raise my head and look toward the window. Darkness there.

I pull my left hand from under the sheet and explore my face with my fingertips. It feels like a terrible mess of a face, misshapen beyond imagining. Dried blood caked under and around my nose. Painful to the touch.

I move my hand to my right side and press on my ribs. Pain there, too, but not so bad that it hurts to breathe. I let my mind travel to the rest of my body, and find nothing else that seems wrong.

I want to start thinking normally, but first I feel a need to clean the blood from my face and actually to look in a mirror, no matter how alarming the sight may be. So, I struggle from the bed, and, a little unsteadily at first, pad barefoot across the rug to my bathroom. Once there, I look into the mirror and see a face I hardly recognize.

Aside from the dark red, almost black, caked blood under and around my nose, the left side of my face is not only swollen, it is a rainbow of ugly colors: black, blue, even a sickly yellow. Somehow this strikes me as funny, and I giggle, a smile trying to form, but being defeated by the swelling. My mouth won't form a smile yet.

I also see that high on my forehead, on the right side, there is a little swelling and a slight discoloration. Nothing compared to what is on my left cheek and around my left eye, but something. And it occurs to me that my head must have hit the floor when I fell, and that the bump and bruise on my forehead are from that.

I reach down and turn on the water in the sink, waiting for it to get warm. I then use a washcloth to wipe the dried blood carefully from my nose and cheek. That done, I look back at myself and find I don't look any better. Just cleaner.

That's when I realize my hair is loose, no longer bound in the ponytail I had managed to set this morning. This puzzles me. Did the man who struck me actually carry me back to my room *and* remove my flowered ponytail fastener?

Neither of those things seems remotely plausible, so I'm left to think that he summoned others to carry me back to my room. And maybe, I think, one of them was a woman. Would a man think to undo my ponytail?

That leads my mind to Dr. Judith Hannerty, the woman I last saw up on the stage in Madison Square Garden. Could she have actually made an exit through all that chaos I witnessed before I was taken? Could she be *here?*

Having no way to sort that out, I give up, and change out of my blue dress and into the white bathrobe that I hung on the bathroom's hook this morning. I select a juice bottle from my refrigerator, and, from the little shelf above the refrigerator, a snack to speak to the hunger I suddenly feel. I cross the room and sit down on the bed. Sipping my juice and munching on my snack, I try to imagine what has been going on outside my room during this long day.

But so many possibilities flit past my brain that I quickly give up on that, too, and decide just to appreciate the fact that I don't seem to be permanently injured, that someone was thoughtful enough to carry me to bed and take care of my hair, and that my questioner has left me alone for ten whole hours. Those are blessings enough.

I finish my snack and go to my window. The scene is the same one as last night. It could be any city in the world. I turn to look for my sandals when, for the first time, I hear voices in my hallway. Men's voices. A woman's too.

I freeze, my back to the window, suddenly fearful again, fearful that my kidnappers will return to try once more to interrogate me, or to threaten me, or to try to claim something terrible about Flurry. I pull my bathrobe tighter around me, and re-tie its cord. The hallway voices grow nearer.

As these yet-unseen people approach my door, fear leaps to the front of my mind and quickly multiplies itself. I shrink back against the window. My breathing becomes shallow: short, rapid, gasping little breaths. My hands go to my mouth, not because I wanted them to, but because they just do. That's when I realize my hands are trembling, and so are my lips. I feel fingertips and lips trembling against each other.

Stop this! I think to myself. *You know how to calm yourself, like you do when you read in church or perform with the school string ensemble. Make yourself breathe slowly. Relax your arms and hands. Stand up straight, Joanna.*

I do these things and, as always, I feel my body correct itself, and I feel my mind beginning to follow along. I do feel less afraid.

But a moment later, I hear a key card at my door and, after some fumbling, I hear the door unlock and begin to open. I see a hand cupping the door edge and slowly pushing the door open. The hand is soon followed by a whole person, and it is exactly the person I do not want to see. It is my questioner.

It is the man who struck me down. The man who abused me. The man who pounded my face and smashed me to the floor. The man who struck me unconscious and who changed the shape of my face into this hideous lump.

That man is in my room.

That man strides toward me, unsmiling. He is followed into the room by another man and a woman, but I don't really see them. I only see my abuser.

He comes closer and stops just an arm's length away.

He's close enough to hit me again, right now, I think to myself. My good eye widens and my breathing changes again and my hands come protectively up in front of my face, my palms facing outward, toward this man, ready to deflect his next blow.

"Go sit down in the chair, Joanna Clark," he says gruffly, indicating my room's one armchair.

He steps aside and I pad across the rug to the chair. I sit down, still pulling my bathrobe tight around me.

I feel terribly exposed in this little garment. But my chief thought is disappointment that I cannot, so far, feel God's presence with me strongly enough to be the confident girl I became early this morning before this man beat me into submission with a single blow from his fist.

Now, standing in front of me as I shrink back into my chair, he leans forward, his face so near that I can feel his breath, just as before, just before he struck me the first time. "You'll answer my questions now, Joanna Clark," he says, threat carried in every word, "and you'll answer them fully and completely.

"Won't you," he says, stating those two words as fact, not as a question.

My answer surprises me.

"No, sir, I won't," I say, my voice soft and calm.

Ah, I think to myself, *you were wrong, Joanna. God is here with you and in you. He is indeed strengthening you.* And then St. Paul's bold assertion comes into my mind: "I can do all things through Christ which strengtheneth me."

And that realization, that God is present with me in this room, with me here in the very face of my abuser, seems to fill me up with a sense of His love. And that, if you can imagine, actually makes me smile.

I'm sure the smile is a pitiful-looking thing, misshapen as my face is. But it is definitely there. I can feel it. Not a big smile. But a smile, for sure.

I see immediately, however, that my little smile seems to have the effect of enraging my questioner. His eyes grow wide and his mouth becomes a snarl. He utters something that sounds like an animal's growl.

His fist rises again.

My good eye is fixed on that fist. I await the pain.

The violent, shattering crash sends a jolt through my entire body. My good eye closes and I cringe in confusion. I realize that glass has been smashed.

I open my eye and see that my abuser has stood up and spun around to face the sound that has consumed the entire room. Quicker than I can follow, I hear the swift padding noise of running steps on the carpet, and I see my questioner, his back to me, hurled to one side, tumbling now into the carpet.

And then I see why.

Lieutenant Luke Manguson, former Royal Navy boarding-party leader — my uncle, the warrior — stands above me, wide-eyed. He is staring in horror at my face.

He is an otherworldly presence. He is huge of chest and bicep, his face blackened, his clothing jet black, his shoulder holster packed with ropes, tools, and knives. And then I see him reach to his waist and un-buckle a clip that was attached to a slender cable.

And then I see that the cable extends to my window, then through the shattered glass of my window. I stare upward at Uncle Luke, and I un-derstand in a flash that he has rappelled from the roof of my building and swung himself through the glass window and into my room at the moment I needed him most.

And I see in his blackened face the outrage of a warrior who realizes that his beloved niece has been abused by his enemy. I see his head turn slowly toward my questioner, who lies on the floor near me, looking up in absolute terror at the apparition staring down at him.

And the thought forms in my brain: *My uncle could kill this man. And I think he wants to do exactly that.*

But suddenly there is another kind of noise from the other side of the room. Uncle Luke turns his head toward the door, as does my abuser from his prone position on the floor near my chair.

And my good eye again widens in astonishment at the sight of a new figure.

My mother.

And behind her, I see Mr. Adelman, then Mr. Belton, and finally, pushing past the two detectives, I see my dad. My parents then run to me, kneel beside my chair, and embrace me from each side. They do this cautiously, aware of my distorted face and of the possibility of other injuries less visible.

"Are you hurt elsewhere, Joanna?" my mother says quietly to me, her voice carefully controlled, but a simmering fury underneath.

"Just a little, Mum, here," I say, gesturing to my rib cage.

"And did they do anything else to you, Joanna? Tell me now," she says, her voice and her gray eyes like hardened steel.

"No, Mum," I say, "it was just one punch, early this morning. I hurt my ribs, I think, when I fell. But nothing else."

Then I realize I should add something.

"But, Mum," I say, pointing to my questioner, "that man's fist was raised to hit me again at the moment Uncle Luke crashed through my window. He wasn't finished beating me. He wanted more."

At this my mother stands and turns, one hand still on my shoulder, and stares at my questioner, who has risen from the floor and moved a few feet back toward the other man and woman who came into the room just behind him. That's when I realize that the room is absolutely silent. Every person in the room has been listening to Mum's questions and my answers.

And it is my dad, his strong, long-fingered right hand holding my left hand, who says evenly, "So it was this man, the man wearing the suit and tie, who hit you this morning, and who was ready to strike you again, Joanna?"

Every person in the room is looking at me for an answer, except for my parents, whose eyes have not left the three strangers who are cringing near Mr. Adelman and Mr. Belton. I find I do not want to answer Dad's question. I fear for the man's life.

I look down, afraid to respond. Then I hear my uncle's voice.

"You were hit with a right hand, Joanna," he says, knowing from experience that a right-handed punch would land on the left side of the victim's face.

He moves quickly across the room to my questioner, seizes the man's right wrist, and raises the man's hand closer to his eyes. He examines the man's knuckles.

"Is this abrasion across your knuckles," he says, his voice deadly quiet, "the result of your striking my niece — a 14-year-old girl weighing less than half what you must weigh — this morning and knocking her unconscious?"

The man looks at the floor. He nods his head slightly.

He says softly, "Yes."

Then he adds, just as softly, "I'm sorry."

I can actually hear the men breathing — my dad, my uncle, the two detectives — their adrenalin pumping, their eagerness to pummel my questioner into a formless jelly fighting against their Christian impulse not to fight violence with violence. It is my mother's voice that cuts through the tension in the room.

"We are not in danger, Luke," says my mother, her voice strong and even. "We have defeated our enemy, at least for now. We are not permitted to do violence against an enemy who has been defeated and captured. Do not strike him, my brother.

"It is not permitted."

My uncle releases the man's wrist and looks at his sister, then at me. He gestures with his hand toward the other two strangers. He looks a question toward me, and I answer *this* question without hesitation.

"These may be the people," I say, "who carried me back to my room early this morning, Uncle Luke, after I was knocked unconscious. I think they were careful with me. And I think that this lady may be the person who was thoughtful enough to undo the ponytail that I set today, knowing the ponytail would make it harder for me to rest. I think she loosened my hair."

The two both look at Uncle Luke and nod their heads. Then the lady looks at me and says, shaking her head sadly and speaking so softly that I can barely hear her, "I'm so, so sorry, Joanna."

"Sally and I," says her companion, apparently referring to the lady, "had no idea what we were getting into. We thought it was a new church. We thought it was going to be an exciting thing. We wanted to be part of something good."

Detective Belton looks at them and says in his rumbling voice, "Then why'd ya let this dirtbag here kidnap Joanna and bring 'er back here t' this place? Y' want us t' believe y' couldn't do anything about that? Hm?"

The lady — "Sally" — looks at him and says, "We were afraid, sir."

My mum interrupts.

"Detective Belton," she says, "did NYPD bring medical staff with them on this action, or just the SWAT officers themselves?"

"They got paramedics with 'em, ma'am," he says, obviously reluctant to turn his attention away from the "dirtbags."

"I'll get 'em up here t' look at Joanna."

With that, he shuffles with his cane over to the hallway and shouts just one word — "medics!" — and I hear running feet in the hallway. That's when I realize that there have been many more people involved in this rescue other than my family members and the two detectives.

My last prayer-dream — my last vision — already told me that my mum might be coming herself on an overnight flight. It told me, too, how I would be so precisely located: by Mum's own vision.

That's how Uncle Luke knew exactly which building and exactly which window to come crashing through.

That's so often the visioners' role, I think to myself, *to give a location when there is no other way to find someone, or to identify someone as a bad person when they have seemed to be good. The visions don't usually give us something we could have figured out ourselves. If it's something we actually can do ourselves, He usually wants us to go ahead and do it; if that's not possible, then there are these Divine Intrusions we have learned to expect and to count on.*

But suddenly I find that I'm no longer thinking thoughts at all. Suddenly I'm simply overwhelmed. They've come for me. They're here.

I'm saved.

And I begin to sob. It's as if someone turned on a water faucet. No preliminary tears welling in my eyes. No isolated tear drops trickling down each cheek. Just a sudden waterfall of tears and sobs of gratitude and relief.

I'm still crying hard a few minutes later when my parents help me out of my armchair, and walk me back to the bed. They help me get myself under the sheets again, while the paramedics — a man and a woman — join my parents at my bedside.

They examine my face. They ask me questions to determine whether or not my mind is clear or still fogged from the concussion. They probe my ribs gently.

Suddenly there is an enormous cracking thud, followed by the sound of a person crashing to the floor. Everyone turns to see what on earth has happened.

I quickly lift my head from my pillow, and I see the beaming face of Mr. Adelman, standing triumphant over the apparently unconscious form of the man who abused me. Mr. Adelman looks happily around the room at my family and Detective Belton, all of them Christians, and says, "My religious guidelines are a little different from yours, my friends. As a good Jew, I'm guided by the book of Exodus, especially the words found in chapter 21, verse 24."

Then, to the paramedics, he adds, "When you finish checking on Joanna, you might come over and take a look at this dirtbag, as my partner Sidney would say. This particular dirtbag is going to have a face that looks a *lot* like Joanna's face does now, and I don't think it will take long for his complexion to develop some of those interesting colors that Joanna has, too."

Mr. Belton, who is not as well versed on Bible passages as my family is, looks at us for help with his partner's reference to Exodus 21:24.

My mum answers him: "'Eye for eye, tooth for tooth, hand for hand, foot for foot.' That's the Exodus passage, Detective Belton. It's quite explicit.

"And, in this case," Mum adds, "it means that if a full-grown man strikes my daughter in the face as hard as he can, then he should not be surprised if another full-grown man strikes *him* in the face as hard as *he* can. Especially if the second full-grown man is a student of the Old Testament."

I look at the expressions on the faces of my parents, my uncle, and Detective Belton. Not one of them appears to be mad at Mr. Adelman. Not even the tiniest bit.

Interesting, I think to myself.

4

It's still Tuesday night, but near midnight, almost Wednesday morning. I'm lying on my bed in my sleeping room in the detectives' office building. I'm wearing jeans and my light blue *I Love New York* tee shirt. I'm holding a small heating pad against my face. Flurry is curled up at the foot of the bed, snuggled against my bare feet.

My little bedroom is amazingly crowded right now, even though it's almost midnight. Standing or seated around the bed are Mum, Dad, Uncle Luke, Reverend and Mrs. Morgan, Samuel, Gareth, and Max. Max would like to be on my bed with Flurry, but, when he looked at Uncle Luke for permission, my uncle shook his head no.

Max then settled for his second choice, lying on the floor next to Samuel.

Everybody, then, is squeezed into my room except for the two detectives, who are upstairs in the conference room, monitoring police traffic and talking occasionally with Aunt Kory at the lodge. My aunt has not left her post all night long. And her husband — our uncle, you know — has noted that, if she had gone to bed at her normal hour, she'd be ready to get up and start her next day, early riser that she is.

It's obvious to me that our adults feel horrible — guilty, even — that we three young people look like we do. You already know how I look.

Samuel looks much like I do, since he was hit in the face in much the same way, except squarely in the nose, and with the hard wooden stock of a rifle, so that *both* his eyes are discolored and swollen nearly shut. He also cracked the back of his head on the Madison Square Garden concrete floor, and was unconscious during the rest of the melee. But I'm told he got a good night's sleep and seemed okay this morning.

Gareth looks worse, though, than either of us. He was struck hard on the side of his face, but the real damage was done when he crashed over a row of wooden seats. His face hit the top of the seat back of the row in front of the seats he fell over. He has a deep cut across his forehead, the sutures plainly visible, and lacerations across one cheek from sliding down and scraping his face on the concrete steps under the seats. It must have been a spectacular and terrifying fall to see.

I'm so glad I missed it.

He received stitches across his forehead Monday night at an ER, and a large bandage covers the concrete scrapes down the side of his face. Samuel and I look like we have been in a fight.

Gareth looks like he has been in a war.

As I said, the adults feel horrible about the fact that it is the young people who have these injuries, though one of grown-ups, Mrs. Morgan, was also slightly hurt, as was Max. Mrs. Morgan's injury is to her forearm; Max's is under one eye.

Mrs. Morgan was hit accidentally by one of the SWAT officers, as he swung a club at one of the fake NYPD policemen. Max received a small cut near his eye from banging into a metal rail in pursuit of another fake NYPD officer.

Reverend Morgan has just finished a beautiful prayer of thanksgiving. He thanked God, on our behalf, for bringing us through the fighting and shooting, for the visions — mine and Mum's — that allowed Aunt Kory to intervene electronically, for Mr. Jonathan Murphy's Christian faithfulness in steeling himself against traitors within his own company and within his failed church, for Mr. Murphy's willingness to change the church into something different — an endowment fund in support of worldwide Christian education — when he saw the need, and for his having so quickly arranged to have my parents flown from Wales to New York in one of his jets.

Reverend Morgan includes in his prayer one of the phrases I love so much, "The blueprint of the universe: My life for yours," a phrase our family has used ever since I can remember. In this case, Reverend Morgan uses the phrase to apply especially to Samuel, Mr. Adelman, Uncle Luke, and Max, all of whom risked their lives to run toward the men who were preparing to use those automatic weapons they were pulling from the golf cart, and also to apply specifically to Gareth, who ran, though hopelessly outnumbered, toward my captors in an effort to prevent my being kidnapped.

When the prayer ends, I look at Gareth with my good right eye. I say to him with my mouth, not my voice, "Thank you. You were so brave."

He, of course, blushes and looks away, embarrassed as always. Samuel, sitting next to Gareth, sees both things — my soundless *thank you* and Gareth's blushing — and reaches over and punches him gently on the arm.

Then Samuel, seemingly proud of the fact that his sister has a boyfriend, says quite loudly, "My sister's right, Gareth, you *were* brave, you know. You ran to save your girlfriend when none of the rest of us even knew she was being attacked. You had no chance, really, to rescue her, but you ran for her anyway."

"And that," Samuel adds, "makes you *my* hero, Gareth. Great job!"

Gareth doesn't know what to do with any of this. Smiling and blushing, he drops his sutured and bandaged face into his hands, trying to hide his embarrassment.

Then, Samuel, not satisfied with the extent to which he has just embarrassed us, decides to make our humiliation complete.

"You'll need to learn," he says, "to be just as brave next time you try to *kiss* my sister. You'll need not to turn chicken just because I'm there with you in the fitness center and ready to make fun of you both."

Mum has heard enough.

"Samuel," she says firmly, giving him the look that mothers all seem to have at their disposal, "that's enough. Just stop."

He does.

Chapter Ten

1

It's Wednesday now, late morning. I slept until 10 o'clock. It seems nearly everyone slept late today, not just me.

The detectives' office building has run out of room for people to stay overnight. Mum and Dad brought sleeping bags down to the fitness room, insisting on not forcing anyone else out of their beds. And, in fact, the fitness room is where we have all assembled right now, for our morning devotions and conversation.

I did my own private reading and prayers in my sleeping room, and the first thing that happened after that was a visit by one of the NYPD physicians. He checked me, Samuel, and Gareth, looking for concussion symptoms.

He reported to our parents that he was satisfied with progress for all three of us. But he added that Gareth and I would probably continue to display symptoms, possibly for another day or two: slight nausea, fatigue, and something he called "mental fatigue." I'm still feeling all three of those, but I was glad to come down one floor and to be led by Reverend Morgan in another set of readings and prayers. It's been a wonderful way for all of us to start this day of midweek rest and thanksgiving.

The fitness room is a good place for our morning session, given the number of people we now have staying in the office building. It's the largest room of all, and a mat — easy to sit or lie on — covers the entire floor. Gareth and I would both prefer to lie down than to sit up.

We brought our pillows.

The K-9 officers have just come for Flurry and Max, but everybody else is present. I'm wearing jeans and, this time, my pink *I Love New York* tee shirt. We never found my dressy sandals, so I'm wearing my everyday ones. We did recover my blue purse, which had my passport inside. That's the important thing.

Mum helped me brush my hair, and she fixed a loose ponytail with rubber bands. My face actually looks worse today, because the discoloration has spread and deepened. My left eye is still swollen shut.

I feel good enough to listen, though.

The grown-ups have been talking this morning, in this session, mostly about the news reports of Monday night's flash event and its sudden, violent ending. The early reports — yesterday's reports — had apparently focused mostly on the violence and on the SWAT officers' timely arrival and apprehension, first, of the fake NYPD officers, second, of Dr. Hannerty, and third, of several others on her team, some of whom were actually on the stage with her.

There were, as well, interviews with Mr. Murphy and Reverend Morgan. There were other interviews with randomly selected spectators who had been present in the Garden.

The more recent news stories, my parents and the Morgans have been saying, delved more into background issues. Such as, for example, the colossal fraud that was to be called The Church of the New Century. And such as the graphic Bibles and the electronic games that were going to depict a very different kind of "god" from the one given us by the real Bible and by real Christian literature. And such as the ingenious plot to have hundreds of thousands, possibly even millions, of people around the world transfer their money into the "church's" bank accounts, a tiny portion of which funding would go to something good, but most of which would go to things obviously evil.

The leaders of the evil plans, they have explained, have all been apprehended, with Dr. Hannerty, of course, among those jailed. Apparently, it will take quite a while to sort out exactly which of her people were responsible for what, and on which side of the ocean each individual person will stand trial.

There have also been more in-depth reports, just today, regarding the violence: the nature of the weapons brought into Madison Square Garden; the types of weapons used to shoot and destroy the gigantic info-board suspended from the arena's roof; the kidnapping and threatened violence directed at Mr. Murphy, Reverend Morgan, and others in their families. Apparently, from Dr. Hannerty's standpoint, no violence would have been attempted had the technical aspects of her plans been permitted to run smoothly.

The fake NYPD officers, both around the stage and on top of the info-board, and the men in the golf cart with their long guns and other weapons, constituted a sort of Plan B, to go into effect if the electronic scheme began to unravel. They apparently intended to kidnap Mr. Murphy, Reverend and Mrs. Morgan, and any of the rest of us they could get, to hold as hostages.

As it turned out, I was the only one they actually got.

We were to be bargaining chips to get concessions from law enforcement, to negotiate with them on not pursuing some of the illicit parts of the shipping business that Dr. Hannerty had set up around the world. And, if all else failed, their Plan B would have focused on reduced jail time for those involved.

A nice bonus has been that some of the news stories have given lots of publicity to the new endowment fund and to the appeal that was made for each Christian person and family to invest time and money in their local churches. That's one of the best outcomes of all, we think.

At one point in the discussion, Detective Belton mentions that the leak in the NYPD precinct office — the one that led to the attack last week in the Brooklyn park — was finally uncovered when the fake NYPD officers were arrested at the arena and later interrogated. A member of the precinct support staff, not the NYPD officers themselves, had been passing confidential information to Dr. Hannerty's team.

At some point during Mr. Belton's comments and the discussion that follows, my good eye closes without my telling it to, and I know nothing else of this entire session. When I eventually wake up, only four people and Flurry are in the fitness room with me: Mum, Mrs. Morgan, Gareth, and Samuel.

I rub my eyes — well, my good eye — and raise my head to look from one face to the other. Suddenly I laugh aloud at Gareth's and Samuel's multicolored, bandaged, swollen faces.

"We all look like clowns," I say happily.

They look at me out of their own damaged eyes. They both shake their heads.

"You think the oddest things are funny, Joanna," says Gareth.

2

It's now been about a half hour since I woke from the rudeness of falling asleep during the late-morning discussion. During that half hour, Mrs. Morgan left us briefly to ride the elevator to the top floor, where she raided the kitchen to bring a midday snack to us. So, here in the fitness room, we're feasting on bananas, apples, granola bars, and the like, while talking about nothing at all for a change.

I seem to be completely well. No longer foggy.

I say this to Mum.

"We saw that as soon as you woke up and laughed at the boys, dear," she says in reply. "Your fog has lifted. I expect your concussion symptoms are past."

"I think so, too, Mum," I say. "It's been the oddest sensation, as though I've been feeling my way from one thought to the next, and then often not even finding a thought at all. But now my mind seems clear as a bell. I'm actually happy, you know? I just don't *look* like a happy human being."

"Yes, you do," says Gareth.

"No, you don't," says Samuel.

"Boys!" say both mothers at the same time.

Laughter all around.

A few minutes of quiet follow, while everyone finishes snacks, including Flurry, whose doggie treats were in the bag that Mrs. Morgan used to bring our snacks down. We deposit all the leavings in the trash bag Mrs. Morgan also brought with her from the kitchen. We wounded ones are now sitting up, no longer prone, with our backs against the wall, which is also padded on this side of the room.

Flurry curls up at my feet.

The two mothers, wearing jeans like the three of us are, and sitting cross-legged in front of us, exchange a long look, and I realize they have something in mind for this time together with us young people.

Mrs. Morgan begins.

"I want to apologize again to you, Joanna," she says, a little hesitantly, "and also to your brother and your mother, for the horrible things I said to you last week in Brooklyn. I've no excuse. I am deeply ashamed."

"Lily," says Mum, "we understand. Your only child had been taken, and that would not have happened had you never known our family."

"But, Rebecca," she replies, "to say the things I said to a *child* was inexcusable. I cannot believe I said all those things to this sweet girl," she adds, looking at me.

Samuel starts to say something smart-alecky in response to Mrs. Morgan's reference to me as a "sweet girl," but Mum sees that coming and stops him with another look. Then she says to him, "Samuel, this is going to be a serious conversation about the future of these two families, and how they plan to relate to each other. You can be serious along with us, or you can go upstairs. Which will it be?"

"Sorry, Mum," he says. "I'd like to stay.

"Sorry, Joanna," he adds, looking at me. "Sorry."

My brother loves me. I have told you. Sometimes he just gets carried away with trying to be funny. Sometimes he is funny. Sometimes not.

"In any case," Mrs. Morgan continues, "I felt at that time that the only way to protect Gareth, to give him a chance to grow up into a man whose life was not constantly being threatened by these incomprehensibly evil forces that seem to swirl around your family, Rebecca, was to separate our families permanently. And that would mean, of course, that my son and your daughter would no longer have any kind of relationship. Not now. Not ever."

My mum nods to Mrs. Morgan. My mother understands this perfectly.

She and I discussed this very thing last month in Wales. We know that close association with us — with visioners who are, of course, seen as threatening to evil people everywhere — is almost the same as *being* a visioner.

If you are in a close relationship with a family that stands in the way of evil, you are automatically in danger that is almost as great as the danger faced by the visioning family members themselves. If you are close to a visioner, you are a possible target.

That's just the way it is.

"But now," Mrs. Morgan continues, "after long, long discussions with Cecil, and after wrestling with this in my prayers, I really do think I'm just wrong about it all. Not *stupidly* wrong, you understand. But wrong.

"I have no doubt God has chosen you, Rebecca, and your family — going back decades now — for a particular kind of service to Him. It's a dangerous service. You've all been wounded at one time or another.

"And yet, here you are, Rebecca, happy and healthy, after all these years. And over there, in England, are your parents and your husband's mother, all of you, and now your only daughter, selected to be visioners. You face danger from time to time, and you are sometimes wounded, but it is all in service to the Lord. *Great* service to the Lord. And, through it all, you're among the happiest people I've ever known."

Mrs. Morgan stops and looks down at her hands, resting in her lap. This is hard for her. All this has been so sudden. And Gareth is her treasure.

"How can I," she says, "in Christian conscience, keep my son from your family? Or myself and Cecil, for that matter? How can I?

"My answer, Rebecca," she concludes, "is that I can't. That I mustn't. That I must trust that God has brought us together and that He is with us, no matter what. Is that not right, Rebecca? Is that not how I must see this?"

My mother smiles, the V-shaped scar on her cheek moving slightly as she does.

"I can't speak for you and Cecil, Lily," says Mum, as I knew she would.

"But I spoke with Joanna last month in Wales about this very thing, Lily. I recalled how Matt, when he first met me, was amazed by the fact of our being visioners. He had not even known that Martha Clark, his own mother, had been chosen as a visioner long before. That she had been given visions even before he was born.

"But he, like you, Lily, came to accept the fact that that is who we are, and that life with us will, from time to time, continue to bring us all face to face with some particular evil that we are chosen specifically to confront. He came to understand that this is godly work. A godly life.

"And, Lily, as you say, we are happy people. A happy family. We know who we are, and we know what we are to do: to live our lives day to day in service to God, like every other family, and when called upon to do something extraordinary, to try to do that as well as we can. It's all quite simple in the end."

As Mum finishes her statement, something jumps up inside me and compels me to speak, and just at this exact moment. And so I do, completely surprised, again, at myself. Sometimes I do feel quite grown-up.

"Mrs. Morgan," I say, aware that she and Mum and the boys all look at me quickly, surprised that I've interrupted such an adult exchange, "I've never had a boyfriend before, and don't even know how to be a girlfriend. But I know that Gareth and I like being together, and like talking to each other, and would be crushed if we couldn't keep trying to learn how to do this.

"If you and Mum were to say our families couldn't see each other any longer," I continue, "then he and I would accept that. But we'd be terribly sad."

"And," says Gareth suddenly, leaping into the conversation and surprising everyone just as I did, "we'd not only be terribly sad, we wouldn't be able to grow up to be as *good* as we have a chance to be. We don't know if we'll be girlfriend and boyfriend in a year or five years or whatever, but we're going to be better people if we're allowed to learn from each other. We *know* that, Mum.

"We're already better people than we were a few weeks ago," he says, "when I met Joanna at my uncle's farmhouse in Wales. We've been through a lot in a short time, Mum, and we already trust each other more than I could have imagined possible.

"It's been amazing, Mum. Let us keep growing up together. Please."

My boyfriend surprises me sometimes. He's a very smart person.

And he likes me just like I am. Too long for my clothes, too clumsy to do anything very skillfully, long hair that won't behave itself, and now, a cheek so swollen and discolored that I hardly look like a person at all.

He doesn't care. He likes me just like I am.

The mothers smile at us, then at each other.

"Well," says Mrs. Morgan, "I'm satisfied, Rebecca. Our children are growing up the right way, and they're going to help each other continue to grow up the right way."

Mrs. Morgan turns to her son.

"Gareth," she says, "on the flight home tomorrow on Mr. Murphy's plane, let's all get together like this and make some plans for the fall. What do you think? Does that sound like a good idea?"

Gareth and I look at each other through our damaged eyes and try our best to smile. We don't succeed very well.

But we know that when we see each other this fall, we'll be better. And a year from now, we'll be *much* better.

And that's enough for now. More than enough.

End

About the Author

Visioners2: Into the City is the sequel to Walker Buckalew's first novel for young adults, *The Visioners: Into the Wilderness.* This second story follows his central character, 14-year-old Joanna Clark, from England to New York City with her brother and boyfriend, where they meet dangers they had expected to leave behind in England.

Walker Buckalew is also the author of the four novels in The Rebecca Series for adult readers. The "Rebecca" in these stories is Rebecca Clark, the young London school teacher who eventually becomes the mother of twins Joanna and Samuel. All six books – adult and young-adult alike – deal with the adventures and dangers faced by one family: mother Rebecca, father Matthew, and twins Joanna and Samuel. Titles of the four stories for adults are: *The Face of the Enemy, By Many or By Few, Such Thy Mercies,* and *Choose You This Day.* Each book has its own storyline, but the constant theme in each is God's hand in the lives of the four members of this family.

Dr. Buckalew, former U.S. Navy officer, high-school teacher and coach, university professor and small-college president, serves now as a consultant to private schools throughout the U.S. and Canada. When consulting with Christian schools, he is often invited to speak to students and to the school community on the themes found in his novels.

He and his wife, Dr. Linda Mason Hall, are residents of South Carolina.

Here's a sneak peek at *Visioners* 3

As she and her family discussed during the flight home from New York, Joanna Clark has made plans to host boyfriend Gareth Morgan during their Autumn break from school, the final two weeks of October. Their plans look much like those the two families had made for the previous summer, when the two young people had read books they hoped to discuss, and had developed lists of London museums and plays they expected to see, before the sudden trip to America derailed those plans.

After three months of long-distance communication done entirely through the mails to avoid risks of electronic interception by the Clark family's enemies, Joanna and Gareth at first encounter the mutual discomfort their shyness produces each time they are together. But suddenly, once again, their efforts to nudge their relationship forward are interrupted by hostile forces from the outside, this time focused specifically on Joanna's mother and uncle: Rebecca, the family's primary visioner, and Luke, the family's greatest warrior.

With her mother and uncle removed from the battle, Joanna, helped by boyfriend Gareth and her twin brother Samuel, will combat these new threats that are thrust upon her thin, 14-year-old shoulders. Can she, for the third time in less than six months, play a lead role in helping to defeat the forces of evil that long ago identified the visioners as their great enemy? And, through it all, can she and Gareth continue "to make each other better people," as they promised their mothers after the terrible events they faced together in New York?